BOOK THREE:
SINISTER SYNTHESIZER

DEAN SWINFORD

ATLATL

Atlatl Press
POB 540
Yellow Springs, Ohio 45387
atlatlpress.com

Death Metal Epic (Book Three: Sinister Synthesizer)
Copyright © 2022 by Dean Swinford
Cover design copyright © 2022 by Scott Cole
Death Metal Epic logo copyright © 2022 by Moonroot Art
Author photo courtesy of James Olon Archive
ISBN-13: 978-1-957504-01-8

Infernal Praise for the Death Metal Epic

"Extremely extreme."
—*Decibel*

"Handled with a pleasing mixture of sardonic humour and deep-seated reverence . . . it's clear that Swinford is onto something special here."
—*Terrorizer*

"An epic hero's journey directly inspired by the music, imagery, and unity of death metal . . . Any metalhead out there who thinks they're alone or an outcast should pick up this book."
—*Indy Metal Vault*

"Cool."
—*Book Riot*

"A fun tale, engaging, interesting and Metal to the core!"
—Metal-Rules.com

"The character development is amazing . . . go read it now."
—CLASH Media

"A worthy sequel . . . engaging and charming."
—CCLaP: Chicago Center for Literature and Photography

SINISTER SYNTHESIZER

The Third Book
of the
Death Metal Epic

Also by Dean Swinford

Fiction

Death Metal Epic (Book One: The Inverted Katabasis)

Death Metal Epic (Book Two: Goat Song Sacrifice)

Criticism

Through the Daemon's Gate: Kepler's Somnium, *Medieval Dream Narratives, and the Polysemy of Allegorical Motifs*

Table of Contents

Part Five

Do not turn to idols or make metal gods for yourselves.
—Leviticus 19:4

*Many years have passed since the tyrant—the guardian
of all keys and the master of the time-walls
was spit out.*
—Mortiis, "Visjoner Av Ev Eldgammel Fremtid"

1.

Metametal:
In the Beginning was the End

The sages say metal began with the first note played by Black Sabbath on "Black Sabbath," the first song of *Black Sabbath*, but the Nekronomikon speaks of those same notes performed, sometimes this way, sometimes that way, in the time before time, the eternal present of endless aeons, cosmic rumblings cloaked by omnipotent crawling chaos.

Metal preexists metal as surely as the Nekronomikon existed in its completed form, a pale rectangle of unblemished flesh, before the very existence of any tangible form.

The music proclaiming the eternity of the void proceeds from the eternal void itself, so that individual notes exist in time while also signaling eternal timelessness.

Endless tales recount this truth. In one, the first musician pipes this song on the first instrument, a flute fashioned from a brother's bone, fashioned by the first betrayer. In another, the ocarina sounds the silence of the void, the instrument itself a paradox of excess and emptiness. Round like a maid's hips, empty as a crone's womb, it contains, then expels, breath, pneuma, soul.

This synthesis of body and spirit, of substance and emptiness, takes its fullest expression, some say, in the pipe organ, in the way that the organ uses its endless breath to surpass the limits of earthly bodies and to express the eternal, the timeless, the divine.

2.
Effigy of Cohabitation

Maria sat, crying, at my door. Her luggage—two suitcases and a roller bag—blocked the doorway. The omnipresent smell of old onions generally suffusing the hallway had been suffocated, overpowered, by a nicotine cloud that hovered, an ominous and black nimbus, over her shaking, heaving form. Six cigarette butts, crushed and spent, lay side by side in a carefully arranged row by the leather jacket she'd heaped on my doormat.

She'd been there a while.

She wasn't supposed to be there. We hadn't arranged to meet. And all her stuff? It didn't look good. The whole scenario did not bode well for my afternoon. I'd just come from the Delhaize. A beer run. I'd sworn off the cheap stuff, the Grafenwouder, the Jupiler. Switched to the real beers. If it was brewed by monks, I wanted to drink it. Holy water. I needed it. After getting dumped by my band. Dumped by Nekrokor, the head of Despondent Abyss records and, now, Desekration's new guitarist.

I had planned an afternoon around the pack of Grimbergen I held in my hands. I had planned a solitary afternoon. My favorite kind. I figured my access to fancy Belgian beers was limited. Ultralimited. Like my money. Which was running out. Barring a parental cash infusion to support their idiot son,

I'd be headed back to Miami within a few months. The money I'd saved from my Booksalot days wouldn't last forever. And even I thought it would be stupid for my parents to help me stay in Europe if I wasn't actually doing anything. At least before, I was playing in a band. Learning a new language. Using my musical talent. Broadening my mind.

I'd never seen her like that. Maria. My sort of girlfriend. My quasi-girlfriend. The girl I'd hooked up with. The girl I kept hooking up with, again and again, because something about her, the novelty of dating a metalhead, a chick who showered less, drank more, and rocked harder than me, stirred my balls with tremulous expectation.

I'd never seen her like that. Emotional. Vulnerable. Clearly sitting there because she needed something from me.

I ticked off the possibilities, my finger drumming a beer bottle as I stood on the landing and took in the scene in front of me. Her sobs had slowed somewhat. She tilted her chin up to me, mascara running like corpsepaint down her cheeks. Tears blotted her gray and washed-out *British Steel* world tour shirt with little black splotches.

She didn't need sex. She didn't need beer. She had all her shit. And she was crying. What did she need? As an emotionally stunted dude, this seriously took some time to sort out. I thought through the whole thing, regarding it all like an incomprehensible calculus equation transcribed, in Latin, as a word problem of the highest complexity. Not sex. Not beer. Plus tears. Then what? She needed ... I had to run through the possibilities again. She didn't want sex. She didn't want beer. She had all her shit. And she was crying. What did she need?

She needed ... and slowly another possibility, a horrifying possibility, came to me. The unthinkable burbled into my mind as I stood on the landing. I clutched the Grimbergen tighter to my chest.

She needed emotional support.

And it wasn't true I'd never seen her like that. It wasn't technically true. I'd seen her crying once before. You know that. She had been waiting for a tram, out in the cold, while I sat in McDonald's and enjoyed America's national dish, a Big Mac combo. With a free Coke refill. It's just . . . that time, I'd been able to ignore her. Been able to back away from the window, McDonald's tray in hand. She hadn't seen me then. She hadn't seen me seeing her. In that way, I'd never seen her like this.

But here, after I'd charged up five flights of steps, delectable monk-brewed beers in hand, I had nowhere to turn. Nowhere to hide.

She wiped her face on her sleeve. Mascara smeared across her cheeks. But she spoke in a clear and direct voice.

"I need your help with something," she said.

I froze. My help? Maria never needed anyone's help. That's why I liked her. She was like a dude. She lived for sex and beer, in that order. She was better than a dude. If she needed my help, it had to be bad. Another horrifying possibility came to mind. This one came faster. I imagined the worst. My mind birthed the worst thing you could think of if your chick is sitting at your door, crying and hauling all her shit. I had a brief vision, startlingly lifelike, of a baby in a Judas Priest onesie. But for a newer album. A onesie as black as India ink, a onesie that hadn't been washed out by a thousand nights at bars, at shows. I had a vivid vision of a baby in a *Painkiller* onesie. With a cigarette butt for a pacifier. A cigarette-sucking headbanger baby that looked . . . like me. I clung to my beers even tighter, the bottle caps pressing hard into my collarbone.

She was pregnant, I figured. Had to be. Some latent paternal instinct took over and I rushed to her. I knelt and held her.

Or really I knelt and held her out of an amplified instinct for self-preservation, heightened by the endorphin rush of my five-floor stair sprint. If she sensed my concern, my solidarity with her plight, I could quickly steer her toward some socialized healthcare service that would make the Judas Priest baby go bye-bye.

"Whatever you need," I said, and that's how she got me.

I hadn't seen too much of her lately. I'd seen her once or twice since that day I'd seen her crying. Both times, I'd seen too much of her. Seen enough of her to fear a baby. But I had never asked her why she'd been crying that day. I never made an effort to spend more time with her. I just assumed our "relationship" was in its landing phase. I'd see her less and less, and then we'd be done.

At least I hoped so. Because of Natasha. Yes, that madness hadn't dissipated in my initial weeks of bandless exile. She obsessed me. She owned me, even though she was thousands of miles away. She owned my time, too. She'd started calling me more and more. At least twice a week, she snared me in hourly bouts of romantic conversation. It doesn't sound like much. What's that . . . like two or three hours a week? I wasn't doing anything else. It's not like her calls interfered with a productive work schedule or exciting nights out with my black metal homies. But it wasn't just the sum total of hours conversing. There were missed calls. Messages on my answering machine. The time spent at the end of each call negotiating a time for the next call. Because I had nothing else going on, her calls provided the only structure to my time. Because I had nothing going on, her calls felt like efforts to control my time.

I never called Natasha. I told her I couldn't afford it. Which was true. She could afford it. Her parents could. We didn't even talk much. I didn't talk much. She talked for me. In her words, I'd been made to apologize a hundred times for my past transgressions. Her words, my voice.

The main thing that stuck in my mind over the last few weeks of long-distance monologues was that she'd resolved to come to Gent to visit me. Sometime soon. Before I ran out of money. But she didn't say it like that. Instead, she'd want to know if some particular set of dates—she planned to come for a week or so—"fit my schedule." I had no schedule. I figured she'd be here soon. Within a few short weeks. As soon as her parents bought her the ticket.

So the sight of Maria and all her earthly belongings on a

fine December afternoon filled me with dread. I feared glad tidings of a child to be born unto us. I feared the undeniable exposure of my latest transgressions.

Maria was smart. She got me to move her stuff into my apartment before revealing anything. I cleaned up her cigarette butts, too. Her sobbing stopped as soon as I piled her bags in the middle of my slaapkamer and shut the door.

"What's going on?" I asked. Glad tidings glad tidings glad tidings. I reached for the bottle opener and popped open a couple of Grimbergens. My hand shook a little as I passed one to her. I downed half my bottle in one sip.

She started by saying her roommate had kicked her out. And you're pregnant, I thought. Zwanger. But that part never came. I drained the rest of the beer once I realized she wasn't pregnant. Glad tidings, for sure.

She couldn't pay her share of the rent. Which was weird because she had a job. She'd never had money problems before. She said her dad had stopped sending the money she needed to afford the rent. Her job didn't quite cover it.

I figured maybe that meant she'd stay at my place for a bit, then be on her way once he sent some more. But then she told me her dad stopped sending the money because he'd been arrested. Jailed for the transit of illegal contraband into Belgium. Drugs. Cocaine specifically.

Apparently he had some kind of mob connections.

This was all news to me, I told Maria and she laughed. I opened two more beers. We sat on the bed.

His favorite party trick, she told me, was to hang a pair of sunglasses between his nostrils. Years of cocaine use had dissolved his septum.

"Yah, he's a little fucked up," she said.

It was the most we'd ever talked.

"So I can stay here a bit?" she asked. "Even though I don't have money."

"I can think of ways for you to pay off your debt," I said.

"You're too good," she said.

The Judas Priest shirt came off first. Then her pants. Within a few short minutes, she was only wearing a black thong.

The straps pinched the flesh on her hips. The black fabric swelled with her sex underneath. I cupped it with my hand. She rubbed against my palm, then reached for my zipper.

A girl moving into my apartment? Maybe it wouldn't be so bad. I figured I'd sort out the details later.

I rolled the thong down her hips, down her thighs, then off completely.

I wadded it up in my palm.

"Make yourself at home," I whispered in my best Fabio voice, then hurled the thong in the air. It hit the wall and slid down into a jumble of covers.

3.
The Loss and Curse of Normalcy

But come on, you're saying. Aren't you forgetting something? Didn't you leave us hanging there at the end of your last book? Just like you did at the end of the first one? It's becoming a habit. Not a good one.

This is supposed to be a story about heavy metal. Not a story about poor David Fosberg's romantic tribulations. A death metal epic. Like it says on the cover.

You got dissed hard by the Master of Darkness himself. You got dissed by Nekrokor. Kicked out of Desekration. But you never told us why. Not really.

And that's all true. The weeks after Desekration's premiere show at the Frontline sent me into a fog of self-loathing. I just spent the last few pages making it seem like Maria moved in completely through her own wiles, that she materialized on my doorstep after weeks of enduring my aloof absence, that I'd coolly nailed her a couple times after getting booted and then spent the rest of the time guzzling Trappist ales, composing mesmerizing electric guitar solos, and, just to stay sharp, conjugating irregular Dutch verbs.

But that's not exactly how it went down. It's hard to admit this. I know you want someone strong. A metal warrior to regale you with epic tales of heroism. To be honest, the weeks after my ousting were unheroic and not epic at all.

Nekrokor kicked me out of the band, off the stage, and into a mire of weakness and shame.

I'm just like you—I had no idea why he did that shit. I wanted to know. As soon as his guitar, his foot, slammed into my chest. I mean, I had a general sense. Before the show, he'd been in town. The boss man checking up on the hired hands. He and Svart had some kind of macho mutual admiration society going down. He'd shat upon my main contribution to Desekration's new songs. He'd besmirched the integrity of my most mesmerizing riff. Recognized it as a derivative twisting of a tired Twisted Sister anthem. He'd belittled my extracurricular activities, my mostly feeble attempts to learn a new language, my small efforts at self-improvement outside of metal's narrow confines.

But that wasn't enough to kick me out of the band, was it? Had any band kicked someone out for so little? I hadn't embezzled money—if there was any—from the Despondent Abyss empire. I hadn't pickled myself, like Dave Mustaine, into drunken incoherence. I hadn't interspersed myself into any awkward love triangles, quadrilaterals, or other sexual geometries. If anyone had done that, it was Nekrokor himself. Or Juan. Both fixated, for some strange reason, on the hills and valleys of Delphine's outstretched landscape. I mean, why hadn't Nekrokor kicked out Juan?

That was my starting point. The question I ruminated on again and again the morning after Desekration's first show. I woke up and lay in bed running through those minutes after Nekrokor kicked me off the stage. The crowd buffeted my fall. The force of Nekrokor's kick pulled the plug out of my guitar. I found myself standing in the pit, my muted guitar in hand. And the rest of the band continued without even a glance in my direction.

No one was fazed. Not Svart, not Tomi, not Nordikron, not even Juan. And definitely not the crowd. After a few seconds, they surged around me, angling to get closer to the stage. I just slowly moved away from the show. No one noticed me, even though, just moments before, dozens of enthralled Belgian teens had clamored to touch my arm, my hair, the little crown of sparrow bones and fishing line pressed down, Björn Borg-style, on my head.

Juan would know, I figured. He'd just kept on playing his guitar—well, trying to play. Maybe struggling to keep up? Maybe afraid he'd be next. Still—out of the two of us, why would Nekrokor get rid of the better musician? Me. Why would he kick me out, but keep Juan? To make it worse, Juan hadn't seemed surprised at all. So he must have known beforehand. And, more importantly, Juan would tell me. He had to. We were brothers. Bound together by our mutual Miami-ness. Our unchangeable outsider status.

Or so I thought.

The day after the show, I got out of bed. Put on some clothes. I picked up the little bone crown, the spiked bracelets, all the other shit they made me wear as manifestations of our commitment to total death, and put them all away. I made a spot on the bookshelf, over by my small CD stash. A total death reliquary. Maybe I'd need them again, I thought. A temporary setback. Maybe I'd find some way to get back in Nekrokor's good graces.

And maybe Juan would know how I could do that.

So I called him. The phone rang and rang, but he never picked up. I figured he was probably asleep or something. Drawing. Sewing a patch on his trench coat. Absently reflecting on a land of apparitions and empty shades as he sat in an armchair, an anthology of graveyard poets on his knee.

Probably he just had a hangover, I figured as I left my apartment and started on the way to his place. When I got close, I stopped at a café and picked up a couple to-go cups of coffee. The old habit of Juan maintenance died hard, I guess.

I stood on his doormat and rang the doorbell. I could hear it from inside the apartment, but at first, I didn't hear any other sound inside. Or outside. A gentle rain started to fall as I waited. The mist muffled the sounds of the street. People walked all around me—Delphine's place, over by castle Gravensteen, was usually pretty busy—but the Belgian winter swaddled everything in silence.

I sat on the doormat for a second—there was an overhang, so I wouldn't get wet. I figured I'd drink some coffee—I'd drink two coffees—before heading back to my place. It surprised me that he wasn't home. I wouldn't have sprung for the second coffee if I hadn't been pretty certain he'd be there. But as I sat there, the back of my head against the door, the mail slot tinkled just the slightest. A few seconds later, it happened again. First, a thump came from somewhere inside, a cabinet door or something, then the flap jostled. The building must have been at least a hundred years old. Stable, but maybe a bit creaky. Someone shuts a door somewhere inside and something outside rattles.

This happened a couple more times before I got on my knees, lifted the bronze flap, then peered inside. I couldn't see much at first. Straight ahead, the staircase going up to the slaapkamer took up most of the view. I smooshed my face against the opening and tried to peer to the right side of the staircase, where the lower level opened up to the kitchen and den.

Right then, an unsuspecting Juan shuffled out of the kitchen and into view. He looked like a marshmallow Peep, his body wrapped in a thick and fuzzy pink bathrobe. Mascara streaks and corpsepaint blotches from the show caked the hollows under his eyes.

I mashed the doorbell again, but he didn't react at all.

He held a bowl of cereal and munched a bite as he headed for the stairs. As he slowly padded past the mail slot, I noticed the headphones he had on, the tinny tap of a blastbeat. A thin black cord disappeared into one of the bathrobe pockets.

At least he wasn't ignoring me on purpose, I thought.

"Hey dude, hey," I shouted into the mail slot.

He still ignored me. He moved up the stairs.

I tried a different tactic, waving the coffee cup back and forth in front of the slot.

"I got you some coffee, man," I yelled again, completely abasing myself on his doorstep. "Right here. It's still hot."

Then he stopped. He turned around and padded down the steps.

A moment later, the door opened. Juan, enrobed in pink, held his hand out for the cup. He grabbed it, then took a long sip. The mouth, the tail, of his heart-encircling ouroboros tattoo peeked above the robe's fuzzy folds. Some furious cacophony still streamed from his headphones. He made no move to take them off.

"David," he said, too loudly. "How you doing, buddy?"

"What do you think?" I asked. "Not good. What the fuck's going on?"

"What?" he said, then slowly took the headphones off. "I couldn't hear you. I was too busy listening to . . . us. *Infernö*. The new Desekration album."

He held the headphones out.

"You want to check it out?"

When he said it was us, that *Infernö*, the product of months of Svart's incessant browbeating, Nordikron's relentless condescension, spun away at 380 rpm in his little Discman, I briefly forgot about my misery, my embarrassing predicament. The rat-a-tat patter coming from the headphones in his hands resolved into "Plaguecorpse Rise" as soon as I slipped them on. Right at the breakdown. The slow part. Where Tomi's bare bones drumming burbled through the riff, Nordikron above it all, an ascendant batlord, chanting "spirit of the past . . . the medieval past . . . plaguecorpse moulders in the soil below" in his most strangled voice, and Juan singing the same lines in the background.

I tapped my fingers against my leg. The timing or something seemed a bit off, a little slower than I remembered. The guitars screeched a little screechier, too. I figured there'd been some knob-twiddling in the studio. When the song ended, I popped the headphones off my ears.

"The mix turned out good. Our guitars sound menacing, dude. Mine and yours," I said. I didn't want to dissect the final mix with Juan.

And then I asked him, "Where'd you get this?"

"Nekrokor gave everyone an advance copy after the show last night. Everyone in the band."

I don't know if he meant that last part as a dig at me, but it stung. It punctured whatever little bubble of wonder or happiness I felt listening to something I'd helped make. It punctured that tiny upswelling of pride I'd felt while listening to the smallest snippet of my work.

"Yeah, everyone but me. Everyone in the band that kicked me out."

I lapsed into self-pity.

"That's why I'm here. You got to tell me, dude. Why'd he kick me out?" I asked. "Is it because I suck? I mean, I sound pretty good on here."

I handed the headphones back to him.

Juan perked up a bit. It was like he realized the enormity of what had happened. The enormity of it for us. Our friendship. No longer was I some metal master tutoring Juan, my unworthy disciple. He turned the Discman off and tucked the headphones into his pocket, the cord dangling out a bit.

"It wasn't anything like that. No one talked shit about your playing. I don't think he had a problem with that, man. You play good—I mean, I've been listening to *Infernö* all morning. You're like a riffing machine on there. Sometimes you're too good—you sound like two guitars at once. No—it wasn't that . . ."

He kind of trailed off. The way he said it made me think he was bullshitting me. Like he knew the real story.

"What?" I asked. "It wasn't that, but what? He must have said something."

"Well . . ." Juan nervously twirled the headphone cord with

his fingers.

"Come on, man. I just want to know. I'm not gonna be pissed at you."

"You sure?"

"Man, I know it wasn't your fault. Besides, I look out for you. I brought you coffee, right? You got to do the same. You got to look out for me."

"Okay. But you can't get mad," Juan paused, took another sip of coffee. "He said you were too normal."

"Normal?"

"Normal."

It probably doesn't sound like much. Normal. A flimsy reason. A meaningless excuse to bump me out. Plus, you might think, what's so bad about a little normalcy, some small level of predictable reliability, in a band presumably dedicated to plumbing the very depths of the abyss, uncovering, in Nordikron's deranged worldview, the spirits of the dead encased in the earth below. If we were actually uncovering the dead, wielding Stratocasters like shovels, we'd need someone normal, someone reliable. A pragmatic Indiana Jones to oversee all nekroexcavating, a good song title, into the Temple of Total Death. Normal—you need someone to make sure everyone's playing in time, to make sure everyone's in tune. You need someone to play the riffs.

"Normal?" I scoffed. "What the fuck does that even mean? That I'm not ..." I trailed off, stopped myself from launching into an insulting diatribe against everyone else in the group. It would have been easy: that I'm not a self-involved prima donna, like Juan; that I'm not an overgrown adolescent, like Svart; that I'm not a misanthropic vampire, like Nordikron.

"Well ..." Juan sighed.

"We're all pretty normal compared to Nekrokor. To Bård," I went on, using his actual name, a Euro version of Bart, and not his imaginary dark emperor moniker. "Nearly every time I see the guy—nearly every time I see fucking Bartman, he threatens me with a knife. What about you?"

I imagined Nekrokor must have admonished everyone else for their shortcomings, too. Svart's too dumb. Juan's too incompetent. Tomi's too . . . Finnish. Nothing like a pre-concert motivational talk. It probably pissed him off that I'd missed it. Forced him to make an example of me. Even though I had a good excuse. I'd been out looking for Nordikron. Bringing him away from the little bird grave he'd dug in a clearing across from the club. Bringing him into the club as he huffed away at a rotting bird corpse in a plastic bag.

"Did he say the same about you?" I asked.

"Come on, David," He gestured at himself, his black finger-nails splayed against his fuzzy pink robe, the sphere of his ouroboros tattoo poking out. "I've been called lots of things, but no one's ever accused me of that."

"Wait . . . you think I'm normal, too?" I was about to recite my resume. Guitarist on Valhalla's underappreciated classic of Florida-style death metal, *Thrones of Satanic Dominion.* Metalhead since 1984, the year that metal itself attained per-fection. Recording artist for Plutonic Records and Despondent Abyss. But I stopped myself.

"Before we came here, you were the most heavy metal guy I knew," Juan said. "You had the hair, the cool shirts. You made me that mix tape. And you were nice to me when lots of people weren't."

"Right. I could tell we had a lot in common," I said.

"In Miami, none of those things are normal," he said.

"For sure," I agreed, in an effort to bolster my weirdo cre-dentials.

"But since I've been here," he went on, "I mean, maybe Bård has a point? You're not really like the other guys in the band. You seem like you can barely tolerate them. Sometimes, you seem like you can barely tolerate me."

I stammered. I didn't have a good retort. I didn't want to argue. Also—though I didn't want to admit it—he may have been right. At least a little bit.

"So what do I do?" I asked.

"I don't know what to tell you, David," he said.

"Wait . . ." I thought of one other thing. "What about Delphine? Did you tell him you knew?"

Before the show, he'd figured out that Delphine once had and, based on all evidence, probably still had, some kind of ongoing entanglement with Nekrokor.

"I . . . that's personal," he said. "That's between me and Delphine . . . and Bård too, I guess. I dunno . . . I've got to go, man."

He was trying to get rid of me. He started fiddling with the door, closing it bit by bit. The message was clear: I'd helped him, but he had no obligation to help me. At least not with this.

Stunned, not really knowing what to say, I found myself thanking him. Thanking him for his total lack of advice. His unwillingness to intervene on my behalf. His inability to involve himself with what he called, several times, my problem.

"Thanks, dude," I said. At that point, he'd shut the door almost entirely.

4.
Some Other Kind of Music

"Thanks again," I said, this time to Juan's closed door. The lock clicked in place. I said it as honestly and without bitterness as possible, even though what I really meant, instead of "thanks," was "fuck off and die," or "eternal demise," or some other total and abysmal rejection of his rejection.

As I turned away from the door and walked away, those thoughts I really thought, "fuck off and die," those things I really felt, "eternal demise," burbled to the surface. I crunched my coffee cup in my fist and, still largely in control of my feelings of rage and betrayal, placed it in the proper receptacle.

"I defecate upon your soul," I muttered, even as I bent to pick up the napkin I'd inadvertently dropped on the ground.

Maybe he was right, I thought. And Nekrokor, too. Too normal. So socially conditioned that I politely cleaned up after myself even as I seethed with rage.

"I defecate upon your soul," I muttered again in a kind of nonsensical appropriation of metal music formulae to express emotional states.

"I defecate upon your soul," I muttered a third time, quietly enough that I wouldn't disturb passersby. It felt good, but I also knew it probably wasn't very helpful or healthy. I hated Juan at that moment, but I also knew, a faint glimmer of rationality reminded me, that I couldn't ever stay mad at him.

Instead, I wandered aimlessly for a while. I circumnavigated castle Gravensteen and eventually found myself moving slowly toward Maria's apartment, even though this same tiny spark of rational thought remained to warn me that visiting Maria might also feel good, but it wasn't bound to be very helpful or healthy.

She lived a few blocks past the castle, past the fantasyland of Gent's city center. She lived closer to traffic, garages, discount stores. "Where real Belgians live," she'd once told me.

She let me in. I didn't have to peer through her mail slot. I didn't have to stalk her. She let me in and held me. Even though I hadn't brought her coffee or anything. She'd just woken up, too. She had on her Judas Priest shirt and that was it. The bottom edge of the shirt hung like a black veil over her beaver. At first, I was too worked up, too upset, to really notice. Even as she pushed it against my crotch. Grinding in slow circles.

I cried like a bitch and buried my head in her bosom. I mopped my face on her *British Steel* world tour shirt like it was a hankie. See—I've been misleading you. When I found her on my doorstep, when I found her crying endlessly, it hadn't actually been that long since I'd seen her. And I knew it wasn't the first time that ragged old shirt had been soaked in tears. It had, and the tears had been mine.

"They kicked me out," I sobbed. "I'm too normal," I blubbered. She just listened. She kept her body pressed to mine. I think she already knew what had happened. She didn't seem surprised. Besides, she was best friends with Tomi's wife.

Maria held me. She let me wipe my face on her shirt, and slowly, with her hand in my hair, she guided my face, my mouth, around to a nipple, somehow both soft and firm, and poking a little tent through the age-worn cotton, right at the bottom of the "J" in "Judas." At the same time, the constant pressure she put on my crotch had roused my body into action. Before long, I didn't feel quite so bad.

I have another confession to make. That shit I said about Natasha? That I never called her? Also not entirely true. After I cried all over Maria's Judas Priest shirt, banged her, then left, I went straight to a nachtwinkel and bought a few telephone cards. I headed home and dialed Natasha up, even though it was like six in the morning for her.

I told her what happened. That I sucked. That everyone in the band—even Juan—thought I was useless, normal, disposable.

I didn't cry then. I'd gotten it out of my system. My body buzzed with a post-coital languor. But I sulked endlessly at the international rate of fifty cents per minute.

"Maybe I shouldn't even be here," I moped. "This is a sign. A sign to go home."

She disagreed. She said I should stay, stick it out. She said I needed to follow my dream, but poetically. In a way that made the eternal dream, my moronic dream, of crushing crowds with chunky riffs sound like some self-actualizing journey of faith and fulfillment.

"You need to be strong inside," she said. "You need to know that you are a musician. An artist."

If you wondered why she persisted in our relationship, this was it. This idea of me as a musician, her little Mozart crafting timeless meisterwerks.

I should have been thankful. Appreciative. She told me I was talented. An amazing guitarist. Creative. And while she told me these things, I absentmindedly touched my balls and sniffed the dank tang of sex on my fingers.

I didn't deserve her support. Her love. I know that now. But then? I didn't see it that way. Instead, I got defensive. I harangued her for insinuating she didn't want me.

"You don't want me to go home?" I asked. "Is that what you're saying?"

"That's not what I mean," she said.

"You don't want me to go back to Florida? Back to you?" I

pressed on.

It took about thirty bucks of phone time for her to talk me down. For her to convince me of my own worth, me, the guy intent on redestroying our rekindled relationship by ejaculating all over its tiny flame. At one point, I emptied all my phone cards. I ran out of money. I had her call me back. So her parents could subsidize her efforts to bolster my fragile self-esteem.

I told her she owed it to me. I told her she'd taught me to expect a certain level of treatment. It's why I'd betrayed her the first time. I had her, and so I deserved even more. At least, this was the bullshit I fed to her over the phone that day. In fact, it was my stream of manipulative claims that got her, then, to commit to visit me. It might have even been my idea, my suggestion.

"If you want me to stay here," I reasoned, "and you really care about me, then you should come here. To support me. Here."

And I encouraged her to keep on talking. Minute by precious international minute. To prop me up and pledge fealty to my musical talent. I made her explain how, exactly, she thought of me as a musician. I made her explain how she could believe all these things about me, but want me to stay far away, on the opposite side of the Atlantic. I used her positive support against her. If she saw me as so important, so worthy of love, then wouldn't she want to be with me, by my side, as much as possible?

I started to insinuate that my current situation could be traced directly to her. That she created this misery I felt, all alone in my slaapkamer. She created it years before, back when we actually had a relationship. My current misery, the emptiness I felt from Nekrokor's rejection, compounded by Juan's confirmation that maybe I deserved it, that deep pit of emptiness wouldn't have been quite so deep if she hadn't been quite so encouraging.

She's the one who built me up. She'd taken me into her parents' enormous house, showed me off at the big parties they had at their Coral Gables estate. Fancy parties—they called them "soirees," something you'd never say in Cutler Ridge unless you wanted to get your ass kicked. She let her mom feed me elaborate Julia Childs feasts when all my other meals were Top Ramen or Taco Bell. She was the one who tried to convince her dad, a well-connected corporate guy with an office high up in some Brickell Avenue skyscraper, that sure, the Valhalla songs she played for him may have sounded like a flooded carburetor, but really I was no different than any of the Miami music icons his company hired for their annual charity galas, no different than local jazz hero Arturo Sandoval, say, just younger and . . . metaller. She's the one who set me up for failure the first time she broke up with me, I somehow managed to convince her. I left out the complicity of my hand, my tongue, my dick in that whole series of situations.

My evil dick. Even as I talked to her, I had the vaguest sentiment of my own dickness. I was an evil dick. I should have been up front with her. About Maria. About my mixed feelings. About us getting back together, despite the distance, physical and psychological, between us. I mean, I knew everything I said was absolute bullshit. I even knew how fucking stupid it sounded to blame her for giving me nice things, for elevating, at the very least, my level of daily nutrition when she let her mom fuss over me. What I didn't understand is how or why she continued to agree with the things I said.

It made me think of Nordikron. The way he persuaded us all to play however he wanted. The way he made us, the guys playing the instruments, into his instruments. As I sat in my recliner, I thought of the last time he'd been at my place. The last time he'd sat in my recliner, playing the keyboard I sold him and gripped by some sort of meditative trance. When he'd come here with Juan, they'd made me invite them in. Like vampires.

Maybe, somehow, I had absorbed this vampiric trait, I thought. Through exposure to Nordikron, I'd somehow picked up the vampire's hypnotizing power of suggestion. As I continued on, somehow getting Natasha to agree that my current situation stemmed directly from her abandonment of me, and the only way for her to expiate that sin was to come and see me, come and comfort me, I took my fingers, the ones begrimed with ball grease, the ones I'd sniffed and snorted at throughout my exhortations, and I pressed my fingertips against my canines, wondering if they'd somehow grown sharper since I'd first met Nordikron. Or maybe my initial contact with Nekrokor had done it. Had my teeth grown sharper since I pricked my finger with a toothpick and bled on a beer coaster for him? Had I lost some part of my humanity by hanging around these dudes?

These musings must have, paradoxically, calmed me down a bit. Distracted me from the more pressing issue of my existential angst. At the very least, it's harder to talk when you're feeling your teeth. It's harder to drudge up the perceived wrongs of adolescent love when you are simultaneously gauging the blood-draining capability of your bite.

I must have been quiet for long enough so she could wrap things up. With the time difference, it was still pretty early for her. Even though I'd kept her on the phone for ages. So we could talk about me.

She said, "I have to go. My mom's calling from downstairs. But I want you to know one thing. If you promise to follow your dream, I'll promise to come and see you."

Then she smacked her lips in a kiss. A sweet and romantic send-off. But something she said distracted me from my absent-minded finger sniffing, my monitoring for vampiric symptoms picked up somehow through overexposure to Nordikron, through Nekrokor's sanguinary contract.

"Wait," I said.

Even though she'd spent her morning—her very early morning—persuading me of my innate value, that last thing she said really shattered it all. The last thing she said brought the truth, the whole hopeless truth, to light.

"You said ... you said that I should follow my dream,

right?" I started.

"Uh-huh," she said, with just the faintest icy edge of annoyance.

"My dream, well, it's music," I went on. "But now, I'm not even in a band."

Here we go again, I'm sure she thought. All the way from the start. It took another five bucks or so of phone time to get me back on track. Before we hung up, she delivered one last inspirational truth.

"It doesn't matter that you're not in that band," she said. "You can still make music."

"What do you mean," I asked, absently testing my tooth with the pad of my thumb.

"Some other music," she continued. "You can make some other kind of music."

5.

Twin Axe Attack

Some other kind of music. Whatever that meant. I had a vague sense she meant something other than heavy metal. An impossible thought.

After that long morning, she left me alone for a while. A week or so without her calls. And I had no real desire to call her. Some other kind of music. That was the advice. Fucking stupid. I could feel better about getting dumped by metal by ... dumping metal?

It made no sense. Like a Zen koan. This disciple, me, was not ready to accept the teaching. Instead, I spent my days in a kind of isolation chamber. A quarantine. Like I'd been exposed to some virus of loserdom and no one wanted to risk infection through exposure to me, my voice. Natasha's parents had probably banned her from the phone. Docked her allowance. Maria and I never saw each other super regularly anyway. And Juan had made it very clear: the Desekration cult shunned me because I hadn't sinned enough, hadn't jumped into the inferno of total death with the right level of enthusiasm. I was the wayward sheep of a wayward flock.

And that morning after the show, when I'd stalked Juan, found him wrapped up in a pink bathrobe, mascara streamlets on his cheeks, he'd said something that stuck with me. Something I returned to in my isolation, walking around Gent, buying beers, drinking them alone. A puzzle I couldn't figure out.

Something I barely noticed that day, when he passed his headphones over and played me the tiniest snippet of just one song from *Infernö*.

He'd said I sounded like two guitars. Just a compliment. Praise for the unerring heaviness of my riffing. A man and his Strat unleashing a twin axe attack. Appreciation for my playing. Some kind words to make me feel better about the whole band expungement situation.

But that was the thing about it. Juan giving me props? Highly unusual. It should have been my first clue. That something was wrong. Something was wrong with *Infernö*.

I had, like, an anxious feeling in my stomach. Some sort of ball-shrinking dread when I remembered listening to that song. The guitar. Something wasn't right with the guitar. The most important part. It sounded like the lead track, my track, had been split. Damaged. Or pushed somehow, the timing just a bit off.

It shouldn't have mattered. I mean, I wasn't even in the band. But I was on the album. I'd helped make the album. I'd written the guitar parts for most of the songs, figured out ways to satisfy Nordikron's stringent demands. I felt invested in the time I'd spent. Besides, maybe someone else would hear it. Someone looking for a guitarist. What if my shit sounded busted?

After seeing Juan, I knew what I had to do. But I resisted. I needed a copy of *Infernö*. I needed to buy a copy. But I didn't want to buy a copy. Not with money. Not with my money. They owed me that shit. For free. I'd signed a blood oath dedicating my fealty. I'd daubed my life fluid onto a flimsy beer coaster. But I couldn't get a free CD? Fuck that.

Juan hadn't had to buy it. And he hadn't sworn his soul to Despondent Abyss records. I had, and he'd just sort of mooched along. Typical. The idea of buying the thing I had made seemed ridiculous. Adding insult to injury. And yet . . .

the tiny snippet I'd heard, a little off, a little wrong, kept playing in my head. The little ear worm humming my riff wouldn't squirm away. Musical embodiment of the sempiternal grave worm or a little scrap of sound I couldn't shake, either way, I knew I could only vanquish it by listening to the whole thing, the whole song, *Infernö* in its entirety. So I resigned myself to the debasing act of buying my own music. And I knew where to get it. The Record Huis. Svart's prestigious place of employment. The biggest indie record shop in Gent. They'd have it, for sure. When I first met him, he'd reconfigured his whole metal section into a career retrospective of Desekration, even though it had been just him, a lonely Belgian with a four track. And now?

That's where I would find *Infernö*. It would be there. Vinyl. CDs. Tapes. In stacks. Unless Svart, vastly overestimating the transformative effect of this record on his economic well-being, had done something stupid like quit.

So about a week or so after I'd gone to Juan's, I woke up with a mission. A purpose. Sort of. I still hadn't convinced myself to buy the thing. But maybe I could look at it. Hold it in my hands. Maybe, if everything felt right, I could buy it. But only to satisfy my curiosity. And not, in any way, to support those fucking bastards.

I knew I'd probably end up at the Record Huis eventually. The universe, Cthulhu and his gibbering pantheon, slithered their tentacles around my shoulders and pushed me out of bed. I woke, startled, to a fire alarm somewhere in the building. Muffled enough that I couldn't pinpoint it exactly, but loud enough to snap me out of sleep. I shuffled to the coffee maker. As I scooped out the old grounds, the alarm finally stopped. And the kitchen lights flickered for a second.

I didn't think anything of it. Just thankful that the ringing had stopped. I measured out my coffee dose, then poured in the water. The lights flickered again, then went out. No power.

I flicked the coffee maker switch a few times, but no dice. Nothing worked. With the heater off, too, a cold chill set into my toes, then slowly moved up my body.

"Fuck," I muttered. Coffee. The most important meal.

The Vooruit, I thought, my mind scrambling for a solution. The hipster café right across from the Record Huis. Maybe they had power?

Plus, I could go big. Take a day off from the Lidl discount coffee I'd been swilling. The Vooruit did it right, fern leaves and shit masterfully baristaed into cappuccino foam.

I put on some pants, then grabbed my wallet. Enough money in there for a coffee. Maybe a pastry, too. I stuffed a few more bills in there. Just in case. I grabbed my backpack and stuck a few things in there. Headphones. My Discman, too, after stashing *Realm of Chaos* back in my CD wallet. I mean, I probably wasn't going to buy anything at the Record Huis. I wasn't going to buy *Infernö*, I told myself. I should wait for a free copy. God knows I fucking deserved one. But if I did, then I could listen to it. Or, another possibility, if Svart hooked me up. He'd probably be at work. Maybe they'd just forgotten to give me my copy.

If I got it, through Svart's largesse or my own cash, then I could confirm my suspicions. About the song. I probably won't buy it, I lied to myself again. And I didn't think I could count on a handout from Svart. The last time I'd seen him, before the Desekration show, he'd called me a wuss. Him and Nekrokor, outside the Record Huis. They'd been plastering the town with Astrampsychos posters. Unlike Svart, who lived with his mom, I was too soft, too weak. That's what he'd said. Nekrokor, too.

I tossed my Nederlandse niveau een book in my backpack. I'd passed my Dutch class, so I wouldn't need it anymore. I sure wouldn't bust out my halting Dutch—alstublief, dank u wel—on the streets of Miami. They'd think I was a German tourist, then rob me. I wouldn't need to consult the book in any future I could imagine. If I swung by the language school, just down the street from the Vooruit, I could sell it back. Add the funds to my beer coffer. Use the money for something more practical. A few pintjes.

In the building lobby, the manager guy fiddled around with a fuse box. He shined a flashlight into a jumble of wires. As I passed him, he said, "Geen probleem." This happened sometimes in the winter, he assured me. The power cuts in and out, sometimes sets off the alarm. Too many people using their heaters. He gave me a shaming look. Probably the American's fault, it said.

Later, I sat in the Vooruit and poured an endless stream of sugar into a perfectly symmetrical tulip of espresso and milk. The Astrampsychos posters that Svart and Nekrokor had taped all across the front of the Record Huis were almost completely gone. The tattered edges of a few letters, an "astra" here, a "chos" there, clung to the window. But, mostly, the posters had been ripped down. Detritus cleansed from the city.

I watched the traffic in and out of the store while I sipped my coffee. All the record nerds. Mostly indie dudes. Some trendy chicks. A fair share of metal kids, too. One of them walked past the Record Huis window, then doubled back. Leather jacket. A Bathory backpatch. He grabbed the biggest remaining scrap of an Astrampsychos poster, the brachiating tangle of letters spelling "Astra," then slowly peeled it off the window. He flattened it out and folded over the sticky parts. He gently rolled it, then slid the scroll into some inner pocket of his jacket.

As I licked the dregs of foam and sugar from the cup, someone stepped into the Record Huis display window. A little door opened at the back and one of Svart's coworkers stepped between a free-standing Stone Roses poster—the one with the lemon—and a hanging mobile of colored vinyl, orange with yellow splatters, translucent green, an *Aladdin* picture disc. Partially bald, a too-tight Jackson Browne shirt barely covering a hairy belly, this guy heaved in some big cardboard cutout. It must have been six feet long. And just about as wide. He leaned it against the Stone Roses thing. He reached through the door again and brought in a big bag of dirt. Some gardening soil. The Bathory guy on the sidewalk perked up, watched him as he shifted some CD stacks aside and set up the new display.

By the time I cleared my cup off the table and left the Vooruit, the shop guy had made some headway on his window display. The metal dude still stood there, watching. I crossed the street and started to head into the Record Huis. *Infernö* exerted its satanic pull, guiding my body through the doorway. I'm not going to buy it, I thought. I'm just going to make sure they have it. I had one foot on the threshold and the Bathory dude kind of yelped. He jumped around a little, too. Did the pee-pee dance.

I stepped back onto the sidewalk, figured I'd see what was up. A thin pane of glass is all that separated me from a gargantuan cardboard Svart looming in the window. Half a Svart, really. Svart from the belly up. The record dude was still in there, positioning the thing on a plastic stand. Then, he took the bag of garden soil and piled it around the base, around Svart's bare chest, all that hair and blubber hemmed in by some silvery He-Man harness. He piled more dirt around the arm that disappeared into the floor.

Cardboard Svart emerged from the inferno itself, left arm outstretched in a claw cursing the heavens, the right arm still caught in earth's stony clasp. A massive nekromole, all fur and flab, this colossal cardboard Svart had tunneled his way out of Satan's vast subterranean cavern. Dug himself right out of the abyss and into the display window of the Record Huis, the best place to buy "*Infernö*: Desekration's crushing magnum opus, available now," cardboard Svart said in the little speech balloon coming out of his mouth.

I just stood in front of the window for a minute. Me and the Bathory guy. Side by side.

I couldn't go in. Not now. Not after seeing this thing. If I did, then the display worked. The fucking Svart billboard. The spell had been broken. The gravitational pull exerted by the album itself. At least for the moment. I'm not giving up my money for this shit, I thought. I touched my wallet, half expecting cardboard window Svart to reach through the glass and pickpocket me right there. The bills themselves recoiled deeper into the wallet. I felt their feathery stirring against my thigh.

It could have been the wind or something.

The Bathory guy turned to me and said, first in Dutch, then, after a second, in English, "Have you got it yet? *Infernö?*"

"Not yet," I said.

"The guitarist," he went on, "I heard he died."

"The guitarist?" I asked. Without thinking, I put my hands over my heart. Still beating.

"You mean . . . they got rid of muh . . . of him?"

I wasn't dead yet.

"No," he said. "They found his body. Nekrokor's dead. That's what I heard." Then he walked away.

6.
A Special Course

I wanted to follow the dude and ask him more, but I held back. Nekrokor's dead? It seemed hard to believe. Maybe the guy was confused, I figured. If something like that had happened, I would have known. So I left the Record Huis behind. I left the Desekration display behind. And I headed down to the language school. It wasn't far. About two or three blocks away. I passed Tomi's gym, the Powerzaal, but I didn't see him, spandex clad and ready to jazzercise into peak drumming condition. Maybe it was his rest day.

On the other side of the street, there was a wooden wall that marked off a construction site. The wall was covered with posters—computer ads, new exhibits at the art museum, topless women slinging yogurt drinks. Before our show, Svart and Nekrokor had lined the whole thing with Astrampsychos posters. Now, there were only scraps here and there. These posters had been pillaged even more than the fragments hanging on the front of the Record Huis. Single letters. Maybe you could get an "A," maybe an "S."

Stolen, I thought. Stolen by fans. It seemed hard to believe. But the guy in front of the Record Huis had done it. He'd taken a scrap of the poster and stashed it away like some rare map, some ancient artifact.

To get into the language school, you had to go through this

archway that set it off from the street. A few groups of students hung around, smoking cigarettes, talking. Probably on break. I waved to an Egyptian guy who had been in my class. When I walked into the office, some Ukranian girl I recognized sat at a table and filled out a registration form. Four or five people were ahead of me in line.

When I got to the window, I asked the secretary for my grades. As I waited, Helena, my Dutch teacher, headed to the faculty mailboxes along the wall. When she turned away from her mailbox, she had a stack of papers balanced on her hip. Some exams, I figured.

I waved and gave her my best Nederlandse greeting.

"Goeiedag! Hoe gaat het met jou?" I said. Hello. How's it going? Conversational Nederlandse executed with authority.

She smiled and waved back. She gestured at me with the stack of papers.

"Very busy," she said.

Then she corrected me. My pronunciation.

"Who HAT, David. Who HAAT het," she said. It must have been instinct. She gestured to her throat with her free hand. I reflexively mimicked her, sticking my chin out, simulating the correct throat gargle needed to say the letter "g." A dry heave. Someday, maybe, I'd get it right.

The secretary pulled an envelope out of a file cabinet, then slid it through the window to me.

Helena came over to the desk. She stood next to the secretary and talked to me some more. She didn't have to, though.

"Are you registering for another course?" she asked.

"Uh ... I just wanted to pick up my grades." I slipped my backpack to one shoulder and pulled out my textbook. "Sell this back, too."

"That's too bad," she said.

"There's a special course you should take," she added. "It's more for tourists. People who aren't living here."

"I'm living here," I said. "I'm not dead."

"Not living here permanently," she went on. "You know

what I mean. You're not trying to immigrate, are you? Leave behind your perfect hamburger world? Anyway, it's a special course. For a special kind of student. I think you'd be perfect for it."

When she said special this time, I got what she meant. A special course for special people. Dutch language halfwits. Americans. Specials.

Even so, I figured maybe it could be good for me. She said she was teaching it. Doing something new. It was a little under enrolled, she said.

Helena insulted me whenever possible. But she was also kind of hot. A little bit older. Sophisticated. She was wearing a purple leather jacket with tight olive-green leggings. She had a real job.

If she wanted me to take the course, it had to be because she missed me. Wanted to spend time with me.

She said the course started after New Year's and lasted a couple of months. Mostly, they'd visit local spots.

"We're learning language through culture. You can think of it this way: we're taking field trips. Like for children," she said. "Americans enjoy this kind of thing, zeker?"

Her little jabs probably weren't super effective sales techniques. But she smiled at me when she talked. And I'd passed Nederlandse niveau een. Proven my worth as a cunning linguist. Even though I couldn't correctly pronounce basic words. Maybe she'd let me prove my worth in other areas?

"You think about it, okay?" she said, then she left.

It wasn't a bad idea, I thought. Better to spend some money on this, on self-improvement, than handing my cash over to the Record Huis. And . . . the idea came to me suddenly, maybe I could hit my parents up for more money? Tell them I'm educating myself. Tell them I need help so I can stay at least until the class ends. Quitters never win, right?

I put myself on the list. I pulled out my wallet and laid down a deposit.

The secretary handed back my receipt and some of the

class materials. A schedule for our trips. A new book with a picture of castle Gravensteen on the cover.

"Do I still need this?" I asked. I plonked the niveau een book on the counter.

The secretary said no. She pulled the book through the plexiglass opening, then tossed it on a textbook stack behind her.

She fumbled in a metal box on the desk, then handed over some cash. About twenty bucks.

I spent the rest of the day dicking around. Walking here and there. Roaming the earth. I passed by some of the spots we would visit for the class. Castle Gravensteen, Sint Michielsbrug, Sint Baafskathedraal, even the Begijnhof near our practice space. Near Desekration's practice space.

I figured I should do some tourist shit while I could. With or without any money I could cajole out of my parents for valuable cultural development, the hour of my unavoidable departure came closer with each passing day. When well-meaning Booksalot customers of the not-too-distant future asked me about my European voyage—what I saw, what I did—I'd be able to tell them about something other than the musty clubs I'd played, the jizz-soaked Svartian couch I'd once called home.

Later on, I passed by the Record Huis again. It must have been six or seven. The sun had failed, defeated by the Belgian winter several hours before. I figured I'd look at stupid Svart another time, then head home. Drink a few bottles of Piraat. The guy who set up the Desekration billboard must have spent the entire day on the window display. A dense forest of trees surrounded Svart. From far away, the window presented an ominous view into a nocturnal forest, its timeless sleep interrupted by a hulking nekrowarrior clawing his way out of the grave.

Cardboard Svart dominated the scene, emerging from the

depths, his body and arm surrounded in mounds of dirt. The whole set up captured what Svart himself would call "the true essence of *Infernö*" and, as I got closer to the shop, I felt the album drawing me in. I was so close, the door to the store just a few feet away. But I resisted. I held back. I tied my shoe. I briefly browsed in a shop down the block that specialized in an incongruous assemblage of leather goods and Rasta gear— Bob Marley shirts, pot leaf hacky sacks. Earlier in the day, meandering by the city's cultural sights, I thought I'd come back here and just buy the thing. It wasn't such a big deal. Step in the store, put down my money, and go. But the closer I got to doing it, the more I thought of my money going to help this guy. Going to help Svart, enshrined here, for all of Gent to see, as the ultimate embodiment of Nordikron's most favorite idea: that those of us blessed to sacrifice our lives to evoke the true tragedy of death would be rewarded with rebirth, reborn in blasphemy, resurrected with—resurrected as—plaguecorpse spirits, it was hard to keep it all straight. All bullshit, of course. That much I knew. I thought of the real sacrifice—my money. And the real resurrection—my money going away from me and going to him. Going, ultimately, straight to Nekrokor. And as I walked by the window, my money on my mind, my hand brushing against my wallet, something happened, a little Christmas miracle, that pushed me over the edge. That pushed me off the sidewalk and into the shop.

I wasn't going to go in the store. I was just staking it out. Stalker mode. "What the fuck?" I muttered, setting down a Rasta flag hacky sack and heading up the street. "That fat fuck," I muttered. I'd check out the window display up close, then go home. My four-pack of Piraat awaited my company.

"Hairy halitosis-ridden Neaderthal klootzaak," I muttered as I passed the door and came face to chest with cardboard Svart.

I knew I was just jealous. Why wasn't the window filled with an enormous billboard of me? I'd done all the work. I deserved a cardboard cutout. Why wasn't the Record Huis window regaled with cardboard David, a true warrior of infernal death?

But then, even as I lost myself in this petty fantasy, a hand reached into the shop window and flicked a switch. All at once, the dark forest, the dense strand of pines arranged around Svart, erupted into a shimmering kaleidoscope of Christmas cheer. Up close, bedazzled by countless strands of blinking lights, I could see that the forest surrounding Svart wasn't really so ominous. The record shop guy had decorated every tree with ornaments and colored vinyl. The *Aladdin* picture disc now took the place of a star at the top of one of them. A Michael Jackson action figure topped another one.

And then some record store guy came out into the window again. Well, a different guy. Someone on the night shift. Scrawny and underfed. He had on a brown Buffalo Springfield shirt.

Anyway, this guy came into the display and plonked a Santa hat right on cardboard Svart's head.

He left the window for a minute, then came back out with another bundle of cardboard cutouts. At first, I thought he had the rest of the band. Cardboard Juan. Cardboard Nordikron. But then he set them up, arranged them, just so, in a semicircle around Svart. They came up to his hairy nipples. It wasn't cardboard Juan, or Nordikron, or even Nekrokor. It was Alvin, Simon, Theodore.

Wait a second, I thought. It slowly clicked. These indie dudes weren't worshipping Jurgen. They were clowning him. It all made sense. They worked with him. They probably hated him. They'd spent the whole day making an elaborate Christmas display mocking him. They'd cast Svartikles, armageddon warrior ov diabolicrusade against Christianity, as the central ornament in their nekrocrèche. Born again from the soil, a babe in the woods visited by three wise rodents.

The hat, the chipmunks, completed the display. They inspired me to buy. I could—no, I would—get it, but maybe as, like, a joke. A gag gift. For myself. For Christmas. Besides, I had the twenty dollars from my Dutch book. Free money. I wouldn't be losing any money by buying the album. I mean, I guess I'd be losing the money I'd spent in the past. But if I bought *Infernö*, my wallet at the end of the day would be no lighter than it had been that morning. I might even come out a couple bucks ahead.

With this highly logical fiscal reasoning, I stepped into the store. Some ambient music, a collage of dub beats and Casio chords, cocooned the store in a web of sound that grew more muffled, but somehow thicker and heavier, as I headed to the back, to Svart's realm, the metal section he aggressively curated as a monument to his brilliance. Silver pentagrams hung from the ceiling.

More than a few people—some alone, some in small groups—ambled through the metal aisles. They dug through racks of Svart's ultralimited selection. Albums by Bathory, Celtic Frost, Destruction, and a few others provided the foundation to guide disciples on the heinous path. On that note, not much had changed since I'd first met Svart. And he'd filled the rest of his metal section with his own shit. With, in his mind, the real shit. The releases that, for Svart, represented the apotheosis of the sounds, emotions, outpourings of Luciferian devotion initially uncovered, initially discovered, by the classics. In other words, Svart's favorite bands: Astrampsychos, Desekration, and anything else released by Nekrokor's label, Despondent Abyss. Some old demo tapes, too.

The racks in Svart's section were surprisingly light, though. When I'd first come to the Record Huis, his metal section was packed to the gills with early Desekration demos. You could pick up multiple copies of Svart-approved classics. But as I walked down the aisle to find *Infernö*, I spotted only one vinyl copy of *The Intrapsychic Secret*, the Astrampsychos album that Svart regarded with such sacred reverence. Partly because he thought they'd stolen one of his riffs. The cover was torn, the rip a white scar across the cover's cosmic pentagram.

And then I saw it—the logo and cover that Juan had designed. It had the plague doctor, his robes emanating black flames; it had the logo, the letters an illegible conglomeration of spikes and curves, a burning pentagram on top and an inverted cross below.

There was only one CD in the rack. I eased my way next to a few dudes sorting through the Desekration stuff, that one copy of *Infernö* and some "To Winds ov Demise" 7-inches. But before I had the chance to grab it, one of the guys added it to a small stack of CDs in his hands. I groaned. I turned to ask the guy if I could have it. Maybe explain the situation. But by that point, they'd started moving to the register.

It just made me want it more. After they left, I wandered around the section in a kind of daze. I'd spent all this time and energy deliberating about buying the fucking thing, and then it disappeared right under my nose. Story of my life, I thought. I flipped through the Bathory albums, spent a few minutes absentmindedly arranging them in chronological order. I ran my finger along the torn cover of *The Intrapsychic Secret*, which just made me feel worse. That one is still one of my favorite albums—unlike so many of the supposedly "essential" and "classic" black metal albums from the nineties, it's held up over time. Would *Infernö* be the same, I wondered?

Finally, I pulled myself out of the metal section. Coming out of that dark corner felt like leaving a cave. Entering the world of the living once more. Even the sluggish ambient beats, the deep bass, felt lighter, more distant, outside of Svart's metal section. Listlessly, I explored the rest of the store, the massive pop section, flipping through all the classic rock essentials, all the alternative cool guys. Everything I'd renounced as lame and cheesy so long ago. Fleetwood Mac. Nine Inch Nails. All that shit. Maybe the rock stars—the real rock stars—had the right idea. Make something that normal people want. Normal people like me, I thought bitterly. Make something about love. About life. Not about the malevolent spiritual powers of the medieval dead.

And all those guys—no matter how fucked up their lives got, no matter how much coke they hoovered up, they'd never had to play along with some idiotic pledge to exchange your soul—whatever that was—for a chance to perform on some obscure nothing that no one would remember in twenty years. Not even Stevie Nicks, who played the witch card better than most of the Satanic losers in my life.

The pop section didn't have silver pentagrams hanging from the ceiling. It had big mylar balloons for each letter. As I stood under a teal "M" with googly eyes, I flipped through Madonna's impressive and consistent output. I remembered Nekrokor's onetime words of wisdom. He'd said, "Don't break the oath," after I'd blotted a drop of blood for him. I needed to buy the album, I realized with an almost frantic urgency. To do just that. To break the oath. The epiphany came to me while I mindlessly held Madonna's *Like A Prayer*. The cover's her belly, her jeweled hands unbuttoning her jeans. The epiphany came to me while I mindlessly stared into Madonna's be-denimed crotch.

By buying *Infernö*, I realized, I would sever the bond between Nekrokor, the master, even from beyond the grave, if that was true, and me, the useless thrall. He'd kicked me out of the band, sure, but he'd never released me from my servitude to his label. And here that most American fount of wisdom came to me: the customer is always right. Once I buy the album, I reasoned, I would be the customer, and not the worker.

I put Madonna down and passed through the used CD section on the way out. And there it was. Nestled next to a "We Built This City" maxi-single and a Duran Duran cover album. A single copy of *Infernö* gleaming like gold among the dross. Immediately, I picked it up and held it to my heart. I didn't even really look at it, not at first. I recognized the title, obviously. The logo that spiked and jagged like Nekrokor's blade. Below that, Juan's ink-drenched plague doctor.

As quickly as possible, I marched to the register and plopped *Infernö* on the counter.

The guy at the counter—the skinny guy who'd set up the chipmunks—smirked ever so slightly as he rang me up. I didn't say anything. I just pulled out my money and handed it over.

He dropped the receipt on top of the CD and said, "This one's been selling a lot."

The receipt curled up and rolled onto the floor.

"We've sold so many. Especially since that one dude died."

"Uh-huh," I said. I took my CD and left. I didn't believe what he'd said. No way Nekrokor was dead.

7.

Session

I couldn't wait until I got home to listen to *Infernö*. As soon as I left the Record Huis, I nestled down on the sidewalk, right underneath cardboard Svart's baleful glare. I wedged my pinky into the folded cellophane on the edge of the jewel case and pried off the wrapping.

In the kaleidoscope of a million blinking Christmas lights—first a burst of bluish white, almost stellar in its brightness, followed by a darker greenish red glow—I gingerly opened the jewel case. And it exploded. One of the plastic arms holding the cover to the case itself splintered off. I caught the cover, but then a hailstorm of little plastic pieces exploded out of the case and fell to the ground. Twenty bucks and I couldn't even get a good copy. A normal copy. Only a fucked up used CD that I couldn't even return.

The little plastic pieces were the tabs meant to hold the CD in the case. No longer secured in place, the disc slid down the case and onto the ground.

"Fuck," I said, scrambling to pick it up just as a group of teenage girls sauntered by, laughing at my awkward lurch.

I grabbed its edges as soon as it settled on the ground and then I raised it off the cracked concrete. I held it upside down and blew a confetti of dirt and, like, little rocks off the playing surface.

Holding it in both hands, the way Nordikron would hold a dead bird or something, I eased it closer to the window to inspect the damage. The white glare of the icicle lights illuminated a pale gash, about an inch long, that started at the edge of the disc. But then, under the green and red lights, the gash disappeared. It was too dark. I thought, just for that flashing moment, that the scratch had faded. Magically, it had healed. Like the disc's silver surface was forged from some futuristic *Terminator 2* liquid metal. An instant later, the gash flashed back into glaring clarity. I could see that, light or dark, white or green or red, it didn't matter. The CD was fucked, for sure. It was just a question of how much.

I unzipped my backpack and pulled out my Discman. Super carefully, moving with the deliberate precision of a bomb disposal technician, I placed *Infernö* in there and pressed play.

It started—surprise surprise—with a cheesy intro. This one, though, wasn't too agonizingly drawn out. Just the sound of a creaking door. A rusted hinge squealing shut. Some droning keyboard from my old Casio. Then Nordikron, his normal voice, no deathshriek or anything, reciting a few lines to set the mood:

Centuries ago, the plague burned through the population,
An inferno of disease and decay.
Eating through the ashes . . .

It cut off immediately into the distorted fury of the first song, which starts with Nordikron's strangled cry, "Plaguecorpse rise." Well, to be accurate, it sounded more like, "Pla. . .pla. . .plague corpse rhiiizeeee." It's the plaguecorpse eating its way through the ashes, eating its way back into the world.

Nordikron had clear ideas about what he wanted to convey, but maybe his ideas about English grammar weren't quite as clear and deliberate. On my first listen, though, everything else about the mix seemed about as perfect as possible. If, by "perfect," you meant a sonic evocation of chaos, of imperfection. Tomi's drums resounded in crisp, deep tones. Svart's bass lines rose into the mix—they emerged here and there like plaguecorpses rising from the ancient loam.

The album started with Nordikron's voice, but it didn't overwhelm the recording. Even though he'd insisted on sonically dominating all of us in practice, the final recording displayed his inhuman talent in measured flashes. He towered above the mix here and there, but not at the expense of everything else. The mix maximized the total effect of his jibbering madness.

I listened, taking it in, slowly turning my attention to the guitars. At maximum volume, with both hands clamped around the headphones, I realized the sound wasn't meant to be perfect. That it made no sense to aim for "perfection" in a sonic evocation of chaos, disease, and death, the very forces driving us all toward imperfection. In this way, the guitars complemented Nordikron's voice more effectively than the rhythm section.

That first song contained two competing forces. Tomi and Svart sounded more technically proficient than ever. Tomi was an amazing drummer, but some studio magic elevated his skill, providing a sound that evoked some genetically engineered drumming prodigy, all hands and feet locked in an eternal spasm. He played with a drum machine's technical competence, but with expert fills pilfered straight from Neil Peart. And Svart's bass showed a range and technical prowess that didn't seem possible for such an oafish imbecile. The final mix showcased their talent. It gave Tomi some extra appendages; it gave Svart that rare gift for bassists—a brain. He'd abandoned the murky bass lumbering of those early Desekration demos and maneuvered himself to shine in the limelight.

The guitars also sounded powerful. When I'd listened to that little snippet of *Infernö* at Juan's place, my first impression was that they'd made our guitars sound heavier than they had in rehearsal. The rhythm pulsed through thick and crunchy riffs. The leads evoked sound turning to static and static to fog. But as I sat on the sidewalk, my full attention turned to listening, I focused on the timing, that initial clue that something about the guitars was slightly off, like milk on the very edge of its expiration date. I turned up the volume, cradled the headphones tightly, and that's when I heard the real problem. There were two discernible leads, one buried beneath the other.

One note, the buried note, murmured and, a fraction of a second later, the same sound resounded from some other guitar situated much higher in the mix. As a result, the lead sounded just a bit late. Just a little disjointed. And the rhythm guitars lurched uncomfortably through the song, sometimes a little fast, sometimes a little slow. This part was Juan, though. He just wasn't as proficient as everyone else. And it was easy to figure out what had happened with the leads. The first one, the buried one, that was me. The one you could actually hear, though, well, that was Nekrokor.

The tracks weren't off time or anything. To be fair, most people wouldn't notice anything at all. It's just that the muscle memory I'd honed through all of our practices didn't match the main guitar sound. The reflexive movement of my fingers tapping against the headphones as I listened came out just the slightest instant ahead. I guess the closest way I could describe it would be if you've ever played *Guitar Hero*. You hit the button right before you're supposed to. Instead of "Hanger 18," you get the clang, the discordant jargle, of a misplaced strum.

My fingers, what I thought of as the "right" way to play the song, matched the muffled track, the buried guitar. If you're reading this, you probably know all about it, though. You've read the reviews on Encyclopaedia Metallum. This disjointed, almost off-time sound, paired with Tomi's polyrhythmic perfection, Svart's best Steve Harris impression, is why obscure metal zine obsessives from Wichita to Guatemala described *Infernö* as an album that showed a genre at a crossroads. It showed two different directions black metal could have gone.

It showed the path that succeeded and the path that eventually ended in unheralded obscurity. The bands that made it big became more proficient. They didn't just practice. They trained. Like Tomi in his Powerzaal. Eventually, they took their rightful place in the pantheon of the rock gods. Those are the bands that you can still worship, summer after summer, at some outdoor festival.

But the other path, the parts of the album that sounded like decay, like a gangrene that seeped deep within the music, that was the forgotten path. Even though those were the parts that sounded like Nordikron's lyrics. That sounded like Nordikron's gospel for humanity: desist and die.

About four songs in, the disc stalled out. I just let it play. I figured it would fix itself. I figured it would move past the scratch or something. But I was wrong. Every few seconds, the Discman rumbled like a malfunctioning droid. A stuttering droid. It paused, primed to eject *Infernö* as a flying buzzsaw out into the Belgian night, out into the crowd of Christmas shoppers streaming by.

It never did, though. It just tracked back and started the song again, disc spinning round and round.

Once, the Discman's lid popped up, revealing a whirling *Infernö* straining to free itself.

Maybe they'd engineered it that way, I thought, even though I knew the scratch was my doing. You can't drop a CD on some sandpapery fucked up concrete. I didn't want to own up to it, though. I didn't want to accept the blame for ruining it. For blowing my cash on some useless piece of shit. I mean, the only reason I dropped the thing was because of the case. The thing had just broken as soon as I opened it.

Maybe they'd boobytrapped the case, I thought. All the cases. On purpose. To illustrate the inescapable grasp of death, decay, and faulty plastic. Maybe they'd added the scratch, too. Maybe it hadn't been my dumb ass. I could see Nekrokor with a stack of CDs and his knife, marking each one.

I knew it was my fault, though. Like everything else. The

guitar track, too. It was my fault they buried my guitar track. I'd done something wrong. I'd fucked up. Or I didn't fuck up enough. Too normal. They kicked me out and Nekrokor played over my track. That's why the timing was off. I'm the buried track. And he's the one you can actually hear.

My guitar wasn't the only thing they'd buried. They'd buried me, too. My name. The back cover had a big photo of the whole band. And below that, a list of the dudes and their trumped-up titles:

𝔑ekrokor: 𝔏ead and 𝔠ommander of 𝔘ndead 𝔏egions
𝔑ordikron: 𝔚ailing and 𝔊nashing of 𝔗eeth
𝔖vartikles: 𝔓ulse of the 𝔖ubterranean 𝔓it
𝔗omi: 𝔍ce 𝔎hazm 𝔗remors
𝔅ard of 𝔘nholy 𝔇esires: 𝔑octurnal 𝔈missions

And there, below the picture, below their pompous titles, below the track listing, and right before an enormous list of international distributors, I read the evidence of one other performer—me. It just said, in tiny, barely legible script, "Azrael Le Fevers: Session." I didn't even get a cool font.

The distribution list swelled like the rotten fruit of Nekrokor's incessant labor. He'd been busy. He'd built a multinational web of contacts, probably through his constant tape trading, his constant global mailings of egotistical self-congratulations, death threats, and wart sludge. The back cover listed so many countries where metal freaks could hear the deeply submerged guitar heroics of this insignificant session player. As far as I could tell, though in the flashing glow of the Christmas lights it was hard to make everything out, you could get *Infernö* anywhere in Europe, as far east as Albania. You could get it in Japan, Australia, even South America. Colombia, Argentina, Venezuela. Guerreros de Muerte in Mexico. More importantly, I thought, he had contacts in the US. And not just some randos slinging tapes at the flea market. He had a distribution deal with Plutonic Records. I put my finger underneath that name and slowly spelled it out in my head, hooked on phonics style, just to make sure: Plu-to-nic. My former label.

That's when I pulled myself off the sidewalk. Session. Barely performing on the long-awaited Despondent Abyss release now available in America through underground stalwarts, Plutonic Records. I slipped the Discman back into my bag and shouldered it. I kept the headphones on as I walked. The disc kept skipping. It would get about halfway through "Plaguecorpse Rise," then cycle back. The Discman jostled and vibrated, like a dryer packed with soggy shoes. Anyone walking behind me would have been convinced I had a ravenous Gremlin or something zipped up in my backpack.

When I got home, I turned it off. Took *Infernö* out of the Discman and put it back in the jewel case. Before I shelved it, I sat on the bed and read it again: "Azrael Le Fevers: Session." I looked at the band photo, too, and imagined myself in there somewhere. Maybe hiding in the web of branches that filled the background.

The first thing you notice in the picture is the coffin. The same coffin from the Astrampsychos live shows. The one they'd used to lock up Goathorn and transport him to the very edge of asphyxiation. The same coffin, but with a fresh coat of matte black paint. And without the lid. The same coffin, but filled with bags and bags of dirt, like an elevated bed for aspiring nekrogardeners.

The next thing you notice is the hand coming out of the coffin. Not quite from the middle. A hand without a body, Thing from the Addam's Family rising triumphant from the soil. A hand, pale and pallid, from a plaguecorpse successfully nudged back into this world. A hand emerging from the inferno itself and bringing with it a silver cup brimming with some bilious black fluid.

But that didn't make any sense. Despite Nekrokor's knowledge of occult glyphs and sigils, the kind he'd intersperse with wart remnants in his ritualized curses, the summoning of a disembodied hand wasn't just beyond his skill level, it was a straight up impossibility. The only reasonable explanation was also the simplest: they'd buried Nordikron in the coffin and heaved endless shovelfuls of garden soil on top of him. And that shit in the cup? Probably burbled blood from Nordikron's dead bird excavations. That, or something even grodier.

Juan, in his overcoat and top hat, stood at the head of the coffin. He held a cross in his left hand. Upside down. A crucifix, I guess. The kind with a gold-plated Jesus sprawled across it. A spray of dirt arced from Juan's right hand and onto the open coffin.

Svart and Nekrokor stood behind the coffin, both of their bodies contorted in rough spasms meant to signify total elite metal status.

Svart, shirtless except for his weird He-Man chest belt, flexed for the camera. With maximal flexion, his flab rolls took on the semblance of rippling muscle. His chest harness held it all in place, working like some sort of medieval Spanx.

Tomi kneeled at the foot of the coffin. The trees in the background wound their branches behind and around him. He cast an expressionless gaze at Juan. Or maybe somewhere behind him. He cast an expressionless gaze at a leaf or something in the trees behind Juan.

8.
Proliferation of Ghouls

The day after I bought *Infernö*, listened to it, pored over the affirmation, the repudiation, of my work on the fucking thing—Azrael Le Fevers: Session—all traces of those Astrampsychos posters had disappeared completely from the streets of Gent.

It was like some hulking streetcleaner ravenous for Astrampsychos posters had scrubbed the land overnight. But as I left the Vooruit that morning with a takeaway cup of good old American style drip coffee, I faced the truth. That rumor—Nekrokor's dead—had transformed all these posters into holy relics. Unholy relics.

And that dude I'd seen in front of the Record Huis the day before, gingerly stuffing a piece of music lore into his jacket, well, that wasn't the last megafan I encountered.

I should have seen it coming, I guess. The writing on the wall. Mene, mene, tekel, upharsin. You have been weighed, David Fosberg, and found wanting. While I'd been sitting around ruminating over the shitty band that didn't want me, brooding over my fragile ego, Nekrokor went and made shit happen. He fucking died. Or at least started a rumor about his death. The latter was the more prudent business move, after all. And as a result, Desekration got big after they ditched me. After *Infernö* came out. Most importantly, after this rumor of Nekrokor's death made its way through the local metal scene.

I guess "big" is a bit of an exaggeration. Some of you know your shit—you're going to tell me that *Infernö* was, like, the 232nd best-selling album released the year it came out. Even that's too big. The 232nd best-selling heavy metal album released by an independent label the year it came out. I'm not trying to lie. I'm definitely not trying to make Desekration or Astrampsychos or Despondent Abyss any bigger than they were. Fuck those guys. *Infernö* got big in Belgium, at least. Well, I guess I mean *Infernö* got big in Flanders. To be absolutely truthful, I'll revise it down even more. Desekration got big in Gent. Hometown heroes for a certain benighted and narrowly constrained segment of the teen to post-adolescent market.

And what I'm telling you, my morality tale of a Florida loser stumbling into an obscure black metal band in a third or fourth tier metal scene, well, that's the kind of scenario where metal exerts its strongest pull. Metal pulls you down, pulls you in, the closer you are to its gaping maw. Its gaping maws, each genre, each subgenre, a portal to the world below. And it seemed important to me because I was in Gent. It seemed important to me because I'd come so close to seeming important. It seemed important to me because that time was the closest I got to escaping metal entirely. I almost rejected metal, pulled myself free from its antitrinity of snapping jaws. I almost rejected metal because it had rejected me. That's what this book is about. That's why I had to write a trilogy about heavy metal. About its pull on my soul. I had to get to the time I almost left it behind.

But in Gent, everyone else was going the other way. Jumping into its jaws. Trying to prove themselves as true minions of total death. The guy who snatched the Astrampsychos poster, he was still just a record nerd. Even all those kids in Astrampsychos shirts that night at the Frontline—they were just people stoked on the music. Stoked on the image, too—I cringed when I thought of all the hands touching me when I'd been all dooted up in my nekrogetup, the spikes, the bone crown. The day after I bought *Infernö*, though, I started to see something different. I started to see people trying to become Nekrokor, to become Nordikron. They wanted to follow Nekrokor into the inferno.

I saw the first one, the first disciple, as I walked away from the Vooruit and back to my place. Crossing the bridge down to the Rooseveltplein, I ran my hand along the rail. A thin crust of ice covered the canal below. On the other side of the street, crossing the bridge at the same time, some corpsepainted dude trudged the other direction. A Nordikron clone, a pale mask with painted circles under his eyes, glanced over at me. The corpsepaint matched the picture of Nordikron in the liner notes of *The Intrapsychic Secret.*

This guy, I figured it was Nordikron because of the way he looked over at me, too. His glance took me in, then spit me out. It wasn't the familiar head nod of brotherhood I normally got whenever I passed some other metal miscreant. It was a withering dismissal. A withering dismissal from some dude wearing corpsepaint before 9 a.m. on a Tuesday.

A swarm of elementary school kids crowded behind him. Some teachers and chaperones, too. Everyone in matching white jackets, the teachers and chaperones hoisting little flags. I couldn't tell if it was Nordikron or not. If he hadn't glared over at me, I probably wouldn't have even noticed. I turned around and headed back across the bridge and up the hill, where the Record Huis perched at its crest. In the morning, the sun shines a bright laser ray on the front windows, making them gleam like the sun itself. Everything seemed sharper, clearer, in the cold morning air. Even the urine tang that wafted from a slushy puddle in front of my local nachtwinkel.

You couldn't wear corpsepaint in the morning. There was a rule or something. Nordikron had told me you could only wear corpsepaint at night, you could only wear it when you felt closest to the dead. You could only wear it on the outside when you had opened yourself up, inside, to the reality of death, the inevitability of eternal negation.

Rules or not, I thought the dude probably was Nordikron. The scathing look of non-recognition. The determined shuffle up the hill. Probably going to the Record Huis. Little Mathias out for a morning stroll. But when he got to the top of the hill, he turned away from the Record Huis, heading instead toward the city center. The crowd of kids followed, too. He looked back at me again, his blackened eyes like wet leaves set in a landscape of field trippers, morning shoppers, and business types.

And when the kids, the teachers, engulfed him, I almost turned back. Headed home. Maybe I'd imagined it, I figured. An incongruous phantom haunting the city center on a Tuesday morning? Probably not Nordikron. Or any other black metal fiend. Probably just some lady executive or something. Probably not corpsepaint either, just some drippy mascara. I'd seen wrong. The cold, the ice, it kind of fucked up my sight, froze my eyeballs in my head. And the scathing look, well, that's the kind of look I generally elicit from fancy ladies. From any ladies.

But then he stared back a second time and I guessed it had to be him. It had to be Nordikron. Summoning me or some shit. I figured I'd tail him. Spy on his dark morning errands. See what he gets up to without his employees, his bandmates, around for moral support.

Maybe he was returning to his lair. After a night of graveyard lurking or something. The only reasonable explanation. To sleep the day away. I had no idea where he lived, but I wanted to see it.

He sometimes alluded to some wealthy family he'd left behind: he'd had a live-in nurse as a kid; on top of that, he referred to his parents' house by a name—like, Himmelsgarten or some bullshit. His parents or, let's be real, some 18th century viscount, looked up at this Gucci ass mansion, then told the stonemason to engrave "heaven's garden" over the front door.

Everyone knew he was rich. Whenever the rest of us bitched about being broke, he just kind of smiled and looked into the middle distance. Probably recalling Himmelsgarten's bourgeois splendor.

It had to be Nordikron, I thought. And once all the kids streamed past him, I could make him out more clearly. The yellow hair. Nearly translucent in the glare of the morning sun. He wore an old denim jacket clutched tight around his neck to brace him from the chill air pushing down through the street. Clutched tight to brace him from the sun itself. The coffee kicked in and I quickly closed the distance between us; about ten feet behind him, I could see the back of his jacket. Any doubts I had dissipated. Of course it was him. Who else would wear a jacket with a full Astrampsychos back patch? I didn't think Despondent Abyss even sold anything like that. As I closed in, I could tell it was the graphic from an Astrampsychos shirt, cut out and meticulously sewed to the jacket. It had the scrawled rhizomic logo right across the shoulders. Below that, the cosmic pentagram from the cover of *The Intrapsychic Secret*. Ptolemy's universe of nested spheres scratched through with the inverted Solomon's seal of Satanic dominion. Running along the bottom, a lyric from "The Inmost Sanctum": "He who is, and was, and always shall be."

The sidewalks on Sint Pietersnieuwstraat swelled with shoppers. I dodged a gang of teenage girls headed toward Shoe's Victim, then darted around an old man smoking a pipe. Passing an Apotheek, I rubbed my thumb against my wart finger's bouldered ridge and resolved to pick up more medicine later in the day. I wasn't in the band anymore, but I still wore the mark.

I hustled through the crowd. I didn't want to lose him. I wanted to see the upscale building where he lived. Catch a glimpse, somehow, of the ultraluxe condo he called home. Probably some high modern fantasy of marble and granite beneath cathedral ceilings. Probably unfurnished except for a coffin filled with Himmelsgarten's nourishing soil.

And that's when he disappeared. I trotted along, my head swiveling in all directions. The mob of students kept going straight, down to the cathedral. And then I spotted my quarry. He'd turned off the main street and followed a lane bordered by a narrow canal. I closed in, his mop of piss blond hair right in my reach. But there, without the crowds around, that's when I knew for sure. It wasn't Nordikron. It wasn't anyone I knew. I should have known, but I'm a little slow. Especially in the morning. I guess by the time all the schoolkids dispersed, the coffee finally got my mind moving.

There were a bunch of clues, but I hadn't noticed them at first. The first clue was the cape. Its absence. The guy didn't have a cape. He had that denim jacket. Still too light and flimsy for me—I had on a wool beanie, my abiban jacket, and at least four layers of shirts underneath—but Nordikron rarely wore anything other than a cape and a shirt, usually Venom, sometimes Hellhammer, maybe a moth-eaten undershirt. And he refused to wear anything from his own bands. That was the second clue. The band merch. Nordikron agreed with Nekrokor on this one. Merchandise existed, Nekrokor liked to say, to mark the fans as yours. That thing you sold them is a sign that you own them. To show that you own them, they own something you sold them.

And that was the other thing, I thought, close enough to the guy to see the even, careful stitching that attached the Astrampsychos picture to the jacket, the perfect line where the perfectly cut cotton met the jacket seam. This guy radiated cleanness. And health. That jacket, I determined, had never been buried in a cemetery. I inhaled deeply. The guy emanated a woodland scented vapor trail that lingered long after he passed. But Nordikron, to my knowledge, never bathed. And he had some total death philosophy to rationalize his filthiness. I remember him once saying the true purveyor of death would never knowingly remove all the dead cells continuously sloughed off by your body, all the flesh starved microbes on your skin, all the flesh starved microbes continuously feasting on your skin as it sloughs off in an endless cycle. Society used cleanliness, he said, to mark a boundary between the living and the dead; anything you did to strengthen that boundary just testified to your unworthiness to play, listen to, or otherwise consume the metal of death.

This guy dressed up like Nordikron did not follow that philosophy. I lifted my arm and surreptitiously sniffed my pit. He smelled better than me, no question. Even filtered through five layers of clothes. He smelled better than any of us. I sniffed my wart finger. He smelled better than Maria, too.

I bent to retie my shoe. Open up a little space between me and my quarry. It wasn't Nordikron, but I still didn't understand why some dude was running around Gent in black metal warpaint. Ahead, he stopped in front of a small coffee shop. A girl in a white skirt and a black turtleneck came out of the shop, a chunky camera slung around her neck.

He gestured to his get up, then struck a stance I'd seen Nordikron do a thousand times before: legs spread wide, a contorted fist held aloft to threaten the very heavens, a constipated grimace of existential agony on his face.

The girl snapped a couple shots, then laughed.

That never happened for Nordikron, though. A pretty girl smiling in his presence. It hadn't really happened like that for me in a while either, I mused.

She took the guy by the hand, the one that, just seconds before, he'd raised as a fist in the face of God, and led him into the coffee shop.

That was the first one. Not the only one. Before long, scores of corpsepainted ghouls—sometimes alone, sometimes in small groups—lurked the Gentian streets. I mean, this first guy, he was no ghoul. He had the gear, the warpaint. He had the Satanic voguing dialed. But a true ghoul, Nordikron or Nekrokor, held himself to a higher standard. Or a lower standard. Hard to keep track. What I mean is that the true ghoul eschewed dress up games to impress the ladies. Juan might approve. He'd never turn down a Glamour Shots session followed by a delightful peppermint mocha. He'd invite himself along. He'd somehow entered the ranks of elite ghouldom even though he didn't know the rules. But he's a special case.

They weren't all so mannerly and well-adjusted, this proliferation of Astrampsychos devotees. This deluge of Desekration adherents. Just a few days later, I was out by De Verloren Hemel, the goth pub. The Apotheek by my place sent me to a bigger Apotheek out on the other side of town. I needed some extra strength shit for my wart finger and that was the place to get it.

A Bardic impersonator stepped out of the goth pub. I raised my hand to wave, then awkwardly shoved it back in my pocket. He had a top hat perched on a mantle of black flowing tresses. He had the corpsepaint, styled just like Juan's in the *Infernö* band photo. He had the trench coat, knee-length and accessorized with spikes. Desekration shirt. Leather pants. The Mad Max boots, too. Thick soled and spangled with silver buckles.

Just like the other guy, though, his costume wasn't completely authentic. It only took me a second this time, a quick moment to play off my friendly wave. He had the wrong hat— that's what tipped me off. It had a big ding on the side. Cheap felt, and not the worn beaver pelt or whatever that Juan affected. Also, it only had a black ribbon around the brim. No dessicated flowers, no mementos of nocturnal romance.

It wasn't that late in the day, not even three, but he teetered down the steps like he'd had more than his fair share of the goth pub's specialty, a cloudy mix of absinthe, juice, and grenadine they called the Disintegration. Well, in Dutch. Het Disintegration. The liquors mixed into a turquoise and purple haze like the album cover. If you had a few, they said, Robert Smith's disembodied hairdo appeared to you in a hallucinogenic vision.

He stepped onto the sidewalk and almost ran into an old woman walking her dog. Het Disintegration was pretty strong stuff. The dog started barking at the guy. I recognized the woman—or I thought I did. Thin and bent by age, like some crooked driftwood, she walked the Rooseveltlaan regularly. She generally rocked tracksuits spangled with beads and bright patches of color. Fashion track suits for the old and wealthy. The one she wore had vast lavender and orange panels topped with unfurling fiddler ferns shaped from thick swirls of golden glitter paint.

I definitely knew the dog. Natasha had the same kind. A spaniel dachshund mix. Long and beige, with fluffy ears and a dustmop tail. A cocker wiener. Every time I passed this lady and her dog, it did the same thing it did to this Bardic clone: it snapped into a steady yapping. Must hate metalheads. I never body checked its owner, though.

The guy glared down at the lady and the dog. No "alstublief" or anything. Very un-Belgian. He tilted on one leg and raised his foot, his fearsome boot, right over the dog's back. The lady's eyes widened. She pulled hard on the leash. But the dog didn't budge. It kept yapping, its legs locked in place.

His foot came down. He stomped the ground. Inches from the dog's fluffy yapping head. Then he bent down. Not too far, though. Hard to maneuver when you're ultrawasted and wearing a giant top hat. He unleashed a reptilian death hiss— not quite up to Nordikron's caliber, but a fair imitation. A saliva tendril spooled from his gaping mouth and onto the cocker wiener's head.

By that point, I was one or two strides away from this situation. The moment for heroism. To make the right choice, stand up for my Rooseveltlaan compatriot, and put this fucking idiot in his place. To be clear: it was the time to help the old lady. Help the dog. Rebuke my metal brother. Even though I was close enough that, still barking, the dog had swiveled its spit-soaked head in my direction.

But I didn't. I walked right past them. The lady could handle this fool on her own. She unleashed a long diatribe against the guy. I don't know what she said. I just know she pointed a curved and rheumatic finger at him the whole time. And it snapped him out of it. Snapped him out of a power fantasy instilled through some combination of absinthe and, well, our fucking music which, to be honest, probably played the larger role in his behavior.

Before I turned the corner, I looked back. The lady kept going. You should never fuck with someone in a track suit. Just common sense. By this point, he'd taken off his top hat.

"Het spijt mij," he said. More than once. I knew that phrase—"I'm sorry," he said repeatedly.

Maybe this guy isn't so different from Juan after all, I thought. The dog stopped barking. It rested its paws on top of his steel-tipped toes. Its pink tongue lapped some stain on his leather pants.

If he'd been temporarily possessed by Nekrokor's spirit, what I'd just witnessed confirmed the limitations of that power.

9.
Overleden

After that, I saw them everywhere. Ravening hordes infiltrating the city. Astrampsychos clones. Desekration drones. I saw them wherever I went. On the square in front of St. Baafskathedraal. Out on the street by the university. Sitting together on the banks of the river running through the city center. Maybe not "ravening." More like loitering. Groups of kids, some corpsepainted, each one clad almost uniformly in either an Astrampsychos shirt or a Desekration shirt. The Astrampsychos shirt for *The Intrapsychic Secret*, with the cosmic pentagram on the front, and the phrase "He who is, and was, and always shall be" on the back. Or an *Infernö* shirt, Juan's new logo and the plague doctor emanating black flames emblazoned across the front. And on the back, just that band picture of them all. The hand rising from the coffin. The hand holding the chalice. And below that, the song title, "Plaguecorpse Rise."

Everywhere I went, the streets were littered with kids in Despondent Abyss gear. It was like Nordikron had commandeered Santa's sleigh. All the disaffected kids in Gent got Astrampsychos and Desekration shirts to rock in the new year. Me? I'd spent the holidays alone. My parents sent me a card.

All these kids, I thought. They must have heard the rumor.

Nekrokor's dead. I wouldn't believe it until I saw some evidence. The kids, though. They believed it. And their belief translated into a massive spike in Despondent Abyss merch sales. The Record Huis had to be cashing in, too. A group of black metal fiends congregated there daily.

I didn't care, though. Or that's what I told myself. Once I saw how I'd been pretty much erased—Azrael Le Fevers: Session—I started to enjoy my new and advanced level of aimless existence. Before Maria moved into my place. Before my fun time Dutch-for-tourists class began. I started to enjoy my aimlessness except when something reminded me of all this band shit, of Astrampsychos, of Desekration. Which was pretty much every hour or so on my aimless days spent wandering the city alone. Still, I settled on a plan. A way to get past this limbo. I'd do the Dutch class, beg my parents for some money, stay around long enough for Natasha to come and visit. And then I'd go back home. Go back to Miami. I'd start something new. I knew I'd probably have to grovel my way back into Booksalot thralldom, but maybe I'd go to school. Maybe I'd ask Natasha to marry me. Maybe I'd let go of the ancient dream. Maybe I'd let go of this metal dream of musical immortality. If I was so fucking normal, I figured, then maybe I'd do just that—I'd embrace my terrible normality.

In those last days before Maria moved in, I found lots of ways to stretch out the day. I began to savor my last days of unemployment. I mean, being in a band doesn't really count as "employment," but it was my purpose. Whatever that means. It was a path I had been employed in pursuing. But this path had diverged from my purpose driven life. Maybe it's better to say I was unpurposed? Anyway, when you're unemployed, unpurposed, or otherwise off the path, you find lots of ways to stretch out the day. Like figuring out the exact right word to describe the plight of your sorry broke ass.

Really, once I woke up, I wondered how long it would take before the sun went down and I could start the cycle all over again. And in the Belgian winter, most of that cycle occurs in a permanent darkness punctuated by the brief gray blur of day. At least, that's how it seemed to me.

So I tried to stretch out all the menial chores of my existence. With few real responsibilities, this was sometimes a challenge. Trips to and from the grocery store took up vast expanses of time. I had a detailed mental map of the store's beer inventory.

One day, I stepped into the store and headed over to the beer section. And as I breezed past all the shit at the front of the store, the flowers, a pasta sauce display, the news rack, I had this strange sensation of being watched. An uncanny feeling, the kind produced by some fatal portrait in a haunted house, one whose eyes followed the movements of the living.

I almost made it all the way past the row of newspapers before I figured it out. About ten pictures of Nekrokor splayed across the front pages of all the local papers. The pictures themselves varied in size and level of grainy pixelation, but all the newspapers used the same photo. And I guess this repetition, paired with my familiarity with the picture, combined to make me feel like I was being watched, judged, on my not-quite-noon beer run.

The picture came from the liner notes of *The Intrapsychic Secret*. Nekrokor, bare chested, his arms covered in acid charred scabs. The headlines were all slightly different, but the message was the same: "Black metaal musicus 'Nekrokor' overleden is." Even though we hadn't encountered "overleden" in any niveau een lesson, I knew what the headlines said. It was what every metalhead in Gent already knew: Nekrokor's dead. Well, everyone but me.

I edged past a tower of pasta sauce jars and positioned myself in front of a rack of local papers.

I stood there with the paper about six inches from my face, my index finger tracing each word. This was important news. I needed to absorb it completely. I wanted to make sure I hadn't missed anything.

The story seemed simple enough. His body had been

found down by the Coupure Links. A woman jogging on the bike path found him in the shallow water at the edge of the canal. After an examination that uncovered no evidence of foul play, the authorities released the body to Nekrokor's legal guardian. I guess once you die, you don't really need an evil pseudonym: the authorities released the body to Bård's legal guardian. And that was it. They didn't haul us all in for questioning. They didn't douse the trees where they found him with fingerprinting dust. None of that CSI shit. They just turned over the body and speculated that he had a weak heart or something. Some weird congenital thing.

The rest of the coverage focused more on black metal itself. They brought up all the stuff that happened in Norway. Some psychologist had an advice column on how to deprogram kids who'd developed an unhealthy fascination with metal. The psychologist suggested replacing the metal discs with something else. Something edgy, but more mainstream, more "normaal."

And as I skimmed through this ten-step guide to de-metalfication, I wondered if the authorities were right. It seemed hard to believe that Bård, so alive in his embrace of total death, suffered from a weak heart. And the place where they found him—the Coupere Links—I knew it well. It was just a block or so from Svart's place. A canal flanked by tall trees and a bike path. It lay just over the bridge from De Verloren Hemel, Juan's favorite hangout.

Somewhere off to my side, a little kid shuffled toward me. She had on a Smurfs shirt, pigtails. I had on my Unleashed shirt beneath my unzipped jacket. I probably reeked of old beer and body odor. I wasn't sure why she'd willingly come toward me. There were some comics on the lower shelf, though, so I figured she was going for those. I scooted over a bit to get out of her way, but she came closer. Her fingers brushed my legs and after a few seconds, she clamped onto my shin to steady herself. I shuffled over to the side some more, trying discreetly to dislodge her.

Then, I lowered my paper and looked around, hoping to locate a parent or something. And over where the newspapers ended and the magazines began, a woman in black jeans and a striped top frantically jammed Belgian *Vogue* into the rack and dashed at me, a look of abject horror on her face.

I smirked. That was the reaction I expected. The kind that had psychologists filling the papers with articles on the dangers of heavy metal. Like I was a monster or something. But when the mom grabbed the girl and hoisted her away from me, she also unhooked a glass jar of pasta sauce from the girl's grasp. In a quick instant, she gently took it from the girl, then put it in her shopping cart.

The mom gave me a conspiratorial grin, then headed off to the produce section. I put my newspaper away, then noticed an empty space, the missing jar, at the bottom level of the pasta sauce tower right beside me.

"Damn," I said. If the girl had grabbed that jar with a little more force, a whole Jenga tower of glass would have collapsed on my slovenly ass.

And then, I thought, strolling away from the newspapers and resuming my beer quest, I'd be overleden, too.

10.
A Better Relationship

When I came back from that beer run, that's when I found Maria on my doorstep. That's when she finagled her way into my place. And the cold fear of paternity that gripped me the second I saw her kind of replaced whatever shock I felt after immersing myself in all available news reports of Nekrokor's untimely demise.

Once Maria moved in, though, the news about Nekrokor—about Bård—helped to bring us together. It's not like I was sad or broken up about him. I mean, I still thought the dude was a dick. Vaguely menacing, even though, overall, he'd helped me out.

A few nights after she moved in, Maria and I sat next to each other in bed. She cradled a Grimbergen bottle between her thighs. I held mine, feeling the cold glass in my palms. A few empties sat scattered across the bedside table.

Maria had just taken a shower, combed her hair. It hung, long and straight, over her shoulders. She had on my Katabasis shirt and a pair of my boxer shorts. Green polka dots.

"If only he'd died before kicking me out of the band," I mused.

"That's an asshole thing to say," she said and then sipped her beer.

I knew she was joking, though. In those early days, I felt

connected to her. In those early nights, we shared so much about our lives.

After she moved in, that became the routine. I'd make dinner, then we'd sit in bed and drink. She couldn't afford her rent, but she still went to work every day. They'd demoted her or something. Cut her pay. She still had a job, she still worked full time, just for less cash. She'd tell me about her job, how she fucked up on a performance review or something, some supervisor had it in for her, and then they moved her down to a different department. After a few nights, her stories went deeper. Into her past. She told me about all the abuse, neglect, and horrible struggles she'd faced growing up in a broken home.

It felt right, sharing the bad shit, caring about her problems. It felt real. A better relationship. More mature than what I'd had with Natasha. Than what I have, I corrected myself, sipping my Grimbergen.

The first couple of nights like that had me thinking I'd get another phone card. Call Natasha when Maria was at work. Call it all off. Call it quits with Natasha. I started to think Maria was right for me. More real. I'd started dating her purely out of sexual desperation. But maybe that was a good thing? Like, she wasn't on this pedestal. I reached over and squeezed her thigh. It felt firm. Real. My dick stirred. A conditioned response. I knew she'd let me do it. I knew she'd want to do it, too. And I knew there was no rush. She wasn't going anywhere. I let her talk. She'd spent the afternoon in a warehouse looking for the wrong part because someone had screwed up an invoice or something. Her supervisor had bitched her out before she left for the day.

The first few nights of living with a girl had been like that. Sitting together. Drinking some beers. Sharing the things that mattered. Sharing the little struggles of each day. She let down her guard. Told me things that no one else knew. I tried to do the same.

I told her about Miami, about the hurricane. How it had

destroyed my house. Hauled away everything from my childhood in one briny surge. All the comic books and Dungeons and Dragons modules soaked into pulp. The keys on the piano so tempest swelled I had to use my elbow, not my fingers, to make a sound. The weird sounds, a random series of drowned notes, coming from inside the piano. Sounds I hadn't made by mashing my elbow down on the keys. The way I opened the lid of the piano and found it filled with water and home to a catfish swimming frantic circles, its tail slapping the strings. I told her how the hurricane had destroyed everything except my music: I'd put all my records, CDs, tapes, in the top of my closet and the storm gods, Cthulhu in his infinite guises, had spared them. I'd stored my guitar in the car and the ancient ones spared it, too.

She told me about her dad. The cocaine cowboy. How he'd raised her on his own. She told me how fucked up it had been. He took care of her, saved her from something even worse that she'd hint at, but never explore. He'd saved her, but then abandoned her, left her to fend for herself. In middle school, she came home one day to see the police guiding her dad, handcuffed, out of their flat. He said, "Don't worry. I'll be home no later than tomorrow," but then he'd spent the next six months in jail. Somehow, the bills and everything took care of themselves. She was too young, that first time, to question it. She just kept going to school, coming home, again and again until one day her dad came back.

Another time, when she was in high school, he'd disappeared for a year. I asked if he was in jail again, but she said it was even worse. He'd gone to South America. Got involved in really shady business. Someday, she promised, she'd tell me all about it. But when it happened, when he fled the country, she hadn't even known. That time, no one, no adult, kept up with the bills. That time, she'd left the apartment for the streets. The landlord came, she said, but not to help. He told her he'd let her stay for a blow job. She refused. He was old and fat, she said. He smelled like cheese. Even though she turned him down, he pulled his dick out and stood in the doorway to her room, jerking off while she packed a bag.

"He splooged on my arm when I pushed past him. All over my bag, too. I lived out of that bag for months. Well," she went on, "I didn't actually live out of it. But it had everything I owned. I lived with anarchist squatters. Gutter punks. In an abandoned factory. It's not far from here. It's still a squat, too. It's around the corner from St. Baafs."

She chugged the rest of her beer, then reached over me and grabbed a cigarette from the pack on the bedside table. The first day she moved in, I told her not to smoke inside. The second day, she came home from work and lit up as soon as she closed the door. I stopped saying anything about it; I figured this was one of those compromises people make in mature relationships.

"The squat. Sometimes I miss the place," she said. She lit up and took a deep drag.

"I started smoking when I lived there. Because there was never any food. When there was, a lot of it was rotten. We hit the dumpsters. And the punks liked it that way. The food . . . it was no longer a commodity item. No longer part of the capitalist system."

She ashed into the empty beer bottle.

The stories about her past made my problems seem trivial, inconsequential.

My parents expressed a glib snarkiness about heavy metal.

Her dad spent her childhood in and out of jail.

I kept getting dumped by bands—first Valhalla, now Desekration—and no one took the time to comfort me, shepherd me in my time of loss.

She got dumped by her own parents, who expressed no concern that their fifteen-year-old daughter shared dumpster rations with a crew of dreadlocked Morlocks.

When you got her going, the stories of all the shit she'd been through just kept coming. At first, we'd been able to match each other, story for story. My sucky childhood versus hers. But I soon had nothing else to add. My complaints seemed so minor. My experiences so limited.

Once, she said, some city government officers barged into the squat.

"To kick you out?" I asked.

"They tried, but they couldn't. The squatters were too smart. One of the guys, he had a law degree. You'd never know it. Wore the same jean shorts every day. Three nose rings. Had a giant Crass tattoo on his chest. But he knew our rights. They couldn't kick us out. So instead . . . since the building was an old factory . . . the city supplied us with food if we spent a couple hours every day working. They put together a little workspace where we made lunches for all the poor people in the region."

"And then they let you stay?"

"Yes. And we didn't have to eat from the dumpster."

"You said your dad wasn't around. In and out of jail. I get that."

"Yah."

"But where was your mom?" I asked. "I mean, fifteen's kind of young to live in a commune."

"My mother," she said, eyes downcast, staring down the barrel of the Grimbergen, a tendril of smoke rising up from the cigarette butt she'd just thrown in there.

"Yeah, your mom. What about her?"

I guess I shouldn't have asked. Maybe that's when I realized all this sharing, all these stories, weren't necessarily the foundation of a strong relationship. Maybe I didn't do anything wrong at all. If her dad was a deadbeat, then you'd figure there'd be a mom around somewhere.

She got out of bed, slipped on her jacket, and took her cigarettes out onto the terrace. She stayed there for hours. She came in once to put on more clothes. It was freezing.

I tried to go out there with her. To comfort her. Because this was a mature relationship. That's what you're supposed to do, right? When I sat next to her, my arms almost on her shoulders, she turned and blew a smoke cloud at my face. She said, "Go away. I need to be alone right now."

I went inside. You're supposed to listen, too. That's another hallmark of the mature relationship. I went back in and eventually fell asleep. She came in at some time in the night. I didn't hear her, though. But I woke up pretty early—like five a.m or something—the next day. She'd just left the patio door open all night. I woke up freezing, a damp cold seeping into my uncovered body. She'd yanked the comforter away from me at some point in the night.

I got up to close the door, then put on my jacket. I stood in the kitchen and made some coffee. While I waited for it to brew, I exhaled, my cloud of breath clearly visible in the frigid air. Around seven, I no longer felt so frozen. Sunlight poked through the windows. I picked up the guitar and started messing around, a series of listless scales, riffs from *Infernö* songs. She should have been up. It was a weekday.

Closer to eight, I shook her awake. Asked her about work. She just groaned and pulled the cover over her head. She stayed in bed like that for hours. I eventually left because it was too awkward for me. She couldn't have been sleeping. Just lying around, unresponsive. I went for a long walk. I must have passed twenty nachtwinkels, but I did not buy a phone card. I'd put my plan to dump Natasha on hold.

When I came back after lunch, Maria still lay there, a lump under the comforter. She must have been up at some point, though. The air reeked of cigarette smoke. A few more empties sat on the bedside table.

11.
Dubbelbuiten

My Dutch class gave me a reason to escape my apartment. We met in the same classroom I'd had before. For niveau een. The desks formed a big square and, when I stepped in, Helena stood in the center with a chalkboard behind her. She had on red tights and a brown leather jacket. I tried to catch her eye, let her know her best student was back, but she was sorting through a stack of papers.

There weren't a lot of students. I recognized a few from my last class. Most of them were older. Some of them looked like retirees.

I sat down and splayed the textbook, a dictionary, and a notebook across my desk. While I waited, I took out my pen and started absentmindedly doodling a Desekration logo. Gouging all those spikes and shit into a piece of paper helped with the tension I was starting to feel from Maria's constant presence at my place.

An Egyptian guy who had been in niveau een came over and sat next to me. He took off a satchel made out of goat hide or something. It had a leather handle where the goat's shoulder blades had been. I recognized the satchel, too. It had also been in niveau een. After he pulled out his books, he leaned over and tapped my shoulder.

"That's a cool drawing, man," he said.

"Thanks," I said, then instantly felt self-conscious for drawing band logos at all. Like a junior high burnout or something. I felt self-conscious for drawing that band logo especially. The logo of the band that rejected me. I started scribbling through it, letter by letter, the whole thing scrawled over in countless ink gashes.

Helena picked up a stack of papers and strutted to the head of the class. Her curly hair hung wet on her shoulders, like she'd just taken a shower. I imagined her stepping out of the shower, water dripping off her hair, her body. My dick swelled slowly, a garden hose filling with water. Maybe I'd ask her out, I thought, then remembered Maria languishing in my apartment, and then I remembered Natasha, only a telephone call away.

And then Helena inhaled or something, some barely perceptible movement that drew everyone's attention to her. She started class by saying, "This is Nederlandse for buitenlanders."

She paused. Then she repeated that last word. It was direct and off-putting. Like Helena herself. I may have had a crush on her, but she also scared me.

"Buitenlanders. Foreigners. Not for people who live here permanently. If you are a native speaker, you should take a cultural class through the local community center."

After she said that, a gray-haired couple got up and left the room.

"Sometimes," she said, "locals sign up for this class to get free admission and tours to the places we're going."

She smiled. "You all are getting quite a good deal with this class. You'll just have to stop by the main school office later today to pick up the pass that you'll use to get in everywhere."

Then, Helena handed out a schedule for the class. A packet of worksheets, too.

She explained that most of the time, we'd meet at the places on the schedule. Our tuition covered all the entrance fees, she said. We just needed to flash the city pass we'd get for being in the class. If we had a problem getting in, we were supposed to say we were from the language school.

"Remember to say this all in good Nederlandse," she said, then laughed as if she'd suggested something impossible.

Basically, we'd go on a tour, answer a worksheet with a bunch of questions about the place, then present what we wrote at the following class meeting. On the face of it, this class seemed easier than the last one. It would take less time. And I didn't have to just memorize a bunch of vocabulary.

But after our first activity, I realized it could be more challenging. We didn't have to memorize word lists, but we had to come up with words on our own. We had to express more complex ideas using words we hadn't covered in our rudimentary lessons on daily routines and states of being.

After she passed everything out, Helena said, "Our first trip later this week is to St. Baafskathedraal. There is a lot there. So much that we're going twice this semester. St. Baaf's is one of our city's most important—most belangrijk—sights."

I knew the word "belangrijk." We'd learned it before in niveau een. Nederlandse is een heel belangrijk taal. Dutch is a very important language. But I quickly saw the difference in her approach for a new class. Instead of endlessly berating our translations, she told us to split the word into its components.

"'Rijk,'" she said, "sounds like 'rich' in English and can mean 'full.' But it can also mean 'realm' or 'kingdom.' Like that store down the street that sells mattresses. The 'slaaprijk,' or 'sleep kingdom.'"

"Some of you should go there. To your local slaaprijk," she said, and then she put on an American frat boy accent. "Instead of getting wasted with your bros every night."

I groaned, loud enough for her to hear.

The Egyptian guy reached over and lightly punched my shoulder.

"Party time," he said, grinning wildly.

"We can learn from the language all around us," she said, then clapped her hands together. "In this class, we are going to some of the major sights of this city. And instead of 'sights,' we might use this word instead: bezienswaardigheden."

She said it a few times, annunciating slowly and writing it on the chalkboard behind her.

"I know it is a long one, but it is made up of smaller parts. Take your dictionaries and see if you can break it into its various components."

I flipped through mine and jotted down a phrase.

"A view-true-ness?" I said.

"Not quite," she said. "Americans—quick to speak up, even when they're wrong."

After the laughter died down, she continued.

"'Waar' is true, but 'waardig' means worthy. The places we're going—some more than once—are very belangrijk. They are very important for their cultural significance. As we go to these places, we are going to encounter many opportunities for improving our language skills. A 'bezienswaardigheid,' then, is a place that has view worthiness. It is worth being seen. This may be a class for buitenlanders—for outside landers—but by exploring these places and responding to them in Nederlandse, you will learn not just language, but also culture."

I'd kind of signed up half-heartedly for the class, but hearing her talk about it more made me think it might help me. Get me out of my funk.

"Alright," she said. "We've got a short introduction activity and then we're done for the day. For introductions, I want you all to make up a compound word that describes you in some way. Put together the words you know. What you come up with doesn't have to be a real word. But it should describe something about you. In a few minutes, I'll want you to tell us your name and your compound word."

When she came to me, I gave her my best invented compound.

"Ik heet David. Ik ben een buiten-gitaar-speler. An outside guitar player," I explained. "I got kicked out of my band."

She smirked.

"Harsh, bro," she said, then moved on to the guy next to me.

"Ik heet Abdul." He rattled off a few more sentences in some heel advanced Nederlandse: he was from Egypt, a small town named Siwa. Alexander the Great went there long ago. It was famous for its oracle of Amon. I perked up, reflexively curling my fingers into the horns. Amon. King Diamond's falsetto came unbidden into my mind: Amon belongs to Them now.

He would have gone on more, but Helena cut him off. Had him get to the point.

"Heel interesaant," she said. "And what is your compound?"

He answered in English.

"I've been here awhile. But I will always be a buitenlander. Sometimes," he said, "the Belgiums make me feel extra buiten. I feel dubbelbuiten. Double outside."

"Dubbelbuiten," she said. "That's . . . that's very deep."

She talked some more about his example, how this class was about broadening our vocabulary, our understanding of language and culture.

As everyone packed up, Helena lifted her voice above the din: "Remember to pick up your city passes later today. And guard yours well—it is your key to the city!"

I kind of felt bad for Abdul. We started talking after class. He'd been here trying to set up a business so he could help his family, all the people in his village. And he regularly encountered bullshit. But he seemed so positive. I kind of felt bad for what I'd said, too. How weak. I'd been knocked down so easily. I'd let a bunch of assholes make me think of myself as "buiten." But Abdul had faced worse things. For higher stakes. And he'd stuck to his goal, stayed positive, learned the language in a place that saw him as dubbelbuiten. By contrast, I'd failed at my pointless and totally self-interested goal of playing antisocial music that most people regarded as noise.

I figured I'd stop by home for lunch. I'd go to get the city pass later in the afternoon. Maria'd probably be at work. I'd have an afternoon alone, maybe play some guitar. Jack off. Listen to some music. Drink a beer. No matter the activity, the prospect of some solo time seemed like an illicit treat.

But when I got home, there she was. Maria. Sitting on my doorstep. Smoking. Again.

"Oh my God," I muttered. I couldn't escape this ... this ... and here my re-immersion in the world of Nederlandse inspired me—I couldn't escape this buitenrooker, this outside smoker.

She eased off the floor.

"You're finally here," she said, then exhaled.

She pulled the cigarette out of her mouth and smooshed it out on the doorframe. The part Nordikron had once smeared with blood. I'd cleared it off. But the paint on the edge, right by your head when you walk through, still had a slight brown sheen to it. And, after Maria finished grinding her cigarette, it had a huge black mark, too.

I kind of glared at her, gesturing at the mark in frustration.

"I got locked out," she said. "I came out here to smoke, but I left my keys inside. The door shut."

"Oh. I've got mine," I said. Since she never acknowledged anything wrong that she ever did, I also started to gloss over anytime she pissed me off. As I reached in my pocket, though, I decided to make a stronger statement about her constant smoking. "It sucks you got locked out, but ... uhh ... I don't think the neighbors like you smoking out here."

I guess I wasn't direct enough. I should have said I didn't like her smoking out there. I didn't like her smoking in my apartment. Or on the balcony. Fucking up my doorframe. The whole floor smelled like smoke. I smelled like smoke. My clothes smelled like smoke, which I really resented because I hated doing laundry.

But she didn't listen. The buitenrooker. She ignored my antismoking message. She didn't even pick up the cigarette butts. Just kicked them closer to the neighbor's door.

She pulled a fresh cigarette out of the pack and lit it.

"My dad, he called me," she said. "I got some bad news."

I guess this was her justification.

"He told me they were going to send him to jail in South America," she continued. "Unless I wire him some money."

I opened the door and she followed me inside. She exhaled across my back as we stepped into the crammed kitchen. There was no difference between the smell outside and inside. She wasn't just a buitenrooker. She was an inside smoker. A binnenrooker. And that was even worse. I heaved out an exaggerated cough. Maria ignored it and told me more about the call. She said she needed a pretty sizable wad of cash to cover some legal expenses. A thousand bucks. To prevent them from extraditing her dad overseas. Or something. I couldn't quite follow the explanation. She wanted to borrow some money, though. That part was clear.

"It wouldn't be for long," she said. "I can pay it back."

I gave a vague grunt. Money I didn't have. For this fucking binnenrooker. Money I wouldn't have if I gave it to her. If she couldn't even pay me rent, there was no way she'd be able to pay me back.

She asked me again. She went on about her dad and his fraught situation. Arrested, now facing stronger charges. Facing the horrors of a third-world prison. Unless I stepped up to help.

"I can't do that," I said. "I wish I could. It sounds really bad. But if I give you that money, I'll go broke. I won't have a place . . . you won't have a place."

I guess we'd gotten to a deeper level of intimacy in our relationship than I was aware of. If by "intimacy," you mean the unfettered expression of negative emotion. Before this, before she'd moved in, Maria had been so cool. So aloof. More distant than me, which is saying something. But now that she'd been living in my place for a few weeks, spending her nights regaling me with dark tales of her horrific past, her coke snorting dad, the time she scored twenty perfectly good tubs of hummus from the Delhaize dumpster, something had changed.

And when I told her I couldn't give her any money, I realized I was no longer dating the old Maria. I was dating someone new. Someone who would immediately burst into tears because I didn't have a thousand dollars lying around for her, someone who stammered through another dark tale of her horrific past, telling me that the time her landlord propositioned her had made her permanently insecure. She confessed she looked tough, but that was all a front. She was always afraid the bottom could drop out at any moment, that one wrong move would have her living on the street again, and my unwillingness to give her money she knew I had just dredged up those old feelings. She told me, her face now as red as it had been that day I'd found her on my doorstep or that other time I'd seen her weeping outside the McDonald's, that withholding this money from her was hurtful, like a violence against her, because it made her relive the abandonment she'd told me about so many times before. Even worse, she didn't understand how I could do that since she'd shared all her experiences of abandonment with me.

I felt trapped. What she said didn't make sense. And the way she acted—this wasn't the Maria I knew. It all disoriented me. I had no way of reestablishing the fundamentals of the situation: I'd let her live with me, I had limited money, I hadn't been the one who made her live on the streets at some point years ago. And yet, as she cried and ranted, I began to believe, somehow, I was to blame. I began to believe I had an obligation to give her the money. To help her dad.

I had nowhere to go. The apartment was tiny, so tiny. If I didn't get away, I knew I'd do what she wanted. I started to think this weird transformation in Maria's personality was all my doing, that she'd become like this because of her time living with me.

Luckily, I still retained some small rational part of my mind. As she talked, I slowly eased away from her. I moved into the kitchen. It snapped me out of her spell. But then she started to follow me. She was in the middle of a sentence—"I came here because I needed your protection, but . . ."—when I grabbed my keys.

"I have to do some shit for my class," I interjected, then headed out. As I locked the door, I could still hear her crying inside. I realized I was locking her in. I was locking her inside. Binnen. Locking her into my place. Locking her, I thought with horror, into my life.

"Dubbelbinnen," I muttered, then fled down the stairs.

12.

It Doesn't Sound Like Scorpions

I headed back to the school to get the city pass Helena had talked about. Then I figured I'd hit the first place on our class list. St. Baaf's cathedral. Anything to get out. To get away from Maria.

A cold rain fell as I walked. Blobs of ice, round and hard as ball bearings, bounced off the back of my jacket as I trudged across the canal and up the hill, my hands deep in my pockets.

I'd left Maria at home, locked her into my home, but I had no idea what to do. I didn't have the money she needed. The money her dad needed. I'd never met him or anything, but I'd heard so much about him I felt an obligation to help. I felt an obligation to Maria. She'd suffered so much. And she just wanted to help her dad. Even though he seemed like a shitbag. Besides, I hadn't passively listened to all her problems. She'd listened to me. To my diatribes about my former bandmates. My mistreatment. Sure, I'd let her live with me, but I recognized she'd been there, she'd been there for me.

Still, I was in no hurry to go back to my apartment. I was in no hurry to face her. If I gave her the money, I'd be done. She'd be done, too. She had to understand that. We might—I might—help her dad, but at what cost? We'd both be on the street, and I'd have no money at all when I got back to Miami. But I knew it would be hard to tell her no. I knew, since she lived with me, that I'd eventually cave to her demand. A well-timed blowjob or something and I'd give her that money, no question. The flesh is weak. I was so engrossed in this problem, I made it past the Record Huis without so much as a single scowl at the cardboard monument to Svart's bare-shirted corpulence.

When I stepped into the language school office, it was silent and nearly empty. The secretary sat behind the glass window. I must have gotten there between classes or something. I went up to the window and, before I could say what I needed, she held up her index finger, then pointed to a chair off to the side of the room.

I went and sat. She came out a second later with a camera dangling around her neck. In an instant, she snapped my picture. Before my vision cleared from the blinding blur of the flash, she'd disappeared back behind the window. Another five minutes or so, and she slipped her hand through the opening in the window and slapped something on the counter with an echoing "Alstublief!"

I walked over and picked it up. The city pass was like a driver's license with my name and photo and nationality. It wasn't so different from my Florida driver's license, at least as far as the photo went: my mouth dangling open, my eyes scrunched together. The dark circles below my eyes magnified by the harsh flash. I had a look of remarkable intelligence. Across the top, it said "Stadssleutel Gent."

"Dank u wel," I said, then asked in English, "This is my city pass?"

"Your city pass," she said. "For Helena's class. Your stadssleutel. The city key."

"Stadssleutel," I repeated. City key. A compound word. It seemed funny to give the city key to an outsider like me. A barbarian at the gate. I slipped the card into my wallet and headed back into the ice rain.

I looked at my watch. One of the independent activities on the class list was a free organ concert at the cathedral. I figured

I'd head there and check it out, maybe start on my worksheet, too. Anything to take up some time, keep me from going home. Going back to Maria. The way I'd left her, it was highly unlikely she planned to go in to work at all that day. It was more likely that she planned to lie in my bed and smoke cigarettes all day.

It seemed funny to give the city key to an outsider, but I'd done the same thing. Maria had her own stadssleutel. The key to my domain. She had the Fosbergsleutel. I'd locked her in. Locked me out. I was the barbarian outside of my own gate. A buitenlander buiten his land.

I had my hood pulled up. I was deep in my thoughts, engrossed in my precious Nederlandse compound words and their hidden wisdoms about my relationship predicament. And then I ran straight into some heap of debris, a tangle of teal and pink, piled on the sidewalk.

Or that's all I saw and felt—my body surrounded by, like, a parachute that drifted in from a Duran Duran video. But firm and unyielding. I had just passed the entryway to the Power-zaal, the power room, another compound, and it felt like I'd run into a pile of abandoned weights. And then Tomi's pale and expressionless face appeared out of the billowing neon, a Scorpions headband cinched around his albino locks.

"Aah!" I shouted, raising my hands to my face. My feet stumbled off the sidewalk, sending me directly into the path of an oncoming city bus, the Z18: Ziekenhaus express.

In an instant, Tomi caught me by the shoulders. He handily set me back on the sidewalk, out of harm's way.

"Gent is a small place," he said. "I knew I would find you."

He kept his hands on my shoulders, restraining me like I was an idiot child who'd dashed into traffic. He had on an over-size tracksuit, an enormous pink gym bag over his shoulder. Two long poles stuck out of the top of the bag. He was un-daunted by the ice rain.

"You'd find me?" I cackled nervously, my heart racing from my near head-on encounter with a bus. "I'm still here. For now."

And then, I don't know why, maybe because he'd spooked me so bad, maybe because I'd nearly died on the street, maybe because, before I ran into him, I'd been ruminating on my Maria problem, I kind of unloaded. Like he was my therapist or something.

If she hadn't just hit me up for money, if I hadn't had to leave my place to escape her tear storm, I probably wouldn't have said anything else. I hadn't seen Tomi for weeks. He said he'd been looking for me, but he hadn't raised his ass off the drum stool on my behalf.

"Maria found me," I said. "And she's living with me."

"Yes. Liza told me she moved in with you," he said.

His lips spread in a thin line, almost a smile, that cut through the middle of his pale goatee. And then he stood there, saying nothing.

"Yeah ... uh," I said, trying to fill the silence. "It's a little weird," I went on. Since his wife worked with Maria, I figured he probably knew all about her crazy past. And then I told him everything. About the money. That she needed it for her dad. To keep him out of South American prison. Because of his international drug dealing. Which had been going on since she was a kid. When she'd had to live on the streets. In a squat. With a bunch of anarchists. And no mom around, either.

I wanted to help her. Because of all she'd been through. But then I'd be broke.

He stood, silent, his grin broadening with each layer of my story. When I got to the end, the part where I confessed that I wanted to help her, even though I knew I'd go broke if I did, his chest rumbled, deep laughter tumbling out through the street.

I stopped.

"What's funny, man?" I asked. "This is some serious shit."

"David," Tomi tightened his grip on my shoulder. "David, everything you just said is a lie."

"I'm not fucking lying," I said.

I tried to flinch out of his hold but couldn't.

"Hmm. You are not," he said. "She is."

"About what?" I asked. Maybe it was even worse, I figured. Maybe her dad was in jail for murder or something. Not just drugs.

He took his hands off my shoulders after turning me away from the street. With one hand, he kind of pushed me toward the Powerzaal so we could get out of the rain.

"Do you have the game two truths and a lie?" he said, his hand between my shoulder blades. It took me a second to know what he meant.

"Yeah—I played it as a kid," I said.

"Well," he continued, "she's playing three lies with you. More, by the sound of it."

"Lies?" I asked. I stuck my hands deep in my pockets and nervously rubbed an old Kleenex between my fingers.

We moved into a covered entryway. There was a short staircase leading up to the Powerzaal. Gym rats of all kinds streamed in and out.

"Yes. No truths," he said. He unshouldered his bag, then adjusted his headband.

"About what?" Even as I asked, I kind of knew. All the stories she'd been telling me. The dense web of her personal mythology. It all seemed too fantastic to be real. But all the stories overlapped so much I couldn't grasp a single strand to start to unravel the thing. I couldn't separate the truth from the lies.

"All of this is lies," he said.

"Her dad's not in jail?" I asked. That one was the biggest part of the whole thing—the dad in jail, the dad who needed my money. But from there, as Tomi explained things to me, I learned that basically everything Maria had told me about herself was all part of an elaborate fiction.

"No, man. Her dad owns the company where she works."

"He's not in league with South American drug lords?" I asked.

"No—he's in league with South American auto distributors. They manufacture parts for work vans. That's a segment of their market, sure. Exporting replacement parts. Quite a boring business, actually."

"Well ... but he was in jail when she was growing up, right? He's gone straight, but that's more recent? She's told me some wild shit about growing up here."

"Wild shit about growing up here? In Gent? You are from the United States, David. From Florida. Does this sound reasonable to you?"

"But," I whined, "the anarchist squat?"

"Did not happen. Liza grew up here, too. They went to school together. They lived on the same street of townhouses on the northern side of the city."

He bent down and took the poles out of his bag.

"All of it's made up? Even the shit about her mom?" I described the black depression Maria entered anytime I brought up her mom.

"Oh—the part about her mother is true. Liza says she's a junkie. Pills. But she keeps fit. From what I have heard, she moves from man to man. Rich men. She takes them for what they have, then finds a new benefactor. She may be a pill junkie, but she's not poor. Her strategy is effective."

It was too much. All this truth. She'd lied about everything. It overwhelmed me. So I changed the subject.

I nodded toward the poles he held.

"You going skiing or something?" I asked.

"I am training," he said. "These are for hiking. They are very different from ski poles."

And then he brought up the band situation.

"It was not my idea to replace you," he said. "I wanted to keep you, but they outvoted me."

His candor took me off guard. If I hadn't brought a coffee, Juan would have just ignored me, pranced around in his pink bathrobe. And Juan agreed with Nekrokor. Told me I was too normal for their band.

Then Tomi asked a weird question.

"What band made you like metal?"

An easy question.

"Motley Crüe. 'Shout at the Devil.' That song. That album." I gushed. No matter what, just saying those words, remembering how heavy that riff shook me as a kid, picturing Nikki Sixx with his black shroud of electrified hair, the football stripes under his eyes, the weird Boba Fett shoulder guard, it all brought me a shot of exuberance, even standing under an awning that held the odor of Right Guard and sweat wafting down from the Powerzaal, even after learning that my live-in lady friend was a fucking liar playing me for my dollars.

"Yes. I figured something like that. Me, too." He gestured at his headband, the airbrushed scorpion, with one of the poles.

"*Love at First Sting*," he said. "'Bad Boys Running Wild.' Have you listened to our Desekration album?"

I told him I'd bought a copy.

"It doesn't sound like Scorpions," he said.

That much was obvious.

"Except in one place. Your classic riff. Paired with my drumming. A reminder of what matters."

"Yeah . . . are you gonna quit Desekration or something?" I asked hopefully.

"No. I would not quit money. An inferno of money," he said. It stung. I knew they had to be doing alright, based on all the Desekration fiends plaguing the city. I knew they were cashing in on some trend.

"Is that . . . is that why you were looking for me? To tell me you didn't want to kick me out? Thanks, dude. It really—"

Before I could go on, before I could tell him his support meant a lot, even though it didn't change anything, he cut me off.

"I did not agree that you are too normal," he said. "Or that it mattered. All the costumes I find tiresome."

He picked up his bag and moved to the stairs going up to the Powerzaal. He turned and said, "A good riff is worth its weight in gold. I heard what they did in the final mix. I may be able to help you. You deserve better. That's what I wanted to tell you."

And with that, he sprinted up the stairs. His hiking poles scraped the doorway as he went in, aluminum on aluminum, clacking like a lobster's chitinous antennae.

13.
The Key to the House of David

I left Tomi behind and started down Sint Pietersnieuwstraat. He said he could help me. He said my riffs were worth their weight in gold. It sounded like he wanted to help me out somehow with money. Which would be great, but I had bigger things on my mind. The whole time I walked, I thought about everything he'd said about Maria.

She was a liar. She lived in my place and made up lies to get my limited money and polluted my lungs with her never ending indoors smoking. She lost her key all the time and cried for no reason.

I didn't know what to do about her, though. Should I dump her for being a liar, for making up some tale about her past? Was that a dumping offense? Or was the money the issue? The fact she had no problem lying to get my money. I'd never dumped someone. Before that, all I'd known was Natasha. And Natasha had dumped me.

The ice rain continued to fall, but a little slower, a little lighter. As I got closer to the cathedral, I moved through a steadily narrowing tangle of streets. Pavement gave way to cobblestones and all the cars and busses, even the sounds of their engines, faded far into the distance. The buildings looked different, too. The plate glass windows and rectangular steel frames of the stores and restaurants of a modern city gave way to a city of an earlier time. A city of odd, off-kilter buildings, a pink cupola here, and over there, a set of three row houses, each house tilting a different direction, one right, one left, one backwards somehow. Further down, I passed a crenellated fortalice with a gift shop on the bottom floor, the threshold into the store sunken six inches or so below the street. In this part of the city, nearly every building bore the subtle but unmistakable mark of the loamy soil below, pulling and pulling for long centuries.

The narrow lane I followed took a few haphazard turns, then spilled onto the edge of a square lined with restaurants and cafes. I stood under the skeletal forms of two trees, their roots hemmed in by paving stones as gray as the sky above. To my right, the cathedral loomed overhead. The ice rain eased up, only to be replaced by a steady wind. Above, so many clouds streamed past. I stopped at a bench flanking the square to get my stuff out of my bag. As I pulled my stadssleutel out of my pocket, I noticed the occasional break in the clouds over the square. A tear here and there hinted at an orange sky somewhere on the other side. Each slight break in the clouds passed like a dead leaf racing down a stream.

Out on the square, I moved to the doorway into the cathedral. Standing on the threshold and looking up, I felt small, insignificant. The wide arched doorway opened at the bottom of a massive Gothic tower. From my perspective, I could see two of its pointed spires flanking the top of the tower. My jacket jostled with each gust as a million clouds rushed by overhead. I felt like the spires were the horns of some stone leviathan and on the ground, far below, the wind itself worked to push me into its mouth.

But of course the tower, the cathedral, would appear to me in that brief moment as a teratomorphic structure. A monster building. My subconscious had been steeped for years in Dan Seagrave's nekroscapes, in Michael Whelan's gape-mawed forests. At any time, dreaming or awake, a steady playlist pattered away in my mind. Song after song. Unclean spirits haunting the chapel of ghouls.

And as I moved into the church, I passed under three statues guarding the entrance. In the middle, an imperious Christ gazed downward at me through flat and pupil-less eyes. The statue on the right pointed at a plate with a sheep on it. I knew enough to figure that was John the Baptist. The other guy had on armor and held a sword. A knight or some shit. And in his left hand, he balanced a book with a plump bird, a stone pigeon—a crappy band name, sitting on the cover.

The Jesus got my attention. That empty stare. Judging judging judging. Jesus was a lot larger than the other two. He glared like some behaloed Yao Ming, one hand pointing up to heaven, the other holding some sphere topped with a cross. The holy hand grenade. Ready to drop it down on the heads of passing blasphemers.

The Jesus was so huge, he could go mano a mano with that other oversized icon ruling my side of the city, with cardboard Svart. He was made of stone, Svart of paper. You'd win, Jesus, I thought. You're a winner. And then, unbidden, the wrong thought: but everyone knows that paper beats rock. I folded my hands as I walked underneath. Hunched my shoulders. I tried to blot my blasphemy out of my mind.

"It was only a joke," I muttered. Only a joke, Jesus. Don't strike me down as I enter your vast domain, your throne of Christly dominion. Amen.

Just then a high-pitched chirping caught my attention. I thought it was some angelic shriek of vengeance, or the cry of the stone bird rumbling to life as I passed. And when I looked up, at first I didn't see anything else. Just the statues. I feared some kind of divine retribution. And at the same time, I realized I'd been under a lot of pressure. The band thing. The Maria thing. The threat of Natasha's imminent arrival. Maybe I was starting to crack. Maybe this phantom cry was the first sign. That I was hearing things. That I needed help. But then I noticed some movement even higher, in the underside of the archway itself, which was decked with a web of some kind of netting, like a ship's rigging. For the real pigeons. A mesh covering to keep them from shitting endlessly down Jesus's neck.

A few sparrows, smaller than pigeons, peeked their beaks out of the mesh. They chirped to each other, scratched at the net with their beaks, then fluttered out from one part of the netting to nestle in somewhere else. They had nests of bundled twigs and plastic scraps scrunched at odd intervals behind the net.

And nothing happened to me when I went into the cathedral. It was just some birds chirping. I guess I carried a lot of weird guilt, which didn't make much sense for someone who hadn't been in a church for many dark aeons. I kind of felt bad. Just a little bit. About my songs, riff after profanatical riff. About an old song, "Zombichrist," the one that, in the Valhalla days, really seemed to irritate central Florida's Pentecostal community. They'd burned a bunch of copies of my first album, *Thrones of Satanic Dominion*. And as I made it through the archway unharmed, I turned back and kind of waved up at the Jesus statue with a conciliatory gesture. Like, hey, maybe I don't really think you're a zombie, statue-Jesus. And maybe, since you know that, you won't try to smite me. I'm just here to do a worksheet. And it was just a song. Just a song.

I shouldn't have feared supernatural reprisal for my music. I didn't come from a religious family or anything. But I'd spent so much time absorbing metal's profusion of nekromantic imagery, of metal's profusion of mystical truths. Nordikron's strangled ravings about medieval spirits possessing the living. Juan's poetic descriptions of a heavenscraping monolith ascended on all sides by the epic heroes of every culture. Even the more primitive Valhalla lyrics I wrote with the Morris brothers. The cartoonish lines we aped from Lovecraft stories and dungeon modules described a supernatural reality where a betentacled Satan ruled from a leaden throne far below and Christ's resurrection was nothing more than a ruse, a trick caused by a paralytic potion.

Maybe I'd internalized all this fantasy so much I'd

somehow become more attuned to religious images. Either that, or all the isolation was finally getting to me. All this time interacting almost exclusively with Maria. Maybe it was just making me too serious, I concluded. It wasn't the first time I'd ever seen a fucking statue. Svart had paraded me around Gent on countless occasions. He was always pointing out this saint and that monument everywhere he went. I mean, his mom belonged to some historical society. I'd never felt watched or anything before. I figured I should call Tomi sometime. See if he wanted to go out for a drink or something. He wasn't shunning me. Not like the rest of them. Just because I was too normal didn't mean I couldn't go out, have a drink, like a normal dude.

Inside the cathedral, the pipe organ marched through the opening strains of a hymn. I went up to the visitor's booth. A blonde lady in a red vest manned a cash register. Over behind her, a black curtain blocked off the entrance to a whole wing dedicated to the church's main money-maker, the Gent altarpiece. I flashed my stadssleutel and tried to say I just wanted to visit the church, not the altarpiece. Helena had lined up an art professor to tell us about the Gent altarpiece later in our semester.

Helena had told us to try to do everything in Nederlandse. It was part of the class. But the whole idea was too much for me to convey. I stood there like a stalled-out robot as I mentally filtered through my limited phrases. A Spanish tour group filed in right behind me. It was a big group. They spread around me and bumped against my back. The swish of jackets and the prattle of all their conversations distracted me. I felt anxious. I needed to finish my business and move on into the church.

"Ik ben een bezorgerer," I began, but I knew it sounded fucked up. A deliverer. Worse than that. A delivererer. I corrected myself, then tried again. "Een bezoeker." A visitor.

"Voor het kirk," I went on, pointing away from the black

curtain for good measure.

She got the gist of my garbling.

"Okay. Do you want an audio tour?" she shot back.

Then, she gestured to a basket of digital tour guides, each black wand emblazoned with a Union Jack sticker.

You know me, though. An intrepid bezoeker of andere taalen. I recoiled from the English audio guide like a vampire from garlic.

"Nee," I said, and saying it renewed my confidence a bit.

"Nee," I brayed again, this time a bit louder.

You don't master Nederlandse voor buitenlanders and swoop your lereress into the old slaapkamer by getting the English tour guide.

"Ik wil een . . . in het Nederlandse," I said and pointed at a different bin, every wand stamped with the three striped Dutch flag.

She kind of rolled her eyes. This whole transaction would have been much easier in English, the jostling of the Spanish group behind me grew louder as they waited, and besides, I'm sure she was thinking, what good would the Dutch wand actually do for someone who could barely even ask for the fucking thing?

But I laid down the rental fee and she passed one over. Before leaving her desk, I snagged a pamphlet in English. Just in case.

I stepped into the main part of the cathedral. It opened into a vast space, the walls rising so high I moved with my head, my face, fixed on the place where all the stone beams of the arched ceiling converged far above. The combined effect of countless marble statues, paintings, and stained glass overwhelmed me. At that point, I'd been living in Gent for several months. I'd seen ancient buildings and monumental art every day. But the total effect of so much art in one place gave me a deep feeling of awe.

And the organ complemented it all. The sound of the hymn filled every inch of this enormous space. When the hymn drew to a close, even the sounds of the organist getting ready for the next song filled the air. The shuffling of sheet music, the tap of fingernails on the keys as the next song began. These sounds came from everywhere all at once.

The organ's pipes stood at the top of an archway leading behind the altar. Not too far from there, a small group assembled around the organ. And when the next song started, I pushed through the group so I could get as close as possible. It was like the beginning of a show. The lights dim and you push up to the front. You push through so you can get as close as possible to the guitarist. To steal some tricks. It's like corporate espionage.

I moved so quick because of the song. It was "Toccata and Fugue in D Minor," that most metal of classical tunes. Maybe the cheesiest, too. I pushed through, expecting to find Gary Oldman in shades or the Phantom of the Opera or some other freak wailing away on the keyboard. But it was just a young guy in dress slacks and a beige polo shirt. Not an organ-playing monster imprisoned in a monster tower. Short hair trimmed respectably around the ears. No stupid costume. Just a normal guy totally ripping. He wasn't much older than me. A year, maybe two, if I had to guess. Fingers flying. He wore a placid smile as he powered through the song. A smile, and not a pained nekrogrimace.

The organ had five keyboards and a million settings. Like the cockpit of the Millennium Falcon. The notes blazed by, but the guy remained so calm, so languid. The notes blazed by, the same way I used to try to play this stuff back in the piano lessons of yore.

I backed out of the crowd around the organist and sat down in a nearby pew. The first few questions on the worksheet were pretty easy. I just read the question, then found the part of my English language pamphlet that had the answer. With a little ingenuity, I was able to put something together in Dutch.

About midway down, the questions got a lot harder. She

had one about the organ concert. Like, how did the music make me feel. The guy still pushed through the Toccata at a punishing pace. When he finished that, he moved into one of my favorites, the "Solfeggietto," by a different Bach. I resisted the urge to rush back to the organ. I still knew this one by heart. I'd ingrained the opening scale in my muscle memory. The song had filled my mind during my recent bout of chicken curry food poisoning. And hearing the guy play it confirmed how the music made me feel.

Hearing him play made me face the obvious. I shouldn't have quit those piano lessons so long ago. The move to guitar was straight up folly. It fucked my life. And when I first got a guitar, these were the kinds of songs I tried to play. I used to sit on my bed, the piano book strewn across my *Empire Strikes Back* comforter. I used to plunk my way through these endless runs. They came to me so easily on the piano, but I had to work to play them on my new guitar.

And when I played them on the guitar, I paid for each small bit of progress. The strings flayed my fingertips. Like Bryan Adams, I persisted. And at the time, I welcomed the pain. It meant I was learning. It meant—and maybe, in retrospect, this had been more important—it meant I was physically shedding the soft skin of the wimpy pianist and replacing it with the hardened callouses of a serious heavy metal dude.

How could I explain this in some heel goed Nederlandse that Helena wouldn't eviscerate? How could I explain that hearing this organist play made me realize how fucking stupid I had been all along? How could I explain, in a language where I could hardly ask for a simple audio guide, that pretty much every stupid decision I'd made since I was fifteen stemmed from the stupidest decision of all, the decision to trade the piano for a sick, repulsive electric twanger?

I just scribbled something short and obvious. The music made me feel good. I liked the music. The organ was big. The organ was uitstekend. And then I moved on. My next few responses came straight from the pamphlet.

I checked my watch. I'd have to go home before long. Back to Maria. And the whole time, despite the ongoing organ devastation, I was still kind of shook by what Tomi had told me. That Maria was a fucking liar. All the shit she'd told me had been completely false. Did she even need to live with me? If her father wasn't actually facing justice for running an international drug trafficking ring, then what did she need my money for?

For the last question, I had to describe some piece of art. Even worse, I had to explain how something in the picture reminded me of something I had experienced. I got up and walked around. The floor was set with these white and brown tiles. It wasn't a checkerboard or even a repeating pattern. It made me think of a dungeon map. The white tiles described corridors and the brown tiles marked off secret walls or something. I could write about that, no problem. I could write about playing Dungeons and Dragons as a kid. I could say the whole cathedral reminded me of some ancient structure bravely besieged by my best character, a tenth-level warrior. Until I realized my severe linguistic limitations.

So I shifted course and tried to find a painting to write about. But they were all covered in this thick brown patina. You could barely see the characters. It was like hundreds of generations of Maria's ancestors had spent their lives exhaling smoke on all the paintings.

Eventually, I turned on the audio guide for inspiration. I hoped it would steer me toward something cool. Besides, the organ guy had moved on to more boring fare—he'd rounded out his set list with some drippy tunes. "Bette Davis Eyes" for organ. Maybe it was the background noise or something—the organ, people's steps, low conversations—but I couldn't make out a fucking word of the Dutch wand. I still kept it up to my ear, though. I figured I just needed to acclimate.

That's when I noticed the windows. Along one wall of the cathedral, a diffuse glow illuminated all the stained-glass windows. The clouds outside must have just broken or something.

And it was just along that one wall. The rest of the windows were still kind of gray and dark. I moved closer. The saints and Biblical characters in the windows emanated an eerie phosphorescence. It wouldn't last long, though. The sun must have broken through the clouds right before dusk. And as I walked up and down this wall, the tour wand at my ear, I made out a word I knew. Sleutel. Key. And I saw a Bible dude with a key. With two big ass keys. They had the length and heft of oars. And it was like the spirit of the Lord spoke to me right then.

Or maybe it was the spirit of this place. The key, it said to me, through its language of light and glass. The sleutel, it said through the audio tour wand. No one could ever lose those big ass keys. Not even Maria. Not like she lost her key. My key, I suddenly realized. It wasn't her key. What if she just, like, permanently lost her key? She'd be a buitenlander. An outside lander. Outside the land of my apartment. Without a key, she'd become someone who lived outside of my door. Someone who stands outside my door. She that hath not the key of David shall openeth his door no more.

I related to this Bible dude with his keys. He held them tight in his arms. So I went back to the pew and answered that last question. I didn't write anything about my revelation, though. I didn't say I was going to take Maria's key. I didn't say I was going to lock her—permanently—out of my apartment. I just wrote that the windows were beautiful. Mooi. The windows were very mooi with the light. I wrote I hoped there'd be more light. That maybe it would stop raining every fucking day. But I didn't write it like that. I used my best heel goed Nederlandse.

As I wrote, a couple dozen senior citizens, bent and silver haired, streamed into the main part of the church. They came from under the church. Out of the crypt. This didn't bother me, though. They weren't the ravening undead. The pamphlet said the crypt held church services except on major holidays. It wasn't a Sunday, but I guess they'd had some kind of afternoon prayer service or something.

That wasn't the weird thing. It was something else. Some-one else. Someone in this group of old people. Someone not as old. Smiling. His scrawny pale arm resting casually across the shoulders of some bunch-backed old hag with a blue perm. It was him. Nordikron. Mathias. Leaving the church service, too.

14.

Metametal:
Chapter for Inscribing the Words of the Nekronomikon on Coelacanth Scales

Seek the eternal essence in the dark of the mind.
Destination ancient city below the seas,
Below the spheres of eternity.
—Liers in Wait, "Maleficient Dreamvoid"

Seek the eternal essence in the dark of the mind. It dwells in the darkest city, sits enshrined in that ancient place. Seek the eternal essence that lies in wait, far below the seas and constrained by seven gates.

Seven tendrils guard each gate. Seven times seven. Seven tentacles.

Are they animal or vegetable? This simple question has driven many to madness.

Seven tendracles sprout from their gates like worms from the hollow eyes of Golgotha, the place of the skull.

Submerged, living, this city calls to me. And I will follow.

My journey begins where sky and sea unite. A holy diver, I plunge from a tower and fall through a brown crust of congealed leaves, splintered branches, and sediment. Each time I fall, I wonder if the city will accept me. The ocean swallows my body, as light and frail as a leaf, but possessed by a leaden mass that carries me down. That pulls me to the center of that city, to the unblinking eyes of seven times seven ancient evils.

My momentum is a downward shuttling arc, yet it traces the curve of coast, a submerged shelf that slips past like a gorgon head shaped from roots and stone. I taste the ocean as I sink, even though some part of me knows I haven't moved at all.

A massive blob of steel gray, like an immense amoeba of ambergris, looms below and rises to envelop me with the sound of an oil derrick shuddering beneath a cyclone assault. Instantly, I sink through its cataract-gray shell, entering a coiled chamber, the internal cavity of this engulfing body, perhaps a monstrous whale shark, some krill-consuming leviathan body. I make out individual bodies, fins, fang-besotten lips, slate eyes, tough and muscled as oysters, that see but do not see.

A thousand fish as ancient as the ocean floor envelop me in their unguent spiral. Fins, spiny calcite tendrils, more like claws or shriveled remnants of vestigial saurian wings than anything capable of propelling this horde of stout granite bodies, trace the surface of my vantage point, trace the surface of my bathysphere eye. In the darkness, their eyes gleam with the matte sheen of a universe of dead planets.

Their jaws clench and unclench methodically, rows of spiny teeth silently intoning the names of the ancient, our overlord, seven times seven in number. I feel their empty stares. If I am here in bodily form, their attention is obvious, but I am just a shade, a soul, an eye seized from below to join the shapeless body of the unseen one. The light of the body is the eye: if therefore thine eye be single, thy whole body shall be full of light.

This dream, this vision, this hallucination holds me away

from external reality. I am aware of its outer edges in the same way I know a painting stops at the edge of the canvas. The frame holding the picture, like the shuffling of footsteps I hear outside in the hallway, is more real than the picture, more real than the dream images that have caught me in an endless descent.

Before, these images were real to me. In the community of my minions and my brothers, the ancient ones, forever far below, were as real to me as my minions, my brothers. Together we crafted words and songs and lives of praise guided by and intended for malevolent forces we knew to be real. And now, this descent, a repeating dream, forms my reality.

Somewhere on the other side, somewhere in a reality beyond the translucent surface of this somnium, I detect paper rustling, the clacking of fingers on keys, the drone of an extended chord, and then the whoosh of an opening door. But in this vision, where I sink through the ocean, then into the city, then find myself again diving from the tower and into the sea, all these sounds, these reminders of the real world, they all transmute into a scratching, a sliding of bodies, these coelacanths now circling me in movements coordinated by whatever dwells in the city far below.

The lines marking the sides of their bodies slide by, and I notice repeated patterns, parallel scars the same in size and shape, perhaps emblazoned by a branding iron coiled within a serpentine grip. Were these fish, undiscovered for so long, once livestock for whatever dwells behind the gates? And yet, the patterns on their sides, an odd conglomeration of dots, triangles, and ellipsoids contorted to various degrees, seem too complex to simply identify this fish from that fish. The distortion of each ellipse had to have been planned in advance, making an entire alphabet from a single shape. The combination of triangles, dots, and loops engraved as a charcoal geometry barbequed into their backs conveys a complex message, an epistle sent from the city below, itself an ellipse traced on the ocean floor, suffused with a pale glow, as though its cratered, fang-gnashed walls were coated in some gloppy glow.

As I see the city, sense myself centered over its crevassed gates, seven times seven, its coral halls filled with the innumerable tentacles of the unnamable, I understand the coelacanth cryptogram, or rather, some consciousness literate in that tongue (if it was ever spoken by creatures with such an appendage) seizes control of my consciousness, coating my mind like the ancient slime coating these ancient fish, coating my mind just as I touch the top turret of this flooded city.

At that moment, the fish break away, disappear into a vast darkness, luring me to contemplate this message, this mystery, engraved on each calcite scale, etched on each outer wall, and carved in enormous hieroglyphs over each gate of this octopoid lair. The same message marks the stone-like skin of the fish and the breathing walls of the city stones.

It is not written in my native language, if I am still indeed that other body and not this invisible eye. I grasp two truths at once: that human body would have collapsed into stringy tendrils of meso-benthic chum much earlier in my descent. And this language I see is one I once knew, yet one indecipherable to those encased in living flesh. The ancient gods—Cthulhu, Nyarlathotep, Dagon—engraved these letters, these words in the steely bodies of each coelacanth.

The message, rearranged as a multitude of bony tendrils gliding over rigid slate scales, changing expression but never meaning, fills the roiling waters: 𝔍 𝔞𝔪 𝔟𝔢𝔠𝔬𝔪𝔢 𝔡𝔢𝔞𝔱𝔥.

Part Six

And, like bright metal on a sullen ground,
My reformation, glittering o'er my fault,
Shall show more goodly . . .
—Shakespeare, *1 Henry IV* (1.2.187-189)

Holy Diver
You've been down too long in the midnight sea
Oh, what's becoming of me?
—Dio, "Holy Diver"

15.
Confrontate the Enemy

I followed him.

And this time, I was certain it was Mathias. Not some paltry imitator regaled in Despondent Abyss gear.

I mean, it wasn't the clothes that gave him away. It wasn't the clothes that revealed Mathias, grand inquisitor of evil, exiting a midday prayer service. He didn't have on his little Batman cape. He had not profaned the sanctuary with the leering Baphomet on the Venom shirt he generally wore.

He was dressed pretty respectably. He had on a white dress shirt. Collared and buttoned. And over that, a denim jacket. Plain, though. Not one single patch besmirched its pale blue surface. He was in disguise.

I could tell it was him by the voice. The Voice. That sepulchral tremor that somehow emanated from within his scrawny chest. He didn't drop his pants, shit on the sacred ground, then gawp the warcry of some Satanic battle lord. He didn't produce a razor and, with a gleeful Nazgul shriek, slice the throat of his senior lady friend. He didn't roar out some noxious death belch to impress his septuagenarian posse.

He just laughed.

The lady he had his arm around, Doris or whatever old ass Belgian women are called, must have said something funny, because he patted her, tilted his head back, and unloosed a stained-glass shaking cackle.

No pretender, no mere fan, could make centuries old glass quake in its leaden framing.

I felt it like a sharp jab to my eardrum, high pitched and bestial. And the glass panel with the key dude twitched with a barely perceptible shiver.

And no one else noticed. Not the tourists. Not his church peeps. They just trudged through the sanctuary, all of them carrying thick black books and photocopied pamphlets. Before they stepped out into the gathering gloom, they stopped at a book rack by the door. It had a wicker basket perched on the top. They lined the books up on the rack and dropped their pamphlets in the basket.

Mathias kept his book. He held the door open for the old lady. It took her a minute to hobble through. Without his arm for support, she moved slowly. He almost spotted me then, too. He turned back for one last look at St. Baafs in all its splendor. Luckily, I ducked behind a pillar. Then, I hunched my shoulders and embedded myself in a jumble of tourists. Together, we dropped off our tour wands at the front desk. And as Mathias left the cathedral, I raced up to the book rack. The books were old and dusty hymnals. I flipped through one. It was all shepherds and wayward sheep. Praises to the kingdom of heaven. For hundreds of pages. And the pamphlets had, like, prayers and shit. Mathias, I thought. A secret churchgoer. And by the way he chummed around with the other congregants, this seemed like something more than a one-time thing.

This all was pretty scandalous to me at that time. Needless to say, black metal cultists generally frowned on church attendance. Unless you're going to the church of total death. The fact that Mathias was feeling that old time religion made my discovery even more delicious. I mean, I didn't really care. It didn't really scandalize me. Hey—I even owned a Stryper tape. But it made me feel vindicated.

And I knew even the most hardened nekrofiends sometimes ended up in places unbefitting their elite status. A little sister's birthday party. A long-neglected trip to the DMV. Even forced attendance at the occasional church service.

I wished I'd had a camera, so I had evidence of Mathias spending his time at church. But I knew it wouldn't change anything. It wouldn't get me back in Desekration.

The old lady, the lady he had his arm around, could have been his mom or something. And, I knew, I must have been missing something. Even the fact that he took the book. Taking what's not yours, that's stealing. And stealing is a sin. So stealing from a cathedral is, like, an extra sin. But I couldn't figure out why he wanted the thing. A hymnal is a book filled with songs he shouldn't like, at least not based on everything he'd ever said to me. But if Mathias took one . . . and here the idea came to my hand before it fully realized in my mind. I grabbed the hymnal at the end of the row. I unzipped my jacket and tucked it in there. Confident in my stealthiness, I zipped my jacket back up and stepped toward the door.

If Mathias took one, then maybe I should, too.

And then I felt an arm on my shoulder. So busted, I thought. Heart pounding, I turned. A church service straggler, an old lady with feathered hair and a cane, held onto my sleeve. I folded my arms across my chest to disguise the telltale rectangular lump of a pilfered hymnal.

She hadn't noticed, though.

"Our next service is Sunday morning," she warbled. "At 10 a.m. We meet in the crypt."

I backed away from the book rack. "Nee . . . nee," I said, like I expected her to sprinkle me with holy water. Force a confession of my hymnal thievery.

I rushed out of the cathedral, still hugging the book to my chest. As I sprinted under glowering Jesus, I ducked my head.

Outside, the rain had stopped. Most of the clouds were gone, too. In the distance, sunset's red gash bled across the sky. And out on the square fronting the cathedral, Mathias broke off from his companion. Before he left, Mathias gave her a hug, which, from what I knew of him, was pretty unfathomable. He held her briefly in both arms. He gently patted her back with the hymnal. And, I realized, he couldn't have stolen it. This lady, his mom or whatever, was fully aware he had it. He'd borrowed it or something because . . . and again, it was hard for me to put this all together . . . because he was going to go back to the church at some point in the near future.

After he hugged her, the lady lifted her face to his. He ran one hand through her blue permed curls. And they kissed. With tongue. Her tongue, as blue and pale as her hairdo, flicked out of her mouth. And into his. He leaned into it, too. Like he was going to chomp down on that old blue gray hunk of tongue and eat her dry parchment skin right off her face. And then they broke away. He wiped his mouth with his denim jacket sleeve and turned down a side street. The lady wasn't his mom. She tottered across the square and on toward the Belfort Tower.

I rushed to keep up with Mathias. On his own, he flipped through the hymnal as he walked. His bony hands, his fingers like ivory blades, marked off several pages in the hymnal.

I followed him, but I stayed on the other side of the street the whole time. That's how they do it in spy movies.

At one point, I really lost him. A tram came up behind me. It passed me, bells clanging, then stopped about half a block ahead. It cut off my view.

When the tram started down the track again, the sidewalk buzzed with people. The post-workday rush. I almost gave up the chase, but then I spotted him, ambling slowly, his hymnal cracked just a bit, his finger tracing the measures of some old hymn.

We passed through the university campus and I kept to the shadows offered by all the trees and bushes. We followed Overpoortstraat, the university party street, for a few blocks. It was still pretty early, though. Quiet. Most of the bars hadn't bothered to fire up their techno machines.

The further we got from the university, the harder it got to hide. There weren't many people. Overpoortstraat petered out into a barren industrial hellscape of warehouses, dusty shops, and the occasional apartment building. On the horizon, the expressway glittered with headlights.

Out here, I couldn't even duck behind any bushes. A few bristly weeds sprung from between the cracked sidewalk, but only streetlights and parked cars offered any cover.

He turned off Overpoortstraat, or whatever they called it once you got past the college bars. He headed to the only building on the street, a bare-bones apartment tower. Stalin style. He lived in a whitewashed brick rectangle. Here and there, small windows broke up the monotonously plain surface. He lived in a tower, but it wasn't a cool tower. Not like the one at the front of St. Baafs. Not like the Belfort Tower. It wasn't sentient and horned and ready to spring to life. No golden dragon stuck to its top. But if Mathias lived there, I thought, then this Gent tower housed a real monster.

On the empty street, he opened the hymnal wide. He sang from the book and, with only the hum of traffic in the distance, his words resonated clearly up and down the street. I positioned myself behind a newspaper box. It wasn't much, but it gave me some cover.

"Signs of endings all around us," he sang, not screamed. And then he went through the line a few times, modulating the notes, the intonation, even altering the order of the words.

"Signs of endings all around us," he sang again, still in a clean and resonant tenor.

"Signs of endings all around," he rasped, filling the street with a reptile hiss as dry and ancient as his old ass girlfriend.

"All around us, signs of endings," and here he spoke the words, a *Masterpiece Theater* narrator with an affected British accent.

"Signs of endings. Signs of endings. Of endings. Endings," he sang, slobbered, shrieked. Each repetition came out in some different voice. The last "endings" scratched the black sky above like some sort of cosmic chalkboard.

As he sang, he moved his arm like a conductor. He threw

out the occasional air guitar strum. And then he stopped and flipped through the pages some more.

"Under the shadow," he sang. And then he went through the same process. Sing. Rasp. Grunt. Screech.

"Under the shadow of your wings," he howled. "I will re-joice."

If I hadn't been in recon mode, I would have cracked my hymnal, too. Just to see where he was finding this shit. In his hands, the dusty church hymnal became a grimoire of total death lyricism. The few times I'd been to church, they'd never talked about wings, shadows, morbid endings. These were metal fixations.

He flipped some more and then moved up the walkway to the building.

"Your right ha ..." he started, then abruptly changed course.

"Your left hand," he sang and raised his left hand in a fist.

"Your left hand," he continued, "Your left hand binds me."

He got to the doorway into the building and jostled his key into the lock. The door wouldn't open, though. He shook the handle. Pulled it. Pushed it. Nothing worked, though.

Eventually, he mashed one of the buttons lined along the side of the door. A few seconds later, someone buzzed him in. The door sprang open, no problem, to a long hallway, its white walls battered and gouged through years of neglect.

The hall had a harsh fluorescent glare, like a truck stop bathroom. It was lined with doors, each one to some miserable and cramped flat. You could tell these weren't palatial digs. Like, I had one slaapkamer, and maybe he had half that. Or less.

That's when I turned and left him. I started walking home. Back to Maria. The monster in my tower.

It didn't make sense that Mathias lived in such a crappy place. In the past, he always talked so much about his family and their wealth. He'd embroidered the tales of his sickly youth with details highlighting his affluence. The servant ministering to his needs. The antique mirror where he contemplated his decaying mortal form. He may have been sick, but he'd been sick in style.

He'd mentioned the name of his childhood home, too. Himmelsgarten. It always made me laugh. Like, what the fuck would my parents have called our broke ass house? Swampmoor Estate. Goonsview Cottage.

One time, he described the stone wall that separated Himmelsgarten from the rest of the town. It's where he used to hang out. He'd sit on the Himmelsgarten side of the wall, suitably blocked from the townie riff raff, and listen to Venom and Dio tapes on his Walkman.

He'd described the four-hundred-year-old timbers that made up the floor of his dining room. That was the oldest part of the whole house. The only thing left from when it had been a rustic hunting lodge for some long dead viscount.

There was a deep gouge in the wood, he'd once told me and Juan. Right under his chair at the Himmelsgarten dining table. A gouge, he once told us, made by the viscount when he axed the foot off one of his underlings. Juan loved this kind of shit. Depraved nobles. The sordid past. But when he'd told us that story, I knew what he really meant. In that story, he was the viscount. Juan and me, we were the underlings. Or just me. I was the underling.

By the time I got back to my place, I didn't care so much about Mathias and whatever I thought I knew about the guy. His hymnal recital. His Pungent Stench kiss. Just to be clear—this lady was no cougar. Mathias wasn't trading up in years for some tightly aerobicized matron. He'd caressed her throat wattle while they kissed.

Let him fuck the dead, I thought as I stepped into my kitchen. I've got my own problems. The place smelled like crushed Marlboros and weed. A haze obscured the slaapkamer. I didn't even know if Maria was there. All I knew was that I needed to confront her. I needed to confront the situation. I needed to fight back. That was the key. And the key, too. The key was the key. She'd installed herself in my place by manipulating my emotions. And she'd tried to take it even further by going for my ultralimited cash.

I needed to assert myself. I needed to do a bunch of things I sucked at. Even though, I guess, that was my problem back then. Playing all these songs about strength and domination, but never showing strength as others dominated me.

And so, I confronted Maria. If "confronted" means awkwardly dancing around the issue.

"Maria, are you here?" I asked into the haze.

She padded into the kitchen. She had on black jeans and an Ozzy shirt. *The Ultimate Sin*. The one with a winged Ozzy lizard. She puffed on a hand-rolled cigarette. Mostly tobacco with a faint hash tinge.

"I talked to Tomi today," I said.

"Mhmm," she mumbled, then exhaled at the toaster.

"He told me about you. About your past."

"Yah," she replied, then took another drag.

"All that stuff you said. About your dad, about you living on the streets."

Nervously, I twiddled one of the knobs on the stove. I clicked it on, then off. I don't know why. It soothed me, I guess. Took my mind off confronting her about her total dishonesty. If she lied about her past, if she lied about her dad, then she didn't really need my money. If she lied about all that, then she was probably lying about paying the money back. She was probably lying about a lot of things.

We stood there in silence, her smoking, me fucking around with the oven knob.

"The anarchists," I said, like that would trigger her memory or something. Like she'd tell me something new, some unassailable fact that would prove Tomi wrong.

"The ones who let you live with them . . ." I went on.

Eventually, she reached into the sink and grabbed a dirty

coffee cup.

"The international drug ring," I said.

I clicked the knob off with steely decisiveness and delivered the damning truth: "And your dad, who's never been to jail."

She tapped her cigarette against the cup's rim. The ash sizzled when it hit the coffee sludge at the bottom of the cup.

I turned away from the stove to face her directly. I folded my arms across my chest.

"It's all a lie," I said. "Tomi told me."

She ashed her cigarette again, then took another long drag.

"Maybe," she said. "It might not be true. Not all of it."

She dropped the spent cigarette in the cup, then picked her jacket up off the chair.

Was this it? I thought for a moment, certain that my brave and forthright confrontation had impelled her to leave in shame.

But that's not what happened. Instead, she said, "We're going drinking."

I said, "I just got home, Maria. I want to talk about this." I really channeled some inner strength and added, "I don't want to go drinking."

And then there was some light tapping at the door. A moment later, the door swung open and some dude walked in.

"You can stay here," she told me. "Joost and I are going drinking."

"Who the fuck's Joost?" I shot back. Even though it was obvious. Joost was this dude standing in my kitchen.

He shot me a smarmy smile. Joost was a normal dude. He had the clean woodland smell of mid-priced cologne. It slowly displaced my apartment's permastench. This was a guy with an office and a designated lunch break. He had short brown hair. Khakis. A blue cable knit sweater. Over that, a brown leather jacket. A yuppie's jacket. Expensive and unblemished. It wasn't a metalhead's leather jacket. Not like Maria's, which she slid on as I stood there trying to figure out what the fuck just happened.

"I've got my key," she said as she slid past me. "In case you don't want to come."

This dude guided Maria by the hip as they maneuvered out of the kitchen and into the hallway. His fingers splayed as he touched her, like he was palming a basketball. He showed a casual familiarity with my girl's ass.

"Oh, I'm coming," I said. "I'm coming with you."

We headed to a bar.

And the Maria I'd been living with—sullen, filled with resentment about her traumatic past—was replaced by her party-time doppelgänger as the first drop of Duvel touched her lips.

As we drank, they answered my profound question—who the fuck's Joost?—in bits and pieces. Maria tried to make it clear to me that this guy was just a friend. A friend with weed. He lived in my building. Basically, he started chatting her up one day when she was getting the mail. He had a good job with irregular hours. Sometimes, like if she didn't feel like going to work or something, she'd stop at his place and smoke out. Or at least that's what she told me.

It pissed me off. She wanted my money, she was a compulsive liar, and she was probably fucking this dude. I drank like a Finn. I drank with Tomi's methodical silence as she jokingly belittled Joost's total ignorance of heavy metal and his musical preference for Oingo Boingo's masterworks.

But somewhere into my fourth beer, I resolved to take action. She knocked my beer glass flat onto the table when she reached over to stroke Joost's perfect, normal hair. She was making a joke, comparing it to her uncombed rat's nest.

That's when I realized she was too drunk to keep track of a key. I realized I was so pissed off that the beers had no effect on me. I remained completely lucid while Maria and Joost lapsed into sloppy drunkenness.

Maria went up to the bar to get me another beer. Joost went, too. But I stayed back. Not like they cared. They stood up there for a while. At one point, she leaned over the bar with arm outstretched. She wanted to get the bartender's attention. This dude Joost immediately moved his hand to her ass to steady her. Keep her from flopping tits first over the bar.

Fuck this, I thought. I slouched down in the seat and slid over to where Maria had been sitting. I leaned over to where her jacket lay all heaped up. I slid my hand into the pocket and pulled out her key.

They came back from the bar without a replacement beer for me. But I didn't care. I had the key.

The next morning, I used one of Maria's moves against her. I feigned sickness. It wasn't all fake. The night out with her and this dude had me feeling queasy. So I just stayed in bed as long as possible.

Normally, I got up first. Brewing coffee. Being useful. But that morning, I stayed in bed longer than Maria.

Eventually, she got up. She had work, too, so that played to my advantage.

And when she left, she didn't even notice her missing key. I'd kept it in my pocket overnight. She left in a rush. No David-brewed coffee. No David-made breakfast toast.

The second she left, I sprang out of bed. I was ready to greet a new and beautiful day. I traipsed around the empty slaapkamer like a frolicsome Care Bear. When I opened the curtains, even the turgid gray sky gave me a little jolt of joy. The sky was slightly less turgid than it had been the day before. I was sure of it.

It took about five minutes to gather all her shit into her bags. I double checked the slaapkamer, the badkamer, all the kamers, and then I dumped that shit in the hall. Just to be a dick, I emptied an ashtray in the top of her roller bag, then zipped it shut.

16.
The Bitterness and the Bereavement

And then I waited. I didn't go out that day. I skipped Neder-landse for buitenlanders, though that action risked earning me Helena's stern disapproval. I didn't even go on a beer run, not at first. I just huddled in my apartment. Every once in a while, I'd get this paranoid feeling I'd left the door unlocked. That Maria would somehow manifest her gross lying ass in my slaapkamer. So I'd pad over to the door, quiet quiet. I'd gently touch the thumb turn, just to triple confirm shit was secure. I'd peer out the peephole until I could see her bags. I'd count them, too. Just to make sure she hadn't come and taken one without me knowing. Even though I knew, deep in my bones, that when she came, she'd make her presence known.

Then, I'd trudge back to my recliner and slip on my head-phones. I wasted the day, and for no good reason. Maria was at work. She wouldn't be back until evening. And even if she'd skipped work, she was probably smoking out with this dude Joost. I didn't need to live in fear. I had many hours until she realized she'd been evicted. Besides, I had her key. She couldn't get in.

I hate-listened to *Infernö*, pulling faces at every slight im-perfection of Nekrokor's flaccid guitar execution. Occasion-ally, the disc skipped and stuttered. When I got to the last track, a fifteen-minute-long Casio symphony called "Omnes

Mortuus Est," I grunted and put the Discman away. All is dead. The pompous Latin title couldn't mask the unlistenable tedium of Nordikron helming some Casios for a quarter of an hour. All is dead . . . of boredom, if you listen to that one.

A light smattering of dust covered my guitar. I picked it up, but it felt unfamiliar in my hands. Heavy and inert. I started in on my standard guitar routine. Unplugged, though. Silent shredding. So no one in the hall—unlikely, but just in case—could sense my presence. I started with some random chords, then interspersed parts of scales in between, so I could warm up my left hand. I followed that up with some rhythmic riffing to get the blood flowing in my right hand. My hands, my fingers, moved, but felt dead.

Like Nekrokor.

Before Maria moved in, I sat in the recliner and played every day. Desekration dickwads may have kicked me out of the band, but it wasn't from a lack of technical skill. But Maria rarely let me practice in peace. She resented the way I stroked it, the way the guitar engrossed my attention. After she moved in, I couldn't play for more than a minute or two before she'd do something to secure her hold on my attention.

Even when she was doing something without me. She could be sitting outside, lost in some drunken haze and oblivious to my existence. The instant I grabbed my guitar, she'd call out from the deck for some random thing, an ashtray or a sandwich. She'd come and ask me for a back rub or something. She'd start into some long-ass story about some problematic co-worker or she'd burst into some fantasy conflict from her imaginary past.

Worse was when she tried to control what I played. Play this song. Play that song. Like a fucking jukebox. She asked me to play shit I liked—that wasn't the problem. It's just that she wouldn't let me zone out. She wouldn't let me meander through evil scales. She wouldn't let me chugg chugg chugg from Phyrgian to Phyrgian dominant and back in an endless, mindless haze. I couldn't get to that place in my head—a brachiating forest, a tower far from humanity, some briny chasm teeming with forms—where I could find an unknown riff, where I could explore an unknown sound.

So I learned pretty quickly not to bother with the guitar. It drew too much scrutiny. Even if I played without plugging in, she still came almost immediately to draw me away.

It wasn't all bad. Once, she was taking a bath. I surreptitiously grabbed the guitar and fingered the opening chords— no strumming—for "Godzilla," a classic for the ages. Just to be completely clear—I had not plucked a single string. But then the bathroom door swung open. She came to me, her body dripping with soapy water. She straddled my leg. Straddled my guitar. She pressed her crotch against my arm and said, "Finger this instead."

I guess you could say I should have learned to play more if it summoned a leg-straddling naked woman. But most of the time, the guitar was a chore magnet. If I reached for it, I'd be making a sandwich for a drunk chick just a few minutes later.

A sandwich. It sounded good. At this point, I guess just touching the guitar unleashed a Pavlovian response. I headed into the kitchen and grabbed a bag of potato chips. Less work. Also, I wanted to break the guitar-sandwich associative chain. The first crunch startled me, even as I chewed. I thought it was the door, crackling with flame, as Maria burned through it one cigarette at a time.

I crunched again. So loud. Like a siren alerting anyone in the hall to my presence. But I was really hungry. I grabbed the bag, then headed back to my recliner. I held my palm over my mouth as I chewed in an ineffective bid to muffle the sound.

Once I finished the bag, I set it on the table next to me. On top of my stolen hymnal. Then I went to swap out *Infernö* with something from my CD wallet. I didn't have much. Morbid Angel. Death. Terrorizer. Primarily the essential cornerstones of death metal as determined by this lone Florida man. A few '80s classics, too. Ozzy. Candlemass. Dio. And that's when I found the first sign of Maria's malfeasance, the lasting damage done.

She'd stolen one of my CDs. *Holy Diver.* Instead of the disc, there was just the booklet: the chain-swirling demon on the cover stared back at me.

That's what impelled my cleaning frenzy. A quest to find *Holy Diver,* maybe tucked away somewhere and not, heaven forbid, lost forever.

I got off the recliner and inhaled deeply. The smoky haze of tobacco and weed choked me. But I breathed it in even deeper. I didn't want to forget it—this is what happens when you let someone take over your space. This is what happens when you let someone steal your favorite Dio album. And then I resolved to scrub Maria, to scrub her fuliginous stink, out of my place.

Standing in the middle of the slaapkamer, I raised my leg and squeezed long and hard. With an urgent fart blast, I declared my independence. With a fart, I began the process of reclaiming my place as my own. Like a flatulent dog marking its territory. I farted again, pushing out the gas with the hope it would displace all the stank air expelled from Maria's charred lungs. Any little clouds of her breath, hovering in the corners like invisible balloons. My farts would push them out.

And then I started cleaning. Putting things back in their place, starting with the half-dozen plates and cups she'd conscripted into service as ashtrays. It wasn't a Martha Stewart level of cleaning. Just enough to help me regain control of my space and possibly turn up a Dio disc. But even my half-hearted cleaning dredged up considerable evidence of Maria's destructive tendencies:

She'd burned a charred black and vaguely triangular shape into the carpet by my recliner. The burn had an uneven depth and shape, as though she'd stubbed out at least fifty cigarettes into the rug, rather than putting them out in the ashtray resting on the table next to the chair. For a brief wistful moment, the burn—its size, its shape, its color—reminded me of her spare and bristly bush. They were roughly equal in size and shape. But then I regained inner mastery. I quickly pulled the recliner over the stain.

She had not left the bathroom untouched. A mass of hair, soap scum, and other suspicious grime the length and girth of a small mouse clogged the bathtub drain. Though, to be fair, the sediment holding it all together, a tenacious blend of splooge and snot, had to be mine. I grasped it with the tips of my fingers and pulled it free. It smelled of Dial soap and decay.

I took it to the kitchen and pitched it into the garbage can under the sink. At this point, the bag overflowed with used napkins, coffee grounds, and empty cans. I figured I'd take the bag down to the dumpster in the basement. A sludge of water and weed residue scuzzed up the bottom of the kitchen garbage can. I noticed this when I hoisted the bag out of the can, something I guess I hadn't done in some time. Stuffed with trash, the bag strained in the can. As I pulled, water sloshed around. I didn't understand where the sound was coming from until I got the bag all the way out of the can. Water and stems and bits of pungent leaves filled the bottom of the garbage can. When I tried to tie the bag shut, the top half of a plastic milk jug flopped onto the kitchen floor. I'd spent enough time with the Morris brothers to recognize the sign—Maria, probably assisted by Joost, had turned my garbage can into a water bong. But they'd never cleaned it out. And in the refrigerator, they'd balanced a paper plate on the top of the remaining half of the milk jug they'd decimated in their bong construction process. They'd finished all my beers, too.

Worst of all, Maria had somehow managed to break my sparrow bone crown. As I dusted the shelf, peering in nooks and corners for *Holy Diver*, I gently bumped the crown with my rag. The thing exploded, though. Bones rained, one by one, onto the rug. The fishing line that should have held them all together fluttered down last of all. Somehow, she'd taken every single bone off the string, then left the bones in a heap. Restringing the thing would take forever, but I couldn't bring myself to throw away all the bones now strewn on the rug. Handmade by Mathias, probably from birds he had caught, the thing was a disgusting artifact. And I hadn't even wanted to wear it. But I wasn't ready to get rid of it. I collected all the bones in my palm and set them in a neat pile on my bookshelf.

At least I thought the bone crown sabotage was the worst thing she'd done. But I was wrong. She also stole my bike.

I discovered this last criminal act after I took the garbage down to the basement. I sneaked out of the apartment and no one jumped out at me. I set the bag down, then quickly rifled through Maria's stuff for my Dio CD. It wasn't there, though. So I took to the stairs—highly unlikely to find Maria clambering up five flights—and dumped the garbage. Afterward, I had a craving for an afternoon beer. It seemed like an ideal reward for my cleaning and a way to soothe the sting of the many insults against the sanctity of my place. I was still on guard, though. Ready for Maria to rage against her eviction. So I figured I'd bike to the store. It would be faster. I could make a clean getaway, beers in hand, if she spotted me out there on the streets of Gent.

I normally kept the bike locked in the building courtyard. The courtyard was empty except for two poles with a clothesline strung between them. Greenish black moss clung to the edges of the concrete pavers lining the courtyard. One of the poles was under a concrete overhang created by the terrace of the apartment on the second floor. I locked my bike to that pole so my chain wouldn't rust in the endless freezing rain.

The courtyard seemed like a safe place to park it. You couldn't even get out there unless you had access to the building. But the bike had disappeared. Even though I registered the bike was gone, I went to the exact spot where I'd locked it. I shuffled around the pole, like I'd find it on the other side or something. No dice. I headed out to the middle of the courtyard, then tilted my head up. Nothing but a gray square of sky far above.

I hadn't immediately fingered Maria as the culprit. Maybe

a helicopter came down. A larcenous, but very strong, bird. Like a raven or something. They go for shiny things. When these explanations seemed increasingly implausible, I studied the terraces above me. A few of them had bikes, but not my bike. No yellow bikes. No rentals. I was probably the only buitenlander in the whole building. Some thieving neighbor could have winched it up to their apartment with a rope or a grappling hook or something, but that didn't seem likely. Besides, the thing had been locked up.

I was sure of it. I felt in my pocket for my keys. The bike key was still there, safe and secure with my apartment key. So I went back to the pole and studied the ground around it. The moss on the pavers had been flecked and scratched by the kickstand. The phantom kickstand. I was in the right place, but the bike was nowhere to be found.

Leaving the courtyard, I wondered if maybe I'd left the bike at the grocery store. I figured I'd check the bike rack over there before I got my beer. That had been the last place I'd taken it, just a few days before.

The bike rack in front of the store had at least ten rental bikes. All yellow, all a little run down. Just like mine. Each time I spotted one, I felt this ecstatic frisson of ownership. Like, there's my bike! But then I'd get a little closer and realize the bike wasn't mine. This one had a Rasta-striped seat cover. That one had white brake cables, but mine were black. Another one had paniers, but I hadn't forked out for such deluxe features.

My bike wasn't there. That's when I started to suspect Maria. I hadn't given her any money, but if she'd learned anything in her imaginary tenure at the anarchist squat, it's that bikes are currency. She couldn't have learned that since she never lived at the anarchist squat, obviously, but what I mean is that she had a motive—my cash, my goods, all for her. And I suspected I didn't have too long before she'd be back at my place. I left all the bikes that weren't mine and headed straight for the beer aisle. Scanning the shelves for something strong and dark, I settled on a pack of Westmalle Tripel to resupply my refrigerator. And by the time I got home, I was even more convinced Maria had something to do with my missing bike. Out of spite, I kicked her bags before I went in my place and locked the door behind me. I cracked a Westmalle and put the rest in the refrigerator. Enjoying the silence of my empty and more sanitized space, I moved over to my recliner and settled in with my brew. And after a few minutes, the silence, the cleanness, started to overwhelm me. Even though I'd worked so hard for these things. I could hear, then feel, a vast void of silence and the orderliness of all my shit magnified its enveloping nature. Complete silence. Or nearly complete. The faint insect whine of nascent tinnitus—hessian's bane—gnawed at its vast silent edges. It was too much. I had wanted this silence, but now that I had it, I couldn't handle it.

I reached for the Discman, put on my headphones, and pressed play. *Infernö* was still in there. The Discman rattled a little, like it did whenever I played Desekration's masterwork. The intro started—"Centuries ago, the plague burned through the population ..."—and then the Discman wheezed. After a weedeater whirring, it jumped to the last track, the one I told you about. "Omnes Mortuus Est." Nordikron and his sinister synthesizer. Fucking bullshit. The worst song. But I let it play.

It started with a breeze—the breath of the tundra, the sighs of damned souls, the hiss of four-track technology—and gradually resolved into Nordikron moaning into the microphone. Up to that point, the first minute or so of the song could serve as the intro for any number of metal albums. After a brief interlude of obscure atmospherics, a barrage of guitars and death barks always comes crashing through. But this one, "Omnes Mortuus Est," just kept going. And after Nordikron moaned for a while, "omnes omnes omnes omnes omnes omnes," a cheesy clarinet melody started in. The kind of thing you might hear in a cartoon. When Robin Hood and Maid Marion join arms and spin through some rustic village dance. An electronic drumbeat came in, too. But not some industrial avalanche, some 808 wall designed to thud you into submission. More like a polka beat, jaunty, replete with cymbals. The sound of the jester's bell-fringed costume as he, too, flailed along with ye maypole dancers of olde.

I jabbed the skip button, but nothing happened. I could have just taken off the headphones, flung the Discman across the room, but instead I sipped my beer. Listening to the song, eyes closed, the Westmalle taking effect, I felt like the sounds described a journey through some ancient landscape. As I listened, the corny pre-programmed synthesizer effects persisted, but they occasionally resolved into some new set of sounds evoking some new landscape. The clarinets and polka beat faded away, replaced by the gentle flute and leaf crunching—possibly Dorito munching—of a single hiker traversing a forest trail. A pipe organ and a stony echo evocative of some ancient building, a chapel or tower, gradually faded into the mournful wail of the wind once more. And then Nordikron chanted, monkish and funereal, "mortuus, mortuus, mortuus, mortuus, mortuus, mortuus," his voice accompanied by the sound of flickering flame. After that, there's a battle or something. Goblins grunt. Trolls on patrol. Coconut hooves. And then it's like the ocean comes and swallows his Casio. Sucks it down deep into the depths. You hear the muffled silence of the underwater world. The shimmer of passing beasts, their scales like fire-forged mail. And again, Nordikron's chants, but deeper and drenched in echo: "omnes" first, and once it fades, "mortuus." A pattern repeating until the end of the track.

It played almost to the very end, then my fucked up Discman seizured back to the troll trumpets and moaning oboes, the part that sounds like whatever anthem goblins might play before a baseball game. It looped back a few times as I sat there sipping my Westmalle. I just let it play and immersed myself in my Discman's Möbius strip of synthesized sound.

Eventually, I finished the beer. The sun shone through the plate glass window, making me feel warm and sleepy. I slid off the recliner and stretched out on the rug. The Discman rested on my chest, its whirring a cat's purr against my heart. And as I continued listening to "Omnes Mortuus Est," I slipped into the powerful grip of a beer-fueled afternoon nap. Still dimly aware of the overlapping layers of Casio sound, I slipped into a dream, a vivid image of Maria floating through my front door and into my apartment.

Do you dream like this? Do your dreams have soundtracks? This happens to me if I'm listening to music when I sleep. It opens a portal to the riff-filled land. But this happens to me even if I'm not actively listening to music when I fall asleep. My unconscious picks some album and streams it for me in the background of my dreams. My unconscious always chooses metal, or something like this, some kind of electric doom synthesis. Mathias would say it was the devil calling me in my sleep. That this kind of phenomenon is just another one of the devil's many marks on my frail frame.

Maybe it was the ocean part, the sound of a coral-encrusted synthesizer controlling the fish and their movements. Maybe it was the Westmalle, high percentage and coursing through my veins on a day where I'd subsisted otherwise on coffee and Triscuits. It felt stronger than a dream. More like a vision. And in it, a spectral Maria, clad in her black thong, floated through the front door of my apartment. I could see the thong I knew so well. I could see the pencil eraser mole right where it gripped her hip. I could see her skin, in this vision as gray and washed out as the leaden sky. She held a massive key. A skeleton key. Like the ones from the cathedral window, but green and glowing. And as she drifted further, over my kitchen table and into the slaapkamer, I could see that a vast translucent cloak covered this phantom Maria. She was a Halloween ghost, clad in a sheet, its edges scraping dust from the floor, crumbs off the table. And as this phantom, specter, maybe succubus, drifted closer, I could see that it—that she—wasn't covered in a sheet. More like a quilt. One stitched together from so many old and worn band t-shirts: Ozzy, Ostrogoth, Priest, Dio. A quilt stitched together from Maria's wardrobe, all her old ass shirts that, in reality, lay jumbled together with all her other shit on my front doorstep. The demon from *Holy Diver*, its insect eyes, its vaguely equine head, spread across her neck. Its coiled whip wound up her cheek and disappeared into her hair which, I guess because she was a flying ghost, undulated slowly like a mass of seaweed, sea serpents, squid tentacles. An airbrushed scorpion stretched under her arm and around her back. At the sheet's draggled hem, Ozzy hoisted Randy Rhoads and the movement of the fabric made this screen-printed madman and his favorite guitarist march jerkily across the rug.

In the dream, she hovered above me where I lay stretched out on the rug. She lowered down and I thought, succubus 69, but she didn't come down all the way to me, all the way to the floor. She lowered just enough to set the key down by my guitar. And then she drifted up again, like a parade float or something, and turned back toward the kitchen, the door, and then out into the ghostly aether or wherever phantom chicks go when they're not delivering medieval dungeon keys.

But without the key, this Maria phantasm couldn't soar through the door, couldn't soar back out into the broader spirit world. Instead, she repeatedly threw her body against it, like a frenzied bird beating its body, its wings, against the door in a useless and spastic bid to escape. And then the dream just paused there, with the ghost Maria, the vampire Maria, now key-less and uninvited, but trapped inside. She kept at her unholy racket.

It filtered through my headphones. The banging seemed, in my unconscious state, to come from floating dream Maria, bashing her gray-sheeted body against my door, and for a moment, I contemplated getting my ass off the rug and grabbing the green glowing skeleton key by my guitar and unlocking the door for her like a proper gentleman. And then I eased a little closer to consciousness. Close enough to know there was no ghost sheeted in concert t's, no skeleton key, and I figured the pounding I heard came from the headphones still over my ears. It was just the orcish war drums or the mesobenthic echo of a coelacanth's gnashing jaws. Something like that. But the banging continued and it roused me all the way awake.

I stripped off my headphones and shut off "Omnes Mortuus Est." The pounding came from my door, just like in the dream. It came from Maria. Just like in my dream. But outside trying to get in, not inside trying to get out. She must have found her stuff. She must have realized I'd snatched away her key.

And if you think this happens to me a lot—people pounding at my door, trying to get my attention, and me, oblivious, inside, well, you are right. I guess you could call that a character flaw, but it's just a symptom of my inherent introversion. Which is why I stayed on the floor, frozen in place. She kept knocking. Harder and harder. Slowly, I crept to my recliner and cowered behind it.

And then the knocking stopped for a while. But she was still there. Camped out on my doorstep. I could smell her. Smoking smoking. The smoke filtered into my kitchen.

I remained steadfast. My cowering continued. About an hour later, she started knocking again, this time in rapid and insistent bursts. One of the neighbors came out. I heard their door. A muffled conversation. Muffled crying. But then the neighbor went back in. She wasn't swayed by Maria's performance.

Much later, Maria got the point. By then, it was totally dark in the apartment. I didn't dare to turn on a light. I heard her shuffle her bags off the floor. I heard the elevator door open. And then I knew I was alone. More than likely, she padded down to dear old Joost's for comfort. But I didn't care. I got up from behind the recliner and went to the door. Peering through the peephole, I confirmed her bags were gone. That she was gone. And then I bravely opened the door. A row of cigarette butts lay on my doorstep. I grabbed my broom and swept them up. When I finished, I locked the door and then cracked open another Westmalle.

17.
Travel Plans

Natasha's calls hadn't stopped during the weeks of Maria's invasion. And Natasha's plan to visit gathered speed, took shape and form, during that time. I think that's part of the reason I was so eager to get Maria out of my place. Sure, the whole Joost situation spurred me into action. Along with Maria's fucking fantasyland of lies. But I also knew the countdown had begun. I knew that, even as Maria lay passed out drunk in my bed on any given afternoon, Natasha was out there, thousands of miles away, getting her passport, highlighting relevant passages in her *Lonely Planet* guide to Belgium, picking out the best money belt for securing her travel documents from pickpockets.

Maria unleashed a whirlwind of destruction in my apartment. Cigarette burns on my rug, hairballs in my drain, the theft of valuable belongings, like *Holy Diver* and my bike. She smote my crown of bones. And I lacked the mental clarity to uncover all that shit until I'd finally taken action, got her out of my place. But I shouldn't have been surprised. She'd flexed her destructive capabilities almost as soon as she'd moved in. She'd leveled the force of her hatred against something I also hated. The phone. She broke the phone just a couple days after she moved in. And I silently rejoiced.

I had been talking to Natasha. Sitting in my recliner.

Receiver to my ear. The phone itself was over by my bed. The cord stretched across the room. Natasha had called at our pre-arranged time. She'd called a little early, even. Well, she always called early. Kept me on my toes. She called earlier than early. In Dutch, that's vroeg. Dubbelvroeg.

And for once, that was fine with me. The earlier the better. That morning, Maria had put on her company polo shirt—white with an embroidered logo—and trudged off for a long day at the office, but I didn't really know when she'd be back. I hadn't even thought about it. I just marveled at seeing her in something other than black, something other than an old band t. And at that point, she hadn't lived with me long enough to reveal the full extent of her work attendance irregularities.

So I sat there talking to Natasha. Well, not really "talking." More like listening. And not very well. Better than normal, though, because she revealed some big news: she had her plane ticket to Belgium. I missed a bunch of the specifics, though. She cycled through a lot of information. I caught her arrival date. Bits and pieces of an extensive list of things she wanted to do. "Accomplish" was the word she used. Something about how stoked she was that she'd convinced her parents to buy the ticket in the first place. A bunch of shit she'd have to do to somehow pay them back, too. Her parents had loads of cash, but her dad always bitched about the evils of the entitlement mentality if he ever had to buy something for her. This was especially true if I was involved. It sounded like he hadn't been too psyched on laying out for a transatlantic flight so his daughter could come and stay with my dumb ass. And who could blame him?

So I sat there listening to Natasha and Maria came home. Maria moved through the apartment, her every move loud and lumbersome. She came into the middle of the slaapkamer and stripped off her work polo. Her pants, too. She threw them in a corner, then slipped on her Ozzy shirt. She went into the kitchen and started clanking all the dishes.

"What's that noise?" Natasha asked.

Cold fear gripped me and, for a second, I shivered like a bald chihuahua. I realized then I wasn't really cut out for this player life or whatever I thought I was doing. I couldn't juggle multiple chicks—not even if they were on entirely different continents.

"Oh . . . uh," I fidgeted in my seat. "The neighbors or something," I finally said.

Maria's every move resounded, loud as fuck, like a jukebox blasting random kitchen sounds. I cupped the receiver with my hand, but it didn't do much to help.

And then Maria came back into the slaapkamer. She had a can of Primus. Half liter. The kind you can get in a vending machine at the train station. She came over to me, closer and closer. The whole time, Natasha went on about rail passes, famous sights, train schedules. I held up my palm to ward Maria away, but it did no good. She held the beer super close to the receiver, then popped it open. The carbonated fizz totally muffled anything Natasha was saying. Maria handed me the beer, then went over to the phone. She picked it up and yanked it really fucking hard. She had one hand on the phone line, too. The whole phone jack just exploded out of the wall.

The last thing I heard Natasha say was, "a day trip to . . ." followed by nothing.

The phone stayed broken for a long time. Getting it fixed was no joke. To get the phone guy to come, you had to sign up for an appointment and then you had to actually go to the phone company office and call them there from a phone bank they had set up in their waiting room. Like, you needed an appointment to go to their office so you could tell them by phone that your phone didn't work. Except no one ever picked up. I went there once and sat on hold for over an hour. Every fifteen seconds or so, some prerecorded message came on. "Het spijt ons," it started. "We're sorry." And then a bunch of shit I couldn't understand. Eventually I left.

I should have been pissed at Maria for breaking my phone. Or at least alerted to the shit that was to come. Her phone destruction should have been a clue. But at that point, my reasoning capabilities had been dulled by several evenings of screwing and post-coital beers. Pre-coital, too. Plus, I was still reveling in her non-pregnancy. I was ready to let anything go.

And, really, the broken phone made it easier for me to live with Maria and still talk to Natasha. I just took my phone card out to some pay phone and called Natasha from there. It sucked I had to use my phone card—up to that point, she'd been footing the phone bills—but I figured I didn't have a better option. I figured I deserved it, too. Penance. And as the weeks with Maria went on, I realized I wanted Natasha to visit. It made me realize I was thankful for Natasha. I was ready to see her. Like, I realized my relationship with her was real, even though she was far away. And that my relationship or whatever with Maria was just a distraction.

I ran into Maria about a week or so after the eviction. I'd gone down to get the mail. After she was gone, I woke up every morning with this rush of giddiness. I felt like Julie Andrews prancing across some Alpine meadow.

The mailman had his head in my mailbox.

"Goeiemorgen," I said and he said "goeiemorgen" right back, the words echoing metallic and droidish. He handed me a letter. From Natasha.

At the end of the lobby, an old guy with a thick moustache unfolded a newspaper.

"Goeiemorgen," I said to him, and he said "goeiemorgen" back, too.

And the guy who rented me the place was right at the edge of the lobby. He had on a chalk-line suit and brown loafers. A paisley tie cinched tight around his neck. He was flipping through a sizable tangle of keys so he could unlock the door to the rental office.

"Goeiemorgen," I said, even though he kind of intimidated me. Any opportunity to flex my skills.

He returned my greeting, but he laughed as he said it. The way you would if a toddler came up and shook your hand.

The elevator opened and I got ready to wish a hearty goeie morgen to whoever came by. It was Maria, though. She had on her work clothes. Her work polo. White and unblemished. Blue dress pants. Her leather jacket on top.

She already had a cigarette going, too.

My goeie morgen froze in my throat. "Goe. . ." I said, then pressed my back against the mailboxes so she could pass. So she could go to work and leave me in peace.

"You," she said. And then she charged me. I caught her by the wrists.

Natasha had slapped me before. I recognized the signs. And when Natasha slapped me, she may have had a point. But this? Maybe I'd been underhanded, but my actions were totally justified. And since I had Maria's key, she couldn't cow me. My good mood fizzled and I kind of lost it. I just said exactly what I wanted to say to her.

"Fuck you, Maria." I pushed her off me.

The mailman, the old newspaper reader, and the realtor guy formed a captive audience.

"You lied to me. You. . ." and here I just laughed. At her enraged charge. At her stupid lies. Her trash can water bong.

"You stole my fucking bike," I finally spit out. "*Holy Diver*, too."

And then I came to my senses. My luxe lobby was no place for some telenovela spectacle. The rental dude hadn't even wanted me to move into his fancy ass building. And I didn't need to invite any scrutiny from him. I already knew next month's rent might be a little late. So I broke away. Before springing up the steps, I turned and addressed the lobby.

"Het spijt ons," I said.

Maria had the good sense to let it go. She turned and walked out of the lobby without another word. When I got up the first set of stairs, I stopped and listened. I heard some muffled chatter. Some laughter, too.

Sinister Synthesizer

I opened Natasha's letter in the locked safety of my apartment. She'd sent a photocopy of her flight itinerary. She'd drawn a big pink heart around the part that showed her arrival time.

18.
Too Good for Metal

The walls of my single slaapkamer home slowly closed in over those short winter days. Closed in like a tomb. For two. The walls of my small apartment closed in over those short winter days with Natasha.

She hadn't come to Gent to stroll along the Graslei or sneak in a covert make-out session somewhere along the darkened staircase spiraling to the top of the Belfort Tower. This was no romantic vacation, I determined when, two days after her arrival, I had yet to get laid. She'd come on a mission.

A mission aimed at self-improvement. At my self-improvement.

The days were short and, luckily, so was her trip. Just one week. Two days in, and I wanted her to leave. So I could romance myself. Alone and with some hand cream.

I woke with a headache. Like a hangover. But it wasn't. Natasha didn't drink. At least she hadn't yet on this trip. And I hadn't either.

She let me sleep next to her. But that was about it. Maybe it was the residual jet lag or something, but she was a deep sleeper. I lay there, unmoving, eyes closed, and wondered what would make her finally forgive me, release me, from the stain of all my sins. I lay there, unmoving, thinking how stupid it was for me to let her come. The long phone calls. The endless bouts of self-recrimination. I should have known.

I should have known the moment I picked her up from the airport. I'd taken the train in to Brussels. The flight arrived pretty early. On a Monday. I rode the express train into the city with all the suits. Then posted myself in the arrival hall. I should have known, but she caught me off guard. When I saw her, dressed in one of those long skirts I knew so well, her long hair down, slightly disheveled from the flight, an immediate sensation of need, of hunger, of fulfillment, all joined together, overwhelmed me.

I moved toward her, toward the long hair I would soon touch. Toward the lips I would soon kiss. I'd thirsted for her, but never thought I'd slake that thirst again.

"Natasha," I squealed, and captured her the instant she stepped into the arrival hall. The moment she passed out of the customs zone.

She stood still while I held her. She didn't hug me back. She didn't kiss me. She tolerated my embrace. But all I felt was a deep gratitude. A deep thankfulness that she let me hold her. That I could hold her again.

"I missed you," I said, and nuzzled her neck.

"I'm here," she replied, "so we can start again."

And that's when her reprogramming regimen began in earnest.

Still lying there, preparing to face another long day of Natasha's visit, I reasoned that my body sent the headache as a message. It needed a drink. My body used the morning headache to convey that urgent truth. Or I just needed some time alone. I missed Maria. The old guilt I used to feel about Natasha had transformed into a fresh and new guilt I felt for kicking Maria out of my apartment. With her, if I had a headache in the morning, it was from an actual hangover. And she'd let me roll over and bone my way back to full health.

Far away, on the other side of the bed, Natasha stirred to

life. She slept late, but that just gave her more energy once she was up. She leaped off the bed, then cast the curtains apart with one quick yank.

"Let's get some breakfast!" she said in a too-cheery tone.

"Urgh," I grunted back.

We'd never spent so much time together. The two of us, trapped, together. We'd never even stayed together overnight. In Miami, her parents torpedoed any possibility of her staying at my place. There was a definite curfew that could not be violated.

And they definitely wouldn't let me sleep in her room. Or anywhere else in the house. After a New Year's party at her parents' house, I asked if I could sleep on the couch in their living room. Her dad pulled me aside and said I couldn't. That I should go home. But as he told me this, he must have realized I was drunk, maxed out on champagne. He didn't want me to hit the road and die. Not if it could be construed as his fault. Instead, he said I could sleep outside. He ushered me to the patio door and gently pushed me out. He pointed to a lawn chair by the pool. I picked up two towels, beige and white and riddled with holes, from the pile they kept for washing the dog.

The next morning, he brought the dog out on a walk. My first thought that year was "The dog sleeps inside, but I sleep outside." Natasha and I broke up just a couple months later.

"I saw a cute pastry place when we were coming back last night. Let's go there!" she said.

I threw on a shirt—plain black, mostly clean—and we headed out. She meant the Vooruit. The techno café. Across the street from the Record Huis. On the walk over, I put my arm around her shoulder. She didn't object. By the time we got to the Vooruit, I'd moved my arm down and around her waist. The soft curve of her hip pressed against my palm with each step. Vooruit. Progress. Maybe this time that word would mean something for my life. First I'd touch her hip. And then we'd progress. We'd move on from there.

After we got our coffee and pastries, we sat at a table by

the window. By the time I'd scarfed down an entire croissant, Natasha had finished her first bite. She nibbled with finesse, exploring the full flavor range in each molecule of her lingonberry turnover. I wasn't used to eating in civilized company. Or any company. I tried to impress her with my mastery of Nederlandse. I translated little bits of Dutch on passing cars and trucks.

I think she got tired of my routine. She pulled a small library of guidebooks out of her purse. Belgium. France. Luxembourg. Each one stuffed with a kaleidoscope of post-it notes.

"What should we see first?" she asked. She flipped through the pages on Gent, asking my opinion on the main tourist sites. By that point, I'd been to each of them many times. I was not as enthusiastic as she wanted. My attention wandered. I stared out the window while she looked up the opening time for castle Gravensteen. She figured I'd like that one best.

"Ooh . . . you've got to see this!" I said. "One of Gent's main attractions. A real curiosity."

She got excited.

"What is it?" she said. She closed the guidebook and scooted closer to me.

"There. That guy," I said. I nodded out the window. "That's Jurgen Svart. Svartikles."

He lurched up the street, at least a head taller than anyone else around him. The morning crowds moved briskly around him as he huffed and puffed his way to work. His shirt—Desekration, of course—rode up past his belly button. His gut, bare and white, cut through the brisk morning air like a beluga's dome.

"The rare Svartikles in the wild. I lived on his couch when I first got here." I mouthed my words. Tried not to move my lips. Hunched my shoulders and eased back from the window. I didn't want to reveal myself. I mean, it's not like Svart would bust into the Vooruit and defecate into my coffee cup or something. Seize my woman and haul her away on his shoulders. It's not like he'd even notice us. Svart was generally pretty oblivious to his surroundings. Hot ladies and heavy metal shirts drew his attention on the street. That's about it. Natasha's a hot lady, but she was safely ensconced behind a plate glass window.

"Oh," she said. Unimpressed. She went back to her guidebook.

"Why do you want to be like him?" she asked.

It was a simple question.

I found myself defending Svart. He'd helped me out. Given me a place to stay. Let me join his band. He was a solid bassist. No Geddy Lee, but skilled. I told her how he coached Juan. How he helped me.

She followed it up with another question.

"Where do you think he'll be five years from now?"

The answer was obvious. He hoisted his camo pants, giving all of Gent a quick glimpse of some tighty whities and the décolletage of his hairy butt crack. Before he stepped into the Record Huis, he scratched his scalp and shook his giant mop of hair. In five years, Svart would be in the same place. A little older. A little sweatier. But here.

"I always thought you were too good for it," she said.

"For metal?" I asked. I set the spoon down.

If she'd said something like that in Miami, if anyone had said anything like that in Miami, I'd have smirked, or snarled, or disregarded them in some way.

I took a long sip of coffee. I didn't know how to respond. Too good for metal? I didn't even know what that meant. For me, metal had an almost supernatural power in a world otherwise mired in banality. Too good for the only remaining path to the ancients? Too good for the only sounds capable of unleashing the rhythmic contortions of the reptilian mind? Too good for the only modern music that laid claim to, paid feasance to, and presented itself as a living oblation to the classical, baroque, Renaissance masters? Too good for the only thing that's consistently comforted me since I was six? Comforted me when my mom hid behind her icy mantle of emotional nonresponse. Comforted me when my dad spewed hostility encased in a whisky breath fog every night after school. Comforted me when my friends abandoned me, abandoned our band, and left me behind. Too good for the only thing that comforted me after Natasha herself left me. After she left me with all my guilt.

Too good for metal? I took another sip of coffee. The caffeine jolted my sense of self-worth. Didn't she know I was David Fosberg, once signed to Plutonic Records?

I put the cup down and started to ask her that same question.

"Natasha, don't you know who I am? I'm David Fosberg. Don't you know I was . . ."

I couldn't even finish my question, though. Its utter stupidity registered as the words came out of my mouth. My ego high flamed out fast, replaced by reality. Yeah, I was once signed to Plutonic. To a small record label barely able to pay the rent on their shitty warehouse. Once signed. Was signed. Past tense. And then I was signed to Despondent Abyss, another tiny blip in the music world. Once signed. Now signed to nothing.

At that moment, her program of reprogramming began to work. I drained my cup, then went up for a refill. If you could think of the music business as J. Lo's big round ass, its cheeks flapping in eternity, then Plutonic was like a flea, hanging on for dear life, its tiny jaws clamped somewhere on the left cheek. Somewhere on its outer edge. Despondent Abyss was like some microscopic mite camped out on the flea's leg, a mite so miniscule it's not even aware it exists somewhere in the orbit of a quivering ass. And me? In this tortured metaphor, I'm not even on that ass. Nowhere close. I'd been dislodged— shaken free. Maybe, just maybe, I thought, Natasha had a point.

When I came back to the table, I sat down and said, "I don't think I'm 'too good' for metal."

And here I unspooled to her everything I'd been thinking about since that asshole Nekrokor booted me off the stage.

That I was useless. That I sucked. That it was cool to be in Belgium, but really, I was just a loser and I guess I was okay with that, but I just wanted to be a loser in Belgium for as long as I could, because I knew I could maybe delay, but never escape, my true destiny, which was to be a loser in Florida.

She never contradicted me. When I said I was a loser. But she did try to steer me on the right path. She asked me why I felt compelled to play metal, to listen to metal, to dress metal, if it wasn't doing anything for me. She suggested that many of my faults probably stemmed from this rigid adherence to metal. She hinted that some of my hygiene defects were probably metal related. I stiffened when she implied that my inability to do laundry, or my covert morning farts, or the gunk under my nails were also expressions of metal identity. But then she backed off a bit, returned to her main point.

"There are other things you can do," she said. "That's all I mean."

"Other things," I said.

"Other things," she repeated. She reached across the table and put her hands on my hand. My gross, nail-gunked hand. The wart hand. It was the first self-directed action she'd taken to touch me since she got to Belgium.

"You're an artist. You get to decide what kind of art you make."

I leaned across the table, too. "I know what kind of art we should make," I whispered.

She giggled. And let me kiss her neck.

"Maybe we could go back to my place?" I suggested, still holding her hands.

19.
Romantic Getaway

It didn't work. My ploy. To get laid. We didn't make it back to my place until later that night. Her Belgium guidebook had set a punishing schedule. We'd spent the day out in Gent. Pastries. Castles. Art galleries. All for naught. When we finally got back to my place, I sprawled next to her on the bed. She lay on her stomach. I put my arm across her back. I eased next to her and tried to kiss her. It wasn't easy. My lips barely reached hers. Eventually, she met my advances with some dry, crusty kisses. Then she said, "I'm not ready." She rolled away from me and fell asleep.

I rolled over too, drew my knees to my chest, tried to ignore the ache tugging away at my balls. Tried to ignore the feeling that this reunion, this going out again, wasn't really what I'd wanted.

It wasn't what she wanted. She made that clear the next morning. She woke up really early, jabbed me with her finger, then asked if we had everything we needed for our Paris trip.

"Our Paris trip?" I asked. "Yeah, after our Alaska trip," I quipped. I thought she was joking.

"I mentioned this," she said. The air grew colder around me. She wasn't joking.

"When?" I asked.

"On the phone. Before I came."

"The phone?" No wonder it hadn't registered.

"Yes. I told you I wanted to travel. That we should go somewhere . . . romantic. That we should go to Paris."

"Romantic?" I asked, like I didn't understand the word.

A pained expression pinched her face.

"It's not too much," she said. "A special trip. Think of everything you've put me through."

Here we go again, I thought, bracing myself for yet another litany of my many sins and defects, past and present, catalogued in full. This is how I missed the Paris plans. On the phone. She'd slipped them in while enumerating my faults.

I mean, she was right. I was far from perfect. I figured I deserved it. The problem, I guess, was that she'd numbed me through repetition. On the phone, she could make me apologize endlessly, mumble agreement to whatever she proposed, unaware that, even though I was unaware of what I said, she was fully aware of my every word.

She described the trip. She pulled tickets, maps, museum passes out of her bag. It was no discount outing.

"Wait. . . you already reserved all this stuff?" I asked.

"Of course. I mean, it's a week in Europe! There's a lot you can fit into a week. Especially if you don't spend all your time lying around."

In bed, I thought. That's what she meant. Lying around in bed. It's what I thought we'd do for the duration of her trip. Lie around in bed. Naked. Except for me. I'd be wearing a condom. Maybe we'd both wear socks. That's how I'd imagined the week. We'd lie around in bed. Recommitting to our love. Over and over again.

"I . . ."

Would I go with her?

How could I put it? When she laid out how much a few days of Paris, Natasha-style, would cost, all I could think was how much faster that would make me broke. Like the doomsday clock or something. At my current pace, I was at two minutes to midnight, but a Paris trip with Natasha would bring me right to the hour of doom.

A few days in Paris in the hotel she booked because the room had a direct view of the Arc de Triomphe, traveling to and from Paris on the fancy high speed train, plus the ambitious marathon of museum visits, concerts, shows, she'd mentioned, all of that money turned to zero a couple of months faster than my current pace, where beers formed the majority of my daily expenditures.

I wanted to stay. At least until summer. I wanted to last longer than Juan. I'd decided that much.

"Are you listening?" she asked.

I'd sort of drifted off into a reverie of the week I'd planned. And how easily we could make it happen. Her. Me. My apartment. Condoms. Fuzzy socks. We had all the necessary components for a good time.

"The train leaves tomorrow morning," she said. "My parents said if you came along, you had to pay half."

"And if I don't?" I asked.

"Don't what?"

"Don't . . . pay," I said.

"Then you can't come," she said. "It's not fair"

"But . . . are you still going if I can't?" I asked. I mean, how could she?

"Of course. It's Paris, David! They said they'd cover it even if you don't come. But if you do come, you have to contribute."

"I don't have . . ." I sputtered.

"You don't have what?" she said. "You have all kinds of time to run away from your life, sit around and hate yourself, but you don't have time to do what I want? I didn't come to Europe to spend all my time in some smelly apartment, that's for sure."

"Uh . . ." I frowned. Kind of sniffed. I'd cleaned the place before she came. Thoroughly. Trust me. It was clean. Not just metal clean.

"Besides," she went on, "all of my friends have been to Europe . . ."

She rattled off their names. I had a vague sense of who they were.

"You know how many have been here? How do you call this place? Gkhent? Guh-hent?" She emulated my throaty, but heel authentik, Nederlandse pronunciation. "You know how many have even gone to Belgium? Exactly none!"

I felt defensive.

"Belgium's the best," I said.

She didn't reply. I thought I was building some momentum. So I continued.

"And my place . . . it's clean. I cleaned it. For you."

"You don't get it, do you?" she hissed. She went over to the bed. She bent over the mattress. On her knees. I stupidly thought things would suddenly change in my favor. Ever so slightly, my balls stirred, ready to relieve their heavy load. But that's when she lost it.

She held something in her hand. Like a bundle of thread or ribbon or something. I didn't know what it was until she waved it in my face. A black thong. A whitish beige stain across the crotch. Maria's black thong. The stain could have been hers, too. Or mine. Or mold. The underwear must have been wedged somehow between the bed and the wall. It had to have been, no lie, like the only spot in the entire apartment I missed when cleaning.

"We weren't going out," I blurted. "You and me—we'd broken up!"

This really set her off.

She threw Maria's underwear at my head. Then followed it with a hard slap to my face.

"I found this last night," she said. "It touched my hand when I was sleeping. Disgusting. You didn't clean so good. I thought maybe you'd show me something different about you. About us. But the whole time I've been here, all you seem to think of is sex sex sex."

"I . . . it's because I love you," I said. "I'm so attracted to you." I tried to move toward her. She raised her hand again.

"You love screwing me," she said. "You think you love me, but you really don't."

At this point, I figured anything I said would just make it worse.

"I thought I loved you," she said. "I went out with another guy, but I didn't feel that connection. Not like we used to have. So I thought we'd try again."

Even though this wasn't going well, what she said, right then, about our connection, it gave me a glimmer of hope.

"Yes," was my brilliant reply. "Our connection."

"But now I know," she went on. "I don't have it with you anymore, either."

She threw the thong across the room, then lay on the bed, her hands wrapped tight against her chest. I picked up Maria's nasty underwear and stuffed it in the garbage can.

At this point, nothing was open. There was nowhere to go. I made some coffee and we sat in awkward silence until the sun came out. We had another day of tourism, sure, but she didn't talk to me the whole day.

We got back after we ate at some pizza place. At one point, she'd asked me to pass her a napkin, but other than that, she hadn't said anything to me.

She got some stuff out of her bag and went into the bathroom. When she came out, she said, "You want me in bed so much, then I get the bed."

I had the slightest idiot glimmer of hope. Maybe the day of silence had been punishment enough? I must have looked not completely miserable for a second. She realized I hadn't understood. She cleared it all up for me.

"I'll take the bed. And you take the floor. I'm waking up at five. A taxi's coming; I already reserved it."

The chirp of her watch alarm woke us up the next morning. She'd slept in her clothes, so she was ready to leave. She didn't say anything to me before she left. She just got up, put on her coat, and grabbed her bags. I slipped on my pants and shoes, checked my pocket for my keys, then rushed after her.

The elevator door closed as I made it to the landing. I took to the stairs, two or three at a time, then ran through the ground floor lobby. She'd already made it down. A red light, a car's brake lights, shone through the frosted glass door of the building. Outside, some guy hoisted Natasha's bags into the taxi trunk. The getaway car.

"Hey!" I shouted. Too loud. Energized by my five-flight sprint. My nasal American voice filled the air all around us. The guy looked over. Natasha, too. They both had the same expression. Untouched. Jaded. They'd seen it before.

She turned to the driver.

"Take me to the train station," she said. And then she was gone.

20.
The Triple Denial

When I evicted Maria, I felt amazing afterward. Full of energy. Like a million frappucinos frothed through my veins. If you'd cut me, I would have bled Colombian supreme.

But after Natasha left, I just felt like shit. I couldn't shake this vaguely unsettling feeling of nervousness that started in my belly and extended through my entire body. I felt it the instant that taxi carted Natasha off to the train station. And after that taxi took her away, I reassessed some things.

I went back in the building and climbed the stairs to my apartment. Then, I closed the door and trudged past the garbage can, the lacy straps of Maria's grotty thong spilling over the edge. The silence overwhelmed me. I had class later that morning, but the sun hadn't even come up. I had a few hours to kill. And I couldn't go back to sleep. I lay in bed and put on my headphones. Some music to fill the silence. Just me and a nasty thong, finally alone together.

The Discman still had *Infernö* in it. I pressed play and it crunched through Nordikron's tortured Tourette's cries: "Pla...pla...pla...plague...pla...pla...pla...plague..."

"Oh, fuck this," I said, then cast the headphones off. I got my CD booklet and flipped through my meager collection. Death metal, death metal, more death metal. Some grindcore for variety. A couple Candlemass albums. But nothing to speak to my lovelorn heart. I pulled out *Blizzard of Ozz*, and, with a little bit of finesse, got the Discman to play "Goodbye to Romance," the closest thing to a ballad I could find. Even that just made me feel worse. It made me think of Natasha even more. And what she'd been trying to tell me on those hours of international calls. Some other kind of music, she'd said. But I hadn't listened. And I couldn't make some other kind of music if I insisted on listening to the same music over and over again. So I popped that shit out and put it away. I zipped up the CD booklet and put it back on the shelf.

That was the first denial.

And for about ten seconds, everything felt right.

Until the silence crept in again.

I figured the silence was my punishment, though. That I deserved it. And when it got too much, I picked up my guitar. When I started warming up, though, it was the same old thing. Automatically, my fingers picked out some evil scales. Automatically, I chugged out some generic riff. Natasha had this faith in me, that I could play some other kind of music, that I could be someone better, but it didn't seem possible.

I stopped playing for a minute.

"Some other kind of music," I whispered. And then absently strummed "Smoke on the Water."

"Aargh," I groaned. I needed to quit metal, that much was clear to me. Everything wrong in my life I could attribute to metal: I'd slept with Maria because she was so metal. I asked Svart to join Desekration so I could keep playing metal. I'd moved to Gent in this hopeless pursuit of a kind of music, a kind of life, that wasn't any good for me.

But quitting metal was not going to come easy. I took a deep breath and closed my eyes. I thought of songs I played before metal. The songs I'd learned as a kid. So long ago. Classical songs. On the piano. Instinctively, I started picking out the opening run of "Solfeggietto," the piano song most deeply ingrained in my memory. On a piano, I could play it blindingly fast. If I ever felt nervous, I drummed the opening notes against my leg. When I'd poisoned myself with a salmonella curry, its vertiginous runs had streamed through my fever addled brain on infinite repeat. C.P.E. Bach was not metal, I determined. J.S. Bach wasn't metal, either. Nothing by any Bach counted as metal.

So I committed to a noble, non-metal task: playing my old piano lesson songs on my guitar. It was a slow and laborious process. I was out of practice. At first, I flubbed many of the notes. Translating my finger positions from piano to guitar took some work. And there was no reassuring chugg-chugg-chugg-ing, no headbanging, at all. I kept at it, chugging coffee between tries. And for brief moments, I was able to ignore the emptiness of my apartment, the way I'd totally fucked things up with Natasha.

That routine worked for a couple weeks. I just didn't listen to music at all. When the silence got to be too much, I took out the guitar and played through "Solfeggietto." As much of it as I remembered.

I had the hymnal, too. The one I'd stolen from St. Baafs. I lacked Nordikron's ability to locate hymns with lyrics and chord progressions that would have sounded just right on an Incantation album. But that was just as well. I picked out the droning chords from the dozens of psalms in the front of the hymnal. I fought the urge to intersperse them with devastating riffs, though it was so easy to do.

"I'm not playing metal," I'd mutter to myself when I got too carried away.

The time and energy it took me to figure out these songs helped me. When I brooded too much on Natasha, on my failure, I just reached for the hymnal and tried to figure out some new song. And after a while, the deep regret I felt about Natasha turned into the smaller regret I felt for selling Mathias my keyboard. These songs and my attempts at renouncing metal would have been easier if I'd kept that thing around. By its very nature, the guitar impelled me toward metal. I had to work hard to stay away from the power chords, I had to actively reject "Smoke On the Water" and its slippery slope to musical slaytanism.

Only Dutch class got me away from my wallowing. Away from my brooding and solo guitar noodling. And I started becoming friends with Abdul. It wasn't like Juan ever stopped by.

I guess Abdul and I really became friends on the big field trip to St. Baaf's. It was the last trip for the class. We had a private tour of the big Van Eyck mural. *Adoration of the Mystic Lamb.* In Dutch, they called it *Het Lam Gods.* Abdul just called it "the magic sheep." An art professor from the local university pointed out all the key details and explained them, in Dutch. We had a worksheet that we had to submit at the end of the class. I had a hard time following along, though. Like, I could see where the lady was pointing when she explained some detail. She'd point at the sheep Jesus standing on an altar, blood streaming like a Slurpee from its side, and then she'd rattle off a bunch of sentences. Then, she'd point at the rainbow haloed dove floating above the sheep and she'd explain some more.

I wasn't getting anywhere on my worksheet, but Abdul scribbled away dutifully. So I moved over next to him and tried to borrow whatever I could.

After the lecture, we walked around together.

When we looked at the panel with the angelic choir, he pointed out the way the organ in the painting matched the organ in the cathedral. When we looked at the panel with the Annunciation, I pointed out the way the buildings outside of Mary's windows matched the buildings outside of the cathedral. The buildings, the city, had endured for centuries.

"The oldest building where I'm from," I said, "is a jail. You know this place is built on an even older temple?"

He agreed the place was cool, but he wasn't as impressed. He said, "You should go to Egypt, to my city, Siwa. The culture there is much older. But so many of the old stories, the myths and legends from all the different cultures that went there, they all say the same thing."

"What's that?" I asked, although I thought I knew. Total death, they all say. The end is the void and the void is forever. A tomb built on a tomb built on a tomb.

"They say to enjoy your life, man," he said. "Enjoy the woman, the drink, the sunshine."

"Wait . . . really?"

"Of course, man," he said. "In my city, people know this. They have all this history, but it helps them to enjoy this life."

"Yeah . . . that's, uh . . . good to keep in mind," I managed to reply.

"You're into that heavy metal stuff, right?" he asked me.

"Ah . . . not so much anymore," I said. The second denial. I half expected the chaos gods to tentacle me to death for yet another transgression.

"You like Metallica?" he asked, ignoring what I'd just said. "They have this one album. The cover's all black."

I tried to keep up my front. I tried to keep the smirk off my face.

He went on, extolling Metallica's extreme-ness.

"Maybe you've heard of it? You would never hear something like that, where I'm from. The music is so, so crazy." He went full Judd Nelson, his fist in the sky.

It was too much for me. I kind of snapped.

"It's not all black, dude," I said. "It has a huge logo. A coiled turd, too." And then I added, just for good measure, "The music's, like, arena rock."

Then I felt bad. About dissing him. About my shallow existence as an elitist metalhead dick. About how illogical it was to espouse elitist metalhead dickhead opinions if I was so intent on rejecting my elitist metalhead dickhead identity. Quitting metal, denying metal, wasn't going to be so easy. So I changed the subject. By complimenting him.

"Why are you in this class? Helena said this class is like for tourists, but your Dutch is really good. Why aren't you in one of the other classes? Like level two or something?"

"I am," he said. "This is all I do. I'm taking all the Dutch classes. I have to learn this language and learn it fast."

He told me more. His parents sent him here for a year. And with an ambitious agenda. To learn the language, get a work visa, and start a business. He'd been in Belgium about as long as I had. Besides the tourist class, he was in level three. And he'd found some potential partners for the export business he planned to base in Gent.

The thing about it was that he didn't seem stressed or overwhelmed by all his plans. If anything, telling me about them invigorated him even more.

"Oh ... I'm staying here until Helena's done," he added. "We're going out after class."

"You're going out?" I asked. "Like ... dating?"

"Yeah, man," he said, then broke into laughter. "I'm dating the teacher!"

"Wait ... how?" I asked.

"I saw her one day. Out for coffee. I just started talking to her. And then ..." more laughter, "one thing led to another."

"Damn," I said. "Good for you."

Helena finished up with the last group of students clustering around her and looked around for Abdul. He waved when she spotted him. Then, he grabbed my arm and brought me in for a hug.

"Okay, I got to go now. I'll call you and we'll hang out."

We exchanged numbers and then he left. He put his arm around her shoulder and headed toward the door. Then, he cupped Helena's ass with his palm, and looked back at me with a wide grin.

I couldn't help but laugh. But as he walked away, my laughter, its echo, just seemed frail and empty in this cavernous space, a tomb, I knew, no matter what Abdul said, and a monument to total death.

Around that time, I got a statement from the bank. It wasn't good. The number shocked me into calling my parents. To hit them up or cash. I'd been planning to beg for money for a long time, but I hadn't gotten around to it. I guess I was in denial. I worried about money, but I stupidly thought the problem would solve itself. Like my parents would magically sense my impoverished state and send a life raft of cash my way. But the bank statement—a number so close to zero—snapped me out of my inertia. Maybe they'd blow me off, I figured, but maybe they'd hook me up. Besides, I planned to tell them I had renounced metal. If anything would get me on their good side, it would have to be that.

So I got out a phone card. My dad picked up and said, "It's the prodigal," before passing the phone to my mom. A Biblical insult. The prodigal son. The one who wastes his dad's cash.

Since they already had me marked out as the leech, I just got right to the point. I needed money, I told her. Bad. And then, I added the stuff about metal. The third denial.

My mom just grunted. I couldn't tell if the grunt meant "fuck off" or "help is on the way."

So I told her again. That I quit listening to metal. She still didn't respond. Just reminded me it had been my decision to quit Booksalot and go to Europe.

I was trying to explain I needed money in my account. And fast. To cover rent. Electricity. Essentials. I mentioned the metal thing again, too.

"But I thought you'd like that," I said. "That it would be a relief or something."

"A relief? Why?" she asked.

I had to really spell it out. "It would be a relief to you, my mother, that I'm not listening to metal. I'm moving on. I'm, like, growing up."

"We don't care what you listen to," she said. She sounded exasperated. "You can listen to acid rock all day. We don't care. We never have."

"But . . . but you always make fun of it," I said. "You call it the belching music."

"Oh, come on." That was my mom's way of saying, "What the fuck?"

She cupped the receiver and said, "He thinks we're out to get his music."

"Which kind?" my dad piped in. "The belching music, the screaming music, or the pointless noise?"

"All of it. The acid rock." My mom had a shaky grasp of modern music genres. "He says he's quitting it."

"I bet it was that girl. She got him," my dad exulted in mock triumph.

I heard the clink of ice in the background.

"She got him whipped," my dad continued.

"Won't spread her legs unless he does what she says," my mom added.

My dad grabbed the phone.

"Son, you listen to me," he said. His gruff voice boomed in my ear. "We don't give a damn what you listen to."

"But, you know, I thought, the deaths heads?" I replied weakly. I brought up the skulls, the gore, the teeming Lovecraftian horrors on all the band shirts I'd worn over the years.

"That's clothes. That's what people see. Like that hair," my dad said. "People see it and immediately think you're an idiot. Give them a chance to figure it out on their own."

And with that, he handed the phone back to my mom. This whole exchange was challenging my very idea of parent and child. Challenging the boundaries of the roles we'd defined over years of conflict. If they didn't really care, then was I still the rebel, the black sheep, the . . . what he said when he heard my voice for the first time in two months . . . the prodigal?

"It's true," my mom added, backing him up. "You're not helping yourself. We never had this with your sister."

"She has common sense," I heard my dad bellow in the background.

I looked at my watch, then did a quick time zone calculation. It was a little after five p.m. for them. Happy hour. No wonder they were so effusive. Almost affectionate in that special Fosberg way. Even when calling me an idiot. Still, I felt like I needed this. I needed them. No one else was going to call me out on my shit.

More ice clinking. My dad, probably in the kitchen, deathgrunted, "Would you like a top up?"

"Yes. I. Wooooould," my mom cookie monstered back.

This was probably the longest conversation I'd had with my parents in several years.

"That girl's got you in the palm of her hand," my mom said. "Some girls are just like that."

"She's got him somewhere else," my dad yelled in the background.

My mom sipped her drink.

"You know what she sees you as?"

A loser. A slob. The miserable ex she'd finally left behind? These were all likely choices.

"A meal ticket," she said.

I laughed, incredulous. I didn't even know what she meant.

"A meal ticket?" I tried to sort it out. "Like . . . she wants my money?"

It made no sense.

"That's the whole point of this call" I said. "I have no money. Natasha's family is . . ."

And here I inhaled deeply, ready to explain the big fat money gap between us and them. Natasha's family lived in Coral Gables. Their driveway had an iron gate. They had, like, soup tureens worth more than my mom's car. If anything, I was doubly stupid for fucking things up with her. She could have been my meal ticket. One of those soup tureens could have been mine.

If I'd turned things around, not wasted my chance, my second chance, not let my evil dick convince me to shack up with Maria, shack up with the thong behind my downfall, then maybe I could have lived, someday, in a house with an iron gate.

My mom talked over me.

"Yes, I know. They have money. We don't. So what?"

"Well ... I just ... I'm not sure how she'd see me as what you said. As a meal ticket."

"Hear me out. You had a good job. At that bookstore. Making good money."

"At the Booksalot?" I couldn't help but whine. My mom had just suggested that working at the bookstore counted as a "good job." What the fuck were they drinking?

Eventually, I persuaded her to send me some economic relief. I had to promise to pay it back. And then some. With money I'd earn when I got back to Miami.

But when my dad heard my mom talking about money coming my way, he just said, "Are you kidding me?" and then the money I'd so tenuously secured faded into thin air. My dad came on and told me I needed to learn how to persist without their help.

When I hung up the phone, I felt confused. I should have been pissed. No money. No help. On the other hand, I kind of felt thankful about what they'd told me. If my own parents didn't really view metal as this pernicious force shitting on my life, then why did I? Still, I held onto my anti-metal pledge.

My path of metal denial grew most challenging when I sat at home. The silence got to be too much for me. I can't just not listen to music at all, I thought. So I figured I'd go and buy something new for the Discman. Some other kind of music. If I was doomed to go back to Florida, it didn't really matter if I wasted a little money on stupid shit.

And if I was really going to quit metal, leave it like it left me, like Natasha had left me, too, then I needed some skin in the game. I figured I'd buy something that wasn't metal. Branch out. Attempt to grow, however modestly, as a human being.

I planned to skip the Record Huis entirely. Too much metal. Too much temptation. Instead, I went to Le Disque, a kind of multimedia superstore deep in the high rent heart of the city. It sat a couple of blocks from the McDonald's. You could buy video games, books, comics, action figures, stereo systems, even blenders and microwaves. You could, of course, find a vast array of music. But it didn't have a metal section. You could get Metallica, but not Slayer. They had Mötley Crüe, but not Celtic Frost.

The problem was I didn't know what to get. Something normal, I told myself. Normal like me. People swarmed in and out of the store. A yellow-vested security guard posted by the entrance checked each receipt.

As I came through the doors, I bumped against a cardboard cutout of Gloria Estefan in a white dress, a magnolia flower in her hair. I could get a Gloria Estefan album, I thought. She's from Miami—I'd be supporting my home music scene. Natasha's mom likes her, too. And then I sighed.

I had to take the escalator to get to the music. It didn't merit inclusion on the first floor, where televisions, microwaves, and video games took precedence. I jammed my hands in my pockets and rested one heel on the next escalator step. On the way up, I passed all these pop music posters. Each one made me think: will you be my pop star?

I escalatored past Harry Connick Jr. and his smarmy smile as he lounged fireside in a holly red sweater. A Christmas album could do the trick, I thought. But then I escalatored past Sinead O'Connor, so bald, so pale, her name written in taupe against an ivory background. Outspoken antipapist with an ethereal atmosphere. Normal, but also kind of metal. I briefly considered it. And then I escalatored past Trent Reznor, a bristly soul patch beneath his lip. One black leather glove. He had on a fur vest, parted to expose a midriff chiseled just so. This was a master of multiple arts—music and fitness. The blurb across the poster kind of sealed the deal for me. It said "hypnotically murky industrial beats suffocated by a cacophony of liquid steel guitar." And it came from *SPIN*, what counted as an authoritative, mainstream source. I knew that *SPIN* would never review any of my shit, they'd never review anything Svart stocked over at the Record Huis, but for normal people, that magazine was about as authoritative as you could get.

As I read the blurb, I thought, "I like murky beats," and "I appreciate cacophony, molten guitar tones." And then the escalator tossed me midway into the music section. Billy Joel to the left. Barbara Streisand to the right.

There were some more Nine Inch Nails posters clustered on a back wall. A Trent Reznor shrine. I followed, prepared to bow down before my new pop master. This was it—the pop music for me. So I grabbed a CD, the best one, then headed down to the cash registers.

With the lunch time crowd greedily buying computers, video games, and, to a lesser extent, music, the line at Le Disque crawled, snail-like, serpent-like, around a large section of the bottom floor. The line moved through the greeting cards section, and as I waited, I read about a hundred Dutch Happy Birthday cards, then it moved past a rack of Garbage Pail Kids cards—Jay Decay, Nasty Nick, and all the rest—and then it moved along a wall of music magazines.

Le Disque didn't really stock any metal, but they had a vast array of Eurometal magazines. The shelf was crammed—everything from *Aardschok* to *Blastbeat* to *Metaalridder.* This last magazine, *Metaalridder,* metal knight, and not metal rider, even though that one sounds cooler, had a Nekrokor tribute issue. A special edition. A profile of Nekrokor's life and times, of the mark he'd made on a burgeoning music scene.

Even in Le Disque, I couldn't get away from metal. Before I knew what I was doing, I grabbed this copy of *Metaalridder* out of the magazine rack and started flipping through it.

I jerked the magazine out of the rack to see Nekrokor and Nordikron. Torburn and A. Hex, too. Hair and shadows obscured their faces. A Dutch phrase emblazoned the bottom half of the cover declared this issue a full on "Nekrokor Speciaal!"

And even though this was supposed to be a special tribute

to Nekrokor, a fallen warrior who had fallen on Belgian soil, Nordikron was the main subject of the cover photo. You can tell that he alone had arranged and framed it, telepathically controlling the photographer through his spectral strangle-hold on the animal nature of the human beast. He had ar-ranged his little minions around him, so their greasy tresses form the sides of a triangle with Nordikron's luminescent face at the center. And even though he was a little dude, the short-est of them all, his head crowded out the rest of the band. Be-sides, you could barely see those other guys. The names and logos of all the other groups featured in the magazine, Beherit, Autopsy, Ancient Rites, and about twenty others, were plas-tered right over their already enshadowed heads.

"Urgh," I muttered, aware exactly of how much fore-thought and human engineering he'd probably put into getting this single photo just right. He was worse than some school yearbook photographer, forcibly twisting heads, shoulders, el-bows, like some sadistic chiropractor. He'd probably daubed his fingertips with saliva to smear the hair out of Nekrokor's brilliant green eyes. A single ray of light, like a security beam but probably meant to evoke a lunar ray, illuminated Nor-dikron's face. The symmetry of the whole arrangement made me think of the pyramid eye on the US dollar, which I had fewer and fewer of by the day.

I skimmed through the pages until I found the interview. The intro paragraph promised, if you can trust my translating, "a rare interview with the most obscure and true occult band." The reporter met Nordikron and Nekrokor in the basement of some record shop after spending a few weeks trying to track them both down. Once I'd flipped through the whole inter-view, I figured I'd just buy the magazine. It would be my little project. An advanced Nederlandse translation activity. Some-thing to keep me busy at home.

The interview started by jocking *The Intrapsychic Secret.* I groaned when I read the first question. Loud enough so one of the cashiers glanced my way. I translated all this stuff later, though. It took me a couple of weeks.

> **Interviewer: I just listened to *The Intrapsychic Secret* and wanted to congratulate you on it. I enjoyed it thoroughly and found it deeply illuminating.**

> **Nekrokor:** We do not care that you "enjoyed" it and, in fact, we would say that to have any kind of positive feeling ... anything close to happiness of one form or another... shows that you have missed the purpose of our work.

> **Nordikron:** Nietzsche remarks in *Beyond Good and Evil* that those who hunt monsters should be fearful lest they gaze in the mirror to find that they themselves have become monsters in the process. We embrace Nietzsche's thinking here, but not in the standard sense. Yes, one may become a monster and that may be clearly visible to that hunter of monsters as he gazes at himself. But we see that recognition as one to be celebrated. We see our own monstrousness, our obsessive and rigid pursuit of evil, as a victory. As a victory over a humanity content to wallow in mediocrity.

> [Here, he pulls out some kind of medical vial filled with what looks to be blood and gulps it down.]

> **Nekrokor:** We see our own monstrousness, our obsessive and rigid pursuit of evil, as a victory over a humanity bound by its own

cowering compulsions.

Nordikron: For those who wallow in mediocrity, we deny them and their power through the ritual of the intrapsychic secret.

Interviewer: And what is the Intrapsychic Secret?

Nekrokor: First and foremost an album that all true metalheads must buy or die! I must tell you, we are not like the punk rockers, the crust punks squatting in an empty hovel and criticizing stores that stock our records. Fuck off and die to them all! And we are not like the bands wearing basketball shoes while singing about politics and the environment. We explore death, revel in its sensuousness, and we revel as well in greed. We do not fool you or ourselves by saying it is bad to sell records or it is bad to be popular. We want to sell records, because in that way we also buy souls.

Nordikron: Yes, every record purchased increases the overall perversion of souls in the world. While ours is not the only path to the damnation of self-knowledge, it is one jagged path, one left hand path. The hand that holds the chalice points the way.

Nekrokor: We are pilgrims on the true *Left-hand Path* . . .

Interviewer: Entombed's first album. I'm surprised you listen to it, given your critique of death metal.

Nekrokor: Of course we know it. We are not reprobates living in some trailer. But we do not like it. Unlike that album, you will not find primary school children able to understand or appreciate our music. See, this is exactly what I mean about death metal. My companion here has often said that death metal is not the metal of death, and I agree with him to the fullest extent!

Interviewer: How do you distinguish your sound from that of more well-known death metal bands like Entombed?:

Nordikron: The songs, the sounds, the words, the riffs—these all come to us in altered states of consciousness.

The magazine had a picture of Nordikron holding out one of his journals. The handwriting was incomprehensible. There were sketches and diagrams—the cosmic diagram on the cover of *The Intrapsychic Secret*—alongside the written scrawl. The interviewer asked them more about death metal, but they used it to congratulate their own amazingness.

Nekrokor: We do not hate all death metal if it is truly about death.

Nordikron: The beyond is an ageless chaos . . . a vast wordless whorl we attempt to constrain with words and fanciful tales.

Nekrokor: I believe in tragedies . . . I believe in desolation. This isn't a fun hobby for school-kids. We praise the evil and we blindly follow its leadings. In that sense, we are no different from Christians.

Nordikron: I would rather spend time with Christians, true Christians, who believe in hell and divine retribution, than any number of idiotic metal fans.

Nekrokor: And here is a place where we disagree ... it's easier selling records to idiotic metal fans than it is to true Christians!

I couldn't translate the part right after this. My dictionary didn't have all the words necessary for their convoluted explanations of total death and infernal chaos. But then the interviewer got them back on track and asked about Nordikron's singing.

Interviewer: How are you able to produce such a voice? Your critics say you must use a vocal processor. Is that true?

Nordikron: The use of any kind of voice modulation would completely defeat the purpose of my vocals. It is not merely about the sound. I am not trying to sound more extreme, more brutal, or whatever stupid words others use to gauge their adherence to whatever they think metal is about. Nekrokor has spoken elsewhere of "total death," and my vocal performance is my attempt to create this experience. And to silence the naysayers, or, rather, to make them gossip even more, I will add this. I do have a tool that enhances the sounds this body produces. It is no studio trick, though. It is an ancient tool, one used long ago, in fact, to bring the voice of the dead to the living. And that is all I will reveal.

Interviewer: This is very intriguing. Can you tell us more?

Nordikron [laughs again; produces a small vial, uncaps it, and drinks]: The key lies in a book you know. One you know but may not have read. Something ancient . . . and evil.

The interviewer listed a bunch of books, trying to guess what he meant. They were books you might expect. *Paradise Lost*, Dante's *Inferno* (no umlaut necessary), the *Malleus Maleficarum*. But Nordikron's responses here were super easy to translate: just "nee" after each one.

At the end of this list, the interviewer threw the Nekronomikon out there. An invented book, but one so central to metal lore. It wasn't the right book, but it got a more substantive response from Mathias.

Nordikron: *The Book of the Dead*. Lovecraft's tome, and not the Egyptians'. Now you are getting closer. I am also speaking of a book of praise. For the forces of chaos that order our existence. The difference is that the book I allude to is real. And it contains within it many stories of the path between life and death. In this way, it is the real Nekronomikon.

I guess the *Metaalridder* guy was tired of trying to figure out what Mathias meant. He moved on to a completely different topic.

It was all stuff I knew. Stuff you probably know, too. Mathias segued into a monologue on the time he'd nearly died as a kid. He talked about his belief that he had died. That he'd somehow soul swapped with some plague-ridden spirit from the Middle Ages. He went on about the Freaky Friday experience that led him to seek solace in metal's crypt.

The interviewer didn't ignore Nekrokor, who explained his megalomaniacal plans for music business domination, took offense when the guy accidentally cut him off as he listed his growing body of international distributors, and hinted at the way he used drugs to secure the affections of unwitting girls.

And then, at the end, when Mathias mentioned the book again, and the path it describes between this world and the next, Nekrokor jumped in:

> **Nekrokor:** I've tried it before and it works. Maybe not for guitar, though, because when I tried it, my arms were too numb to play for days afterwards. And perhaps this is not for everyone. I have seen some . . . problems happen with those who were not prepared for its effects. If you discover his method, try it and die! But it drew me closer to the kingdom of death. I sank through an ocean, my soul surrounded by swimming monsters, the scaled sides of each creature marked with a single letter of the ancient one's true name. I have tried his method several times, and each time, I find myself sinking through this same ocean, my soul surrounded by these same beasts. The only difference is that the name spelled by their swimming forms is different every time. These experiences have been enough to convince me that Mathias is telling the truth, and it is just one reason why everyone reading this must purchase all Despondent Abyss records, all Astrampsychos albums, all Desekration albums, everything we release that supports our

growing empire of total death. He has found a way to bring that dead and rotting plague spirit out through his voice in ways not even possible through his talent alone. He has studied this method in an ancient book that I detest, though perhaps he is right that it is not totally useless. If it helps him in this way, then he is right that it is the most evil book of all.

I still have that magazine. It's in some shoebox with the rest of my Belgian mementos. But I sold the NIN CD about a week after I bought it. I listened to it more than once. I listened in vain for the murky industrial beats. I waited, to no avail, for the liquid steel guitar. I suffered through some acoustic pouting sessions, some industrial fuck ballads, and I pondered the blurb that had drawn me to the disc in the first place. By liquid, had it meant diffuse? Watered down? Liquid like a thin gruel?

I gave it time. Repeated listens. The best music always sounds shitty at first, I thought. Because it's too complex. There's too much for the feeble mind to absorb. There's nuance. Layers of tracks shifting and colliding in impossible combinations mastered with full intention by some magisterial overlord. Trent Reznor wouldn't let me down. But in the end, knowing full well that I'd blown twenty bucks, I hocked it for just enough to cover a couple cans of Jupiler.

21.

Nekrokorus Mortuus Est

It wasn't enough, though. I hocked the NIN CD, but I was still approaching total brokeness. So I did the unthinkable. I hocked my guitar, too. At the time, I figured it didn't matter. If I no longer listened to metal, no longer played metal, then why did I need an electric guitar made for playing metal?

I'd had my guitar since high school. The same guitar. When my parents realized I was serious about quitting piano, they'd made me a deal. They'd help me get the guitar if I paid half. And promised to graduate high school. I'd kept up my end of the deal, and I'd kept the guitar in good shape.

It wasn't perfect, though. The black paint had worn away around its edges, revealing a mottled brown beneath. The edges of the paint jagged this way and that like some rocky coast meeting the sea. The plastic plate had once been white, but now it had a gauzy sheen, a kind of plaque yellow. The knobs spun a little too freely, like they were just going to spin off with even the slightest adjustment. The spot where I'd scraped off the old Valhalla sticker left a rectangle of dust and hair encased in glue.

I took it to a music store over by the laundromat. The owner considered my guitar's many flaws. He plugged it into my amp, an equally beaten down relic. He strummed a couple chords, held his ear to the neck as he plucked the strings. The guy looked severe, no nonsense. His brow furrowed while he listened to the notes he could get out of the thing. He had on a flannel shirt and dirty black jeans. He had a brownish yellow moustache that he stroked after he unplugged the guitar and laid it, like an etherized patient, across the glass counter.

And then he made me an offer. It wasn't great. I knew what I'd paid. What my parents had paid, too. But I also knew the hour of reckoning had come. Het rekening. In Dutch, that means the bill. I was broke and rent was due.

I considered just leaving. Leaving the store. Leaving Belgium. Immediately. This was a few weeks after my ill-fated attempt to become a Nine Inch Nails fan. A few weeks after picking up the *Metaalridder* memorial issue for Nekrokor. It's not like I was doing anything. I wasn't in a band. My Dutch class had finished. I spent my day dicking around Gent, walking around the city all day, and at night, playing scraps of all the non-metal songs I knew.

I probably should have left. Kept my guitar and headed straight back to Miami. But I took the guy's offer. It wasn't great, but it was enough. I wanted to stay in Gent. At least until summer. At least until Miami pulled Juan back first. And selling my guitar would help. That's what I thought, anyway, when I took my guitar to this dusty old music shop by the laundromat. It was no Guitar Center. A range of medieval stringed instruments, lutes of various sizes, proto-violins, some weird recorders, hung from the front window. They had a wall of trumpets and French horns, too.

The guy handed me the money and I stuck it in my wallet. Before I left, I ran my finger one last time along the guitar's curved body.

That night, I headed to Abdul's for dinner. He was my only friend for a while there. Even though our class had ended, he still called me to hang out. He regularly hosted dinners at his place. Sometimes other people from our class went. Sometimes people he described as "potential investors" for some nebulous export venture, usually business majors from the university. Sometimes, it was just me and Helena as his guests.

He lived in a pretty spartan complex of student apartments. The entrance was ringed by hundreds of bicycles, most rusty enough to transmit tetanus. His apartment had gray linoleum, cheap Formica cabinets, and impossibly thin walls. By the time I came in and put the beers I brought in the refrigerator, I could make out the Flintstones theme coming from one neighbor and a football match from the other.

"When I try to sleep, I hear babies crying from over there," Abdul said and pointed to the Flintstones wall. "And then I hear sex noises from over there," he added, pointing to the football wall. "It's like I'm living in the middle of the cycle of life," he finished, then started laughing.

He stepped over to his boombox and turned up the volume.

"This should drown out the noise," he said. Then he went over to the stove to mix the paella he was cooking that night. He wasn't like me, a one dish guy. Left to my own devices, I ate burritos of some form almost every day. But Abdul always had some new recipe. Sometimes stuff from Egypt, sometimes recipes he learned from his other friends. And he had so many friends. He was my one friend, but every day, he made, like, twenty new friends. I liked hanging out with him because he had this openness and positivity that, growing up in Miami, I'd never encountered.

Whatever music he had did little to drown out the background noise, though. He was playing, like, a video game theme song or something. Simple keyboard tones ploinked through bombastic and repetitive tunes that might accompany some 16-bit quest to save Hyrule. Occasionally, the rolling blast of a synthesized drum roll interrupted a high-pitched calliope squeal.

By this point, he'd been dating Helena for a couple of months. She knocked on the door after I'd been there a few minutes. I always talked with her in Dutch at first, but gradually reverted to English.

She carried a wooden bowl with a big Greek salad. After she set the bowl on the counter, she hugged Abdul from behind. He stood at the stove, making final preparations on the meal.

"You liking this music, David?" he asked, then turned around and shot me a wide grin.

"Why?" I asked.

"I picked it up just for you," he said, a slightly affronted edge to his voice. The song sounded like a music box, the kind with a ballerina on the top, mixed with the chimes of a cuckoo clock and interspersed with beats from the world's cheapest drum machine.

I couldn't tell if he was serious.

"I'm not really a video game guy," I said. "What game is it from?"

"I picked this up the other day," he said. "Since you said Metallica was too soft. I wanted to see what you meant. This is your friends."

"My friends?" I asked. I didn't recognize it.

"This isn't David's friends," Helena said. "It doesn't sound like noise."

"No, I'm not joking," Abdul said. He went over to his desk and picked up the CD case.

"It's called ..." and here he followed the words on the cover with his index finger.

He was having trouble reading it.

"Neck... neck ... row ... core... us," he paused. "And then it says: more too ... toos ... more toos est."

He took it over to Helena, then gently rubbed her shoulder.

"Eh, Helena ... what means this?" he asked.

She took the CD and squinted at it for a second.

"Nekrokorus ... Mortuus ... Est," she said. "Hmm. Well, it's kind of a mixing of Greek and Latin. Nekrokorus isn't really a word, though. You said these are David's friends? With errors like that, it doesn't surprise me."

Helena excelled at insulting me.

"I guess I believe it," she went on. "This guy on the cover kind of looks like you, David."

She held the jewel case up and pointed at it.

"David makes this same expression whenever he takes a test," she explained.

It was a Desekration album. And the cover was a picture of Nekrokor looking supremely fucked up. Looking like me taking a Dutch test.

The cover showed him lying in an open coffin. He had his hands crossed, Bela Lugosi-style, over his chest. He held a silver key. One I'd seen before. It locked the coffin that had dominated the stage at the Astrampsychos show when they opened for King Diamond. It locked the coffin that had nearly asphyxiated their singer.

A spasm or something wracked Nekrokor's face. His head met his neck at a sharp, unnatural angle. Swollen and purple, his tongue protruded from his mouth like a sea cucumber. His eyes were wide, his pupils dilated like black marbles. A stream of snot flowed from his nose, down his cheek, and pooled somewhere by the tip of his distended tongue.

"That's not me," I said. "That's Nekrokor. My former boss. Not really a friend."

The happy keyboard tracks continued while we talked. Where "Omnes Mortuus Est" had been ambient, almost atmospheric in a low-tech kind of way, these songs seemed deliberately frantic and childish.

"He looks pretty messed up," Abdul said.

"I agree," Helena said. "Like David conjugating verbs. He looks dead to me."

And they were right.

"That's what it means," I said. "*Nekrokorus Mortuus Est.* It means 'Nekrokor is dead.'"

Helena chimed in. "I thought it sounded vaguely familiar. This is the heavy metal guy. The one who died."

"That's the one," I said.

At that point, the keyboarding stopped. I fought the urge

to bound over to the boombox and hit stop before the inevitable. If this was a Desekration album, the fanciful video game music wouldn't last forever. There'd be a deluge of sound, of noise. Grating noise. I didn't want Helena to make fun of me. I didn't want to explain the noise to Abdul. I wanted to protect them from the noise. These were my new friends. My normal friends.

But the next track started without an electric guitar. Without a blizzard beat. Instead, it was just a voice. A groan. Barely intelligible, too. Not theatrical or powerful enough to come from Nordikron. It was a rambling groan that sounded like someone choking out the words "I am become death" over and over again.

Abdul started laughing.

"It just does that for, like, half an hour," he said and then headed over to the stove.

Helena got down some plates and moved everything to the table. On the boombox, the groaning continued. Like someone had plugged Nekrokor's corpsefinger, or maybe his corpsedick, into a light socket. I flipped over the jewel case and read the back:

No Living Musicians Used on This Recording

Desekration are Nordikron and Nekrokor Eternally
All Other Lineups Hereby Null and Void

Recorded Under Full Moon
Winter Solstice, Anno Yersinia Pestis Spiritus

They'd taken over Svart's band. Kicked everyone out. But then I set the case down and turned the music off. Nordikron had taken it over. He was only dead in his twisted imagination, but this proved that he'd been more thorough with his "bandmate." I turned off Nekrokor's agonized croaks, the sounds, more than likely, of his death.

Sinister Synthesizer

Abdul looked up from the stove. I didn't want to dampen the party atmosphere with *Nekrokorus Mortuus Est.* So I clicked on the radio, where Jacques Brel sang about my temporary home, Abdul's adopted home, with its canals and endless mist.

22.
Total Infernö

Not long after that, Tomi called me.

I wasn't surprised by the call, or even his urgent insistence that we meet. *Nekrokorus Mortuus Est* had no real drums. And, if you believed the hype, no living members. Clearly, they'd fired his ass, too. The phone startled me at first, though. It could have been Natasha, ready for a detailed postrelationship postmortem of my many flaws. That sharp pang of fear dissipated after about the third ring, though. If it was her, I realized, I could just hang up. The magic of phones. Besides, it was probably just Abdul, the only person who ever called me. But it wasn't him. Instead of his bright and friendly "Heeeyyy maaan!" I got Tomi's spare, clipped summons. Seven o'clock at De Verloren Hemel.

I wasn't surprised by his invitation. But I was surprised when I walked into the De Verloren Hemel that night to find Tomi and Svart sharing a velvet-pillowed corner booth. Svart had been a true believer of Despondent Abyss and all the shit they peddled. The last time I'd seen him, Nekrokor had belittled me and Svart had just laughed. It must have taken a lot for him to come out. It must have taken Tomi a lot of convincing to get Svart out to see me.

The booth sat under a framed poster of Siouxsie Sioux, a woodcut of her face, her expressive eyes, her electric hair.

174

Strident industrial beats emanated from the jukebox. The whole bar hummed with the mechanical rhythm of an ass slapping session deep in some stahlwerk.

Tomi radiated strength and vitality. He wore a sleeveless Kreator shirt, the better to display his biceps, rock hewn and pale as a marble Adonis. He had his long blond hair drawn back and secured by a purple scrunchie. Svart loomed behind him in the corner of the booth. The shadows enveloped him like a cloak. He had four or five studded bracelets on one wrist. His other arm, cinched into a spiked vambrace, rested on the table like a sedated hedgehog.

A trinity of occult amulets—Leviathan cross, pentagram, Mjolnir—hung from his thick neck. He had on a Desekration shirt. The one he always wore. From "To Winds ov Demise." The one with an enormous photo of his ugly mug across the front.

He may have been in a goth pub, but Svart made it very clear that he himself was no goth and, lest anyone think otherwise, solid metal to the core. But his excessive show of metalness was completely unnecessary. No one, least of all actual goths, would ever mistake Svart for a card-carrying member of the Cocteau Twins fan club.

"Svartikles!" I said. "Long time."

Some of Abdul's chipper and positive demeanor must have rubbed off on me. I leaned into the booth and held out my left hand. It was the only way I could reach him. I held out the leprous and cootie defiled hand of the outcast. And Svart shook it. He grasped it hard and a spasm of pain shot through my arm as his handgrip crushed against my warts.

Tomi held up his beer, then drained it to salute my arrival.

I brought my hand back and flexed my fingers. Stimulate some bloodflow. Something else surprised me. It had to do with Juan. His absence. I thought for sure a meeting at De Verloren Hemel just implied Juan's presence. The bar was close to Svart's place, and he came a lot to leer at the barmaids, the goth regulars, and various passersby, but Juan actually hung out there.

"Where's Juan?" I asked.

Tomi and Svart exchanged a brief, conspiratorial glance.

"He's not here anymore," Tomi finally said.

"Did he die, too?" I quipped.

"He left Belgium," Svart said.

And when Svart said that, I suddenly felt light and free. Like I'd won some endurance contest, a triathlon made up of guitar playing, beer drinking, and dealing with fucking weirdos. Juan had left Belgium . . . before me. He'd left Belgium. Which could only mean he'd gone back to Florida. As I stood there in a goth pub, every surface decorated in an ink-drenched shabby chic of leather and lace, he was probably languishing in some endless Miami traffic jam. Despite the isolation, the total rejection, of the past few months, I suddenly felt victorious. Unless Svart meant he'd left Belgium for somewhere better.

"Like, you mean he left alone or he went somewhere with Delphine?" I asked. We'd met her in Trondheim. He could have tagged along on some northward trek. He could still be in Europe, insinuating himself more into her life. Meeting her parents or something. Setting himself up for a cozy life as a kept man.

"He . . . he ditched her," Svart said. A lascivious grin spread across his flat, wide face. "But I helped her overcome her grief."

"Oh. Damn," I said happily. "That's too bad."

I figured she would have dumped him, not the other way around.

"Well," and here I thought of my own numerous failures in that department, "long distance relationships are tricky. I guess it was easier if he just broke it off."

"It's easier for me," Svart said. He dry humped the table once or twice. "Nice and easy."

He chortled, then guzzled some more of his beer.

I went up to the bar. I recognized the girl slinging drinks;

Svart had pointed her out every time I'd come here with him when I was living on his couch. He claimed he'd slept with her, but she never showed the slightest awareness of his existence. I figured I'd go with a Duvel, but I got distracted. She had on a low-cut halter top. It was made of leather or something. Maybe vinyl. It had fringes that flapped against her ribs when she moved. She had a bunch of piercings, too. Tattoos sleeved both arms. Fish and waves and shit. While she waited for me to order, she sucked on a long silver barbell in her tongue. Its round tip slid in and out from between her lips. She wasn't my type or anything. I wasn't her type. And after my experiences with Natasha and Maria, I was not trying to make a move on anyone. But the tongue stud—in and out, in and out—transfixed me.

"Uh ... I'll have," and after stuttering for a bit, I guess I wanted to impress her, get something fancier than a beer, I said, "I'll have Het Disintegration."

That was the house special. A mixed drink. Kind of pricy. Maybe I picked it in memory of Juan.

She slurped the barbell back into her mouth, then turned to the bottles arrayed behind her. Immediately, she slammed a shot of this, a jig of that, into a silver shaker. In the background, Lisa Gerrard wailed like a spirit wild in the woods.

A large blue circle took up much of the bartender's back. As much of it that wasn't enclosed by her skimpy top. It had waves around the edges. A big blue ball. Her ocean tattoo extended from the top of her ass to the bottom of the fringes on her halter top. A globular tattooed ocean covered most of her back like an inky blue turtle shell.

Inside the circle, a robed Medusa, viper haired, breasts exposed, stood on the left side. She had her arms stretched out, casting a hex or beckoning an embrace, to a warrior on the right side of the circle. The warrior sat heaped and huddled behind a shield and his gray skin crackled like crumbling stone.

Both figures danced as the bartender jiggled the shaker.

She really put her back into it. I couldn't help conducting a careful assessment of the revisionist history cast in ink on her back. Jiggling, jiggling. Medusa wins. She turns Perseus to stone. From what Svart told me, this chick had the same power. She turned Svart to stone. His dick, at least. Though that, too, I figured, belonged to the realm of myth and untruth.

As the bartender poured the fully mixed Disintegration into a chilled glass, I felt a brief sadness wash over me. I hoped I'd feel better once I let the Disintegration wash into me. Her tattoo, of Medusa petrifying Perseus, reminded me of the first time I'd met Juan. He had been a questing hero, too. Questing for a book. *The White Goddess.* And the cover had the same hapless mortal on my bartender's back. Perseus beseeching the Fates for some weapon or wisdom. In the story, the real story, Perseus wins. But we were more like this tattooed re-telling. Petrified, shattered, useless warriors. I felt just a little guilty that I was still in Belgium and he'd been sucked back by Miami's tractor beam of lameness.

When the barmaid turned back to the bar with my drink, she gave me the faintest glimmer of a smile. The tongue barbell poked in and out as she grabbed a pink swizzle stick with a grape at the end. She gave the mixture one last stir, then pushed it my way.

"Smakelijk," she said and when I took the glass, her cool fingertips brushed against mine. I pulled back like she'd shocked me, but it was just because I didn't want her to inadvertently touch my wart hand, which still kind of tingled from Svart's vice grip.

When I sat down at the table, Svart immediately gave me shit about my drink.

"Are you on your period or something, David?" he asked. He poked one beefy finger at the swirl of purple, blue, and red in my glass.

Svart came to De Verloren Hemel enough to recognize a Disintegration when he saw one, but he would never order it. Mixed drinks were not meant for virile Him-Guys. Plus, the beer was much cheaper.

I ignored him and stirred the drink with its hot pink swizzle stick. I pulled it out of the glass, and liquid dripped from the grape stuck to the end. It was not a manly drink. But I didn't care.

Svart hoisted his Duvel and slugged it back. Tomi repeated the gesture, then repeated it again. Properly fortified, he got down to business.

"They cut us out," Tomi said. "I went to cash a check from the label, but the bank said it had been cancelled."

"It happened to me, too," Svart said. "To my mom. She took my check to the bank."

"'They' cut you out?" I asked. "You mean 'him'? You mean Mathias? Isn't the other dude dead?"

Svart sat silent, his hands folded on his belly.

Tomi nodded imperceptibly.

"Dead," he finally said. "Nekrokor is dead."

No one said anything else for a few minutes.

Tomi finished his beer, then went to the bar for another. As he brushed past me, he said, "Or so they say."

Svart leaned up, his elbow on the table. He rested his craggy head in his palm and all the spikes in his armband poked within mere millimeters of his face.

"I have heard some things," he said when Tomi came back, beer in hand.

Tomi joined in, "When they returned the body to him. That's when I grew suspicious."

"You mean they returned the body to Bård's family, right?" I said.

"Mathias is his family," Svart said. "They're brothers."

I coughed, a wave of acrid half-swallowed Disintegration filling my mouth.

"Bruh . . . bruh . . . brothers?" I choked out.

"Half-brothers," Tomi corrected. "The same dad. A wealthy guy. A true patron of the arts."

"I thought," and then I didn't know what to say. Mathias

and Bård were brothers. Somehow, I hadn't known that. Instead of revealing my ignorance, I sipped my Disintegration. It stung my lips, then my throat, like the fermented juice of some impossible fruit, a mango-lingonberry hybrid.

"You would not think those two are related," Tomi said. "And they rarely disclose this fact."

"They both are . . . were . . . so talented, though," Svart said. He couldn't quite break his devotation to that cultic Despondent Abyss mystique.

"Mathias claimed the body, and then must have had Bård buried," Tomi went on. "Perhaps to hide how he did it."

"I thought they'd ruled out foul play," I finally said. "You think he killed his own brother?"

"He'd done it before," Tomi said.

"Killed his brother?" I asked. I whispered it, though. A few groups of goths fluttered around De Verloren Hemel, and they all fluttered a little too close to our table. Fluttered a little too quiet for my liking. Even Siouxsie Sioux, hanging above Svart's head, seemed more spy than sentinel.

"Well, killed someone," Tomi quipped. "As far as I know, he only had one brother he could kill."

"I have heard that theory, too," Svart said. "That this was not his first time." He kind of dragged out the word "theory," though. Like he didn't believe it.

"What theory?" I asked.

"About that Astrampsychos live album. *Live in Brno*," Svart lingered over the title. It was one of his favorites. "People talk sometimes about the original pressing. The one with the printer's error. All pink. Like that dog dick in your drink. And the guy who made the mistake, he died not long after. Some say that was all Mathias. That he poisoned this guy."

"Right," I said. Svart had told me this legend as part of his black metal indoctrination efforts.

"Yes," Svart said. "But nothing was ever conclusive about poison. Those who know better say it was a spell. That's what really happened. He killed the guy, sure. But through his power. Through a powerful spell of destruction."

"You think, like, magic?" I asked. "Death by magic?" It sounded implausible to me, but not impossible. After my dealings with Mathias and Bård, I had a healthy fear of everyone associated with that band. If anyone, living or dead, possessed occult powers, they'd probably have a spot on the Despondent Abyss roster.

The beers loosened Tomi up. He disagreed.

"Death by magic," he scoffed. "Bullshit, of course. There are only powerful spells of destruction in your Dungeons and Dragons campaigns, my friend, and not in reality."

"But you said he killed the printer guy. That he got away with it," I said.

"Yes, just not with a magical spell," Tomi said. "This is the real world."

"Wouldn't the cops have figured it out?" I asked.

"Not necessarily," Tomi said. "Your American cop shows are just another kind of fantasy."

"It's true," Svart insisted. "I've had the chance to talk to some of the other guys in Astrampsychos."

Here, he beamed.

"They admire the excellence of my early Desekration tapes."

"So what'd they say?" I asked. "I mean, why would Mathias kill his own brother."

Svart told us everything he'd heard from the other Astrampsychos guys. He kind of got off on telling us who said what. Like, "A. Hex said . . ." and "Torburn told me . . ." as he recounted his story. According to Svart, it all had to do with metal fame and currying favor with "unholy forces of evil," a phrase Svart muttered with awed veneration. Judging by the trinity of trinkets looped around his neck, though, he had a hard time identifying how these evil forces fit into any discernible belief system. Mathias killed Bård for some dark spirit, but whether this was Satan or Thor or some gaggle of crusty witches, who could tell. Svart said that Mathias killed

Bård as an offering to these same ill-conceived spiritual forces and, when he tried to explain why, things got even murkier. Basically, Svart thought Mathias killed Bård to make our record more evil. Or something. Which explained, of course, those swollen royalty checks. The spirits rewarded sacrifice with album sales. This all was well and good, according to Svart, until Mathias got a little too evil and cut everyone else away from the cash. This, for Svart, was one evil step too far.

Reluctantly, he admitted killing Bård was pretty bad, too, and that it would have been better to keep Bård alive—he was a genius and of more benefit to these unholy forces as a living thane of the eternal diabolicrusade. If Mathias had just found some other sacrifice, maybe someone more expendable, Svart wondered, and cast an ominous glance in my direction, then the whole situation wouldn't be so fucked up.

Before Svart got too worked up about this idea of sacrificing some expendable and worthless fool—it wouldn't take much for him to figure he had one right in front of him blithely sucking down a Disintegration—Tomi shut him down and offered his take.

"All bullshit," Tomi began, then waved his heavily muscled forearm over the table to dispel the bullshit-befouled air streaming out of Svart's jowly mouth.

"This happened because of money or sex," Tomi said, and of the two, all signs pointed to the former. In Tomi's more clearsighted view, the surge in album and merchandise sales probably had something to do with it, but simple greed is always more powerful than nonexistent spirits. Generally, people think of Finland as a pretty safe place, a place where people keep to themselves. But at midsummer, he said, all that shit comes out and there's always a spate of fights, stabbings, and mysterious deaths.

"They're not caused by spirits, my friend," Tomi said. "Especially not the ones between family members."

Tomi had enough Finnish midsummers under his belt to put two and two together: this was about money, plain and simple. Bård might have run Despondent Abyss, but Mathias was involved, too. Tomi suggested one other possibility, which was that Mathias accidentally killed Bård, perhaps while helping him to produce the tortured cries that passed for vocals on *Nekrokorus Mortuus Est.* But even in that case, money played the key role: they clearly made that sorry excuse for a record as a way to take over Desekration and the money that rightfully belonged to Tomi, Svart, and even me.

The mere mention of that album shifted Svart's attention away from murder motives and the malign influence of evil spirits.

"Such shit," he sneered. "*Nekrokorus Mortuus Est.* After my mom told me about the check, we got a shipment of those at work. We still have many copies. They are not selling like *Infernö.*"

All this talk of treachery for infernal spirits and limitless money got to my head a little bit. I was down to the dregs of my Disintegration, too, each sip a futile attempt to elicit more alcohol from the ice cubes at the bottom of the glass. But when I thought a little bit more about treachery, spirits, and limitless money, something didn't add up. The limitless part.

I left Svart fulminating about all the shitty keyboards on *Nekrokorus Mortuus Est* so I could head back to the bar and get a Duvel. The bartender chick wasn't there. Some guy in a black dress shirt instead. I got the Duvel because it was much cheaper than another Disintegration. I didn't have limitless money and I couldn't foresee any unholy forces pushing some my way.

When I got back to the table, Svart had settled down. He and Tomi were deep in conspiratorial talk.

"Is this even worth pursuing, guys?" I asked. "I mean, how much money do you think they're keeping from you?" I recalled my own royalty checks, few as they were, from the Valhalla days. Good for some beers, maybe a couple pizzas, too. Probably not good enough to get tanked on Disintegrations.

"They have been sizable," Tomi said.

"And getting bigger," Svart added.

"No way," I said.

"They secured an American distributor for *Infernö, The Intrapsychic Secret*," Tomi said. "They have international distribution."

I knew this, though. My old label, Plutonic Records, was their American distributor.

"That doesn't mean much," I said. And then I reminded them about *Thrones of Satanic Dominion*, the criminally underrated masterwork of Florida death metal that I helped make and Plutonic had released.

Svart drummed his fingers on the table and feigned disinterest. But he didn't cut me off. Somehow, he'd become slightly more open minded.

"I barely got shit from that thing, man," I said. "And any time I asked for more, they gave me some rundown of all the money I should have been paying them. Production costs. Shipping costs. Studio costs. Their fucking warehouse rent. They acted like it was a major favor anytime they kicked twenty bucks my way. Mathias, Nekrokor—dead or alive, they're not getting any money from those Plutonic dudes."

Tomi and Svart exchanged a brief glance. Tomi coughed, then drank his beer.

"What?" I asked.

"That may have been what happened with you," Svart said. "But we have seen something very different."

"There is enough, I am sure, to let me quit my job," Tomi added. "At least for some time."

"From *Infernö*?" I asked, incredulous.

"From *Infernö*," they said in unison.

The merchandise too, they explained. Some grunge guy had worn one of our shirts somewhere. Tomi thought it was on the cover of *Rolling Stone*. Svart was certain it was on MTV. They both agreed it was some grunge guy, though. Someone who should know better, I guess. So people trusted his taste. They allowed themselves to be influenced, to seek out

Desekration merchandise. To buy *Infernö*.

The grunge guy might have worn the shirt as a joke. So other people wanted it, too. Wanted to be in on the joke. And it might have been a joke, a lot of jokes. And all those jokes turned into a lot of shirts, a lot of tapes and CDs. Which turned into a lot of money. A lot of money for Mathias.

"And we both think you . . ." Svart continued, then paused for a second, like it was hard for him to admit. He scratched his chin, then finished his thought.

"We both think you were treated unfairly," he said.

"Together," Tomi said. "If we work together, we can get what is ours." And in the amount of time it took the jukebox to switch from industrial spanking to ethereal 4AD glossolalia, I was back in Desekration.

"How do you think I can help with this?" I asked.

"You knew Nekrokor first," Svart said. "Even though they knew of me. They knew of my commitment to the true ways."

Before I met Svart, he sent those guys copies of every rehearsal tape he'd ever made.

"Yeah, but that was totally random," I said. "I just ran into the dude after a show."

"If I have learned anything about Mathias and Bård," Tomi said, "it is that nothing they do—alone or together—is completely random."

And he may have been right. I ran into Nekrokor after a show, but he had arranged it that way. But I didn't have any way to find those guys. To find Mathias, I corrected myself. Nekrokor's dead.

"You want me to find Mathias," I said. And then I had a vivid memory of Mathias making out with some grandma out in front of St. Baafs cathedral. I recalled the moment I spied Mathias, sallow and lank-haired, ascending out of the cathedral's crypt. And then repairing to some dismal apartment block.

"You want me to find Mathias," I said again. "And you may be right. I know where he hangs out. The building where he lives, too."

And then I told them everything about that strange encounter.

Tomi nodded, like Mathias as a choir boy made perfect sense. He harbored no illusions about Mathias as the chosen one of unholy forces, and metal songs brimmed with depictions of holy rollers engaging in truly nasty behavior. But the news of Mathias willingly at church kind of rocked old Svartikles. He inhaled deeply and folded his arms around himself. This was more painful than the possibility that Mathias killed his own brother. Svart's massive frame sank into the cushions of our cozy corner booth. He fingered his amulets one by one as I talked, fingered the Leviathan cross, the pentagram, his silver Mjolnir. As though he needed all the powers of witchcraft and the abyss and the whole firmament of fucking Nordic gods to process the news that his nekrohero was singing hymns and sharing the peace with a contingent of dowdy senior citizens.

"But even if we do find him," I asked, "what are you going to do? Frog march him to the bank or something?"

Tomi sat with both hands flat on the table.

"Killing someone is a crime," he said. "And someone may be willing to pay to keep that action secret."

"You really think Mathias killed Bård?" I asked. "I mean, even if that's true, you can't prove it. I don't think tracking down the little fucker will solve anything."

"We will see," Tomi said. "But my money says yes. Perhaps yours, too. There is another matter to discuss. Another reason for you to join us."

Svart got excited. He leaned in toward me, close enough that I caught a whiff of gym shorts soaked in stale beer.

"We're going to release the real version of *Infernö*," he said. "*Total Infernö*. And keep all the money."

"Like, you want to do a new recording or something?" I asked. I hadn't told them I'd hocked my guitar for rent money.

Tomi cut in. "Svart has the rough mix," he said.

"I kept copies of everything before sending them off to Nekrokor," Svart said. "Because of their historical significance."

"The rough mix," Tomi said. "From before it got to Nekrokor. You know what that means. This version . . ."

"The correct version," Svart said.

"This version," Tomi went on, "it will have a different guitar sound."

"By 'different,' you mean I'm not drowned out of the mix," I said.

"Zeker," Svart said. "Besides, I think they fucked with the bass sound, too. This isn't just about money. It's about preserving metal's legacy."

"The drums, too," Tomi said. They each had their own beefs with *Infernö*'s mix, Nekrokor's final knob tweaks before venturing into the great beyond.

"And best of all," Svart went on. "There will be no fucking keyboards on this version."

"No keyboards?" I asked. "The last song is, like, fifteen minutes of keyboards."

"Gone!" Svart said. "The intro, too. Straight into the songs. No pussy bullshit."

"We're doing Mathias a favor, anyway," Svart said. "His vocals sound better on the tapes I have. Deeper, more echo."

"So you're going to pay him his part of the royalties on our bootleg version?" I quipped.

"Fuck no," Svart said. "Not unless he gives us the money he owes us. And it's the correct version, not a bootleg."

"How you going to pull this off, though?" I asked. By their account, *Infernö* was everywhere. And not just in Belgium. It was all over the world. Pulling in money. Moving off the shelves. Fashionable people in London, Tokyo, Los Angeles were clad in our gear. I had no idea how to get an album made—CD, tape, or vinyl—and then get all those copies out to stores. And I doubted Svart had a clue, either. The closest thing Svart had to a production studio was a double tape deck, battered and abused after dubbing hundreds of early Desekration demo tapes. To Svart's fevered mind, a hand dubbed version might be the only offering suitable to lay on metal's immortal altar.

And, I thought, maybe they just wanted me to spend my time making copies of this thing. Like some unpaid intern. They both had jobs, but I had time to kill. As I contemplated this dismal possibility, I slugged down my Duvel.

Tomi, sensing my unease, rested his hand on my shoulder.

"I know someone who can help us," he said. "Someone with much experience in the music business. From the band Unicorne."

"The name is familiar," Svart said, then stifled a belch. "This is a Belgian band?"

Tomi reassured him the guy was legit. He told us this band—Unicorne—was playing later that week. And that he'd told this dude we'd all be there. He'd met the guy when he was getting some shit fixed on his drum kit. Just like his body, he liked to keep that thing in optimal condition.

At that point, the lights in De Verloren Hemel dimmed even more. The bass line on the industrial tracks started thumping extra loud. While we'd been talking, the bar had filled. Over in the corner, colored lights spiraled above a small dance floor. I looked at my watch. Late enough for the bats to leave the belfry.

We all agreed it was time to leave. We headed down the Coupure Links. Not far from the spot where they found Nekrokor, his body anyway, floating in the canal.

Tomi told us more about this Unicorne show. We had to go. He'd put us on the guest list. And with this guy's label contact, we'd probably be able to get our pirate version of *Infernö* out into the world. Maybe not as far out into the world, but enough for us to soak up some of the cash people were supposedly spending on our shit.

Svart seemed kind of distracted. Drunk, probably. He'd thrown back a heavy load of Duvels in De Verloren Hemel. As we walked, though, he came back around. Fresh air, movement—it all cleared Svart's head. And before we split off, him to his mom's, Tomi out past Gravensteen to the townhouse he shared with his wife, and me back to the Rooseveltlaan, he suddenly stopped in his tracks.

"Unicorne," he muttered. "In the eighties, there was a Belgian band called Unicorne."

Tomi nodded.

"In the eighties, there was a Belgian band called Unicorne," Svart repeated, but then he sneered, big and ugly as the portrait on his "To Winds ov Demise" shirt, "and they played Christian metal."

Tomi nodded again.

23.
The Heart of the Dragon

In the past, I had assessed Tomi's silence as evidence of a mental emptiness, his head a cavern devoid of words, thought. But with this plan to reclaim Desekration, to unleash *Total Infernö* upon the land and siphon the resulting royalties, Tomi was revealing himself to be shrewd and calculating.

I guess it shouldn't have surprised me. It wasn't so different from his approach to the drums. Like, to an unseasoned observer, Tomi at his kit resembled a spastic blur, and the sounds he produced a euphonic barrage barely distinguishable from the tumult of a parade of garbage trucks cruising past a construction zone. But when Tomi played, his body a blaze of muscle and sinew slamming some drumhead, some cymbal, up to 300 times a minute, he played with mechanical intention: the beats, and the barely discernible silence between each one, remained distinct, yet part of a logical pattern, a coherent whole.

He was no braindead beatmaster. And he brought that same level of distanced scrutiny to his efforts to secure his rightfully earned cash.

So I just had to trust him. Even though, in his mind, the pattern necessary to get back his cash led him, led us, to a Christian metal show somewhere out in the villages surrounding Gent. I had to trust his plan, even though I no longer owned

a guitar, had undergone a sustained period of metal absti-
nence, and wasn't entirely sure of my place in his plan. Still,
when he had invited me and Svart to this Christian metal
show, I said I'd go. It's not like I had anything better to do.

We stood in the lobby of Gent-Sint Pieters station and
waited for Svart. When I walked into the station, I found Tomi
planted right in the middle of the lobby. Feet wide. Shoulders
back. Super fit. It was late afternoon; commuters and students
filled a lobby that, in another hour or so, would revert to the
empty shell it was for most of the day. Like rats swarming
away from potential danger, all the travelers gave Tomi a wide
berth. He just stood there, arms crossed and unmoving. He had
on a plain black shirt, extra tight to expose his swollen guns.

Tomi handed me a train ticket. The town was somewhere
between Gent and Antwerp. It was scheduled to leave shortly,
but Svart was nowhere to be seen. The revelation that we
were going to a Christian metal show hadn't sat well with him.
But I didn't expect him to flake. I mean, he wasn't Juan.

As I studied the clock, a commotion of cursing and rattling
beer cans came from the station's main entrance. Svart made
his entrance. If we rushed, we'd make the train no problem.
But Svart was in no condition to rush. He held a cardboard
twelve pack box in his arms. Smooshed empties spilled out
onto the floor; a couple cans got stuck in the station door
where Svart stumbled in. He had pre-partied to excess.

And he'd arrived fully kitted out so no one would mistake
him for a drunken youth pastor. He'd strung even more occult
amulets around his neck—Doctor Strange meets Mr. T: along
with the evil cross, the pentagram, the Mjolnir, he'd added an
ankh, some Celtic jumble of knots and dragon snouts, and a
trio of inverted crosses. Strapped around his head, he had a
bone crown just like the one I'd worn at Desekration's first
show; just like the one heaped on the bookshelf in my flat.

"You break into my place or something?" I asked, gesturing to my own head.

He stared back uncomprehending and through glassy

eyes.

"Your crown. The bone crown. I have one of those, too," I explained. Even though Maria had broken the thing.

Tomi put his hands on our shoulders and firmly herded us toward the train.

Svart touched the crown, then gingerly moved it over so it rested just right atop his out-jutting brow ridge.

"I got it from Mathias. He gave it to me," he explained.

Explained a little sheepishly, too, since our whole Christian rock journey was about taking Desekration back from Mathias.

I tried to make a joke.

"He took your band and ate your lunch, then left you with some old chicken bones, huh?"

"Ate my lunch?" he asked.

Tomi shrugged, too.

I forgot sometimes that idiomatic expressions didn't always work with my Eurofriends.

"Ate your lunch," I repeated.

I mimed raising a fork to my face, like that'd clear it up.

"It means he took your money. He took some shit that was yours, then left you with the scraps. Chicken bones. Lunch scraps."

Svart touched the crown again.

"These are not chicken bones," he said, hyperliteral even when plastered.

Tomi marched us up the stairs to the train platform.

"They come from sparrows," Svart said and fished a new beer out of his box. "Mathias told me they are part of a magic rite."

Tomi groaned. He had failed in his efforts to disabuse poor dumb Svartikles of the mistaken notion that Mathias was some secret magician, some high-level nekromancer escaped from the Temple of Elemental Evil.

I groaned too. Our groan duet echoed in the stairwell.

I'd caught Mathias fucking around with some dead bird

and there had been nothing magical about it. Just a jumbled ball of rot and feathers stuffed in a plastic bag and buried in the dirt.

No point arguing with Svart, though. Especially not drunk Svart.

"Hey, we can use all the magic we can get," I said.

Tomi propelled us into the train and, as soon as we stepped in, the doors shut behind us.

The train was nearly empty, so we found seats around a table. A few minutes after the train left Gent-Sint Pieters station, the outer suburbs dissipated into a landscape of flat fields. Tomi leaned back in his seat, eyes closed, softly beating his fingers against the table in what were, probably, a complex and ever-changing polyrhythm of Neal Peart proportions.

Svart drained his beer, then rooted around in the box for another. He poured a bunch of crushed and empty cans onto the table. He had tapped his stash.

Some train guy rolled the snack cart down the aisle. Tomi cracked an eye, then closed it again, lost in his finger drumming. As soon as the cart passed, Svart pushed past me, his hairy belly briefly smearing across my cheek.

Once in the aisle, he gripped my arm rest and glowered over me.

"Cough up," he said. "We need more drinks for this trip."

"Here," I said. I dug out my wallet and slipped him some cash. By this point, the drink guy had moved on to the next car. Svart stalked down the aisle after him.

Once Svart left, Tomi sat up.

"He's pretty wasted," I said. "I hope he doesn't go crazy at this show or something."

"Yes. He cares too much what others think of him. I always thought of that as an American trait."

I figured he had a point, but that one cut a little too close to home. I changed the subject.

"Is Unicorne, like, super religious?" I asked.

"Who cares what they sing about," Tomi muttered.

"Hey, I don't care," I said. "I have a Stryper tape," I added. But I hadn't brought that one to Belgium. Hadn't listened to it since middle school. It was somewhere in my sister's house. In a shoe box full of wack tapes. Hall and Oates. The *Miami Vice* soundtrack. I didn't tell him that, though. I wanted to seem open minded. Unconcerned about my metal credibility. Even though I told him about the Stryper tape because I guess I cared what he thought of me.

"In the eighties, they had a couple of songs that charted in a few countries. They were like Ostrogoth, but more commercial. Like White Lion or something. Svart hates them because their biggest song had religious lyrics. A ballad, but about Jesus. When you hear them, you will know. It charted in Finland. I never cared about the lyrics. It could be a ballad about artichokes, but you will feel it."

We slipped into silence for a few minutes. I contemplated the possibilities of a vegetable-themed concept album. The train, paired with the countryside at dusk, gently lulled me.

"There is a woman," Tomi said, right as I drifted into a nap. "A woman at my work."

"Uh-huh," I replied and shifted up in my seat. Tomi was married. I thought things were good with them, but I had a feeling I knew where this confession was going. A ballad, but about sex.

"I was submitting my time forms. Then something happened," he went on. He stroked his goatee, then looked away from me, looked out the window at the fields, the trees, the tiny houses in the distance. I braced myself for some scandalous details. Heavy petting in the utility closet or something.

"She told me she wanted to kill herself," he finally said.

"Oh," I replied. I wasn't sure how to respond.

"Then I told her I wanted to kill myself. Also."

I'd known Tomi long enough to realize this was some serious shit. Some relationship advisor would see this as the danger sign of an emotional affair or something. Still, I had no idea what to say to him. Where to start? The people around me talked so much about death, emptiness, eternal suffering, that his casual admission of suicidal ideation didn't faze me. I mean, that's why they'd all booted me to begin with. Too mentally stable. Not committed enough to the true life goal of destroying that life. Plus, I was no expert at relationships.

In the end, I just ignored that last part, the part where he told me he wanted to off himself.

"So what happened?" I asked. "What did she say?"

Tomi was about to divulge more, but he stopped when he heard two airy whishing sounds coming from the other end of the car. The first came from the doors, the second came from a beer. Svart, fortified for our journey, bumped and shuffled his way down the aisle, a new and full box of Jupiler cans in his arms. Tomi's silence made sense; Svart was not the best person to confide in.

When Svart got back to us, he set the box down on the table and fished out some cans. He tossed one to me and another to Tomi. He made no move to get back in his seat, though. He stood in the aisle and leaned his thighs against the table. Occasionally, he grabbed my armrest, and sometimes my shoulder, if we hit a bump or something.

"You owe me," he said once he drained his first can and went for his second. Of this box.

"Train prices," he explained. "Total rip off."

"I didn't ask you to buy a fucking twelve pack," I said.

"You might not have," he said, then wobbled, either from a slight bump or his heavy inebriation, it wasn't clear. "But I know these beers won't go to waste."

"I'm broke, dude," I said.

After that, the trip wasn't too long. It was far enough that we needed to take a train, but the whole trip took about twenty minutes. Long enough for Svart, with our help, to make a significant dent in his new beer stash. When the train eased to a stop, he grabbed the box and cradled it in his arms, leaving a smattering of spent cans on the table.

We got out on a lonely platform and passed through a white steel gate. A few other people got off, too. Commuters. Business dudes. Each one with a leather shoulder bag strapped over a black suit jacket. None of them, it was clear, were here to track down some long-forgotten also-rans from the eighties.

The only sound came from the squeal of the gate as Tomi pushed it open. A sign pointed to the city center. It had a high street, a tower or two, a steeple. Kind of like Gent, but smaller. A micro Gent.

But Tomi motioned us to follow him the other way. Away from the town, which was small and, even at sunset, mostly empty.

"Uggh," Svart exhaled, then took a cavernous swill. "Fucking Unicorne. Unbelooflijk."

It wasn't even dark yet, but the owner of the nachtwinkel across the street was already pulling down his shutters. Svart kind of gasped, handed me his beer box, then rushed over and ducked under the half-closed door. A few minutes later, he came out with a plastic bag of beer cans for his nearly depleted supply. I gave him the box and he topped it off, then threw the empty bag on the ground.

It didn't take long to leave the town behind. We passed some apartment blocks, all slightly different tones of beige. We crossed a stone bridge over a small stream and then we passed a desolate playground.

"You know where the show is?" I asked Tomi. He just nodded. Svart reached in his box and distributed the next round.

Tomi guided us through a neighborhood of detached homes. He never looked at a map or anything. Once, he paused at a bus stop to read the route map. But other than that, the way he guided us made me think he'd been here before.

When we walked along a chain link fence fronting an elementary school, Svart said, "This reminds me of where I grew up. Before my dad left."

He chugged the rest of his beer, crushed the can, then tossed it over the fence.

The show wasn't in a club. It was in some community center on the outskirts of town. Like a warehouse or something. The main entrance was just a big garage door. Svart panicked before we went in. He figured Christian rock in a community center guaranteed an alcohol-free experience. So before we all walked in, he had us stuff his remaining beers in all available pockets. The good thing about Christian rock in a warehouse is that no one frisked us on the way in, so our beer smuggling went undetected.

We hadn't needed to be so covert, though. It wasn't what I imagined: group prayer, Bible reading, maybe a robed choir. The whole set up wasn't that different from any other show. It wasn't in a club, but I'd played countless Valhalla shows in Miami warehouses.

They had a makeshift bar, a merchandise booth, and a stage at the far end of the warehouse.

The only thing that stood out was that most of the people were pretty old. Thinning hair, gray hair, flappy underarms. I was surrounded by bodies in decline. Well, "surrounded" isn't totally accurate, since there weren't a lot of people there. More than at a Katabasis show, but that wasn't saying much.

Svart continued his quest to drink all the beer in Belgium. And Tomi disappeared right after we walked in. I'd spot him behind some silver mane or a swollen beer belly, and then he'd be gone. So I eased a can of Jupiler out of my back pocket and made my way over to the merchandise booth.

There were a bunch of CDs in cardboard boxes. A stack of tapes. A battered green milkcrate filled with old records.

I picked up one of the CDs. It said "Advance Promotional Copy" across the top.

On the cover, an armor-clad knight sat astride the back of a unicorn, its front hooves pawing the air. The knight clutched a crystal guitar. A stream of ice or some blue shit, a firehose stream of glacier flurry Glucozade, ejaculated out of the guitar head and into the airbrushed star system overhead.

Yeah, ejaculated. There's no other way to describe it.

The guitar knight had this look of orgasmic rapture on his face. The way he sat astride his steed, the slightly skewed perspective of its twisted neck, the iridescent purple of his armor and its horn, made it look like he'd popped a steel boner right through its skull.

The guy running the booth came over. He'd been at the bar with a group of other old dudes. He had a lined face, tired eyes. He had on a rumpled plaid shirt and jeans. The guy could have been a middle school teacher or a world-weary dad.

His hair was magnificent, though. He ran his fingers through it. Light brown, feathered with frosted edges. It was short, but just long enough to suggest a glorious past.

I must have been doing something particularly un-Belgian, because right off the bat he spoke to me in English.

"That one you're holding, it was going to be huge. Their breakout to a global audience."

"This?" I asked. I pointed at the skull-splitting boner horn.

"The label got bought by a big American company, though. They dropped all the Belgian groups."

"That sucks," I said.

"What can you do? I grew up with these guys. Thought they were the best. Now, sometimes my wife lets me come and help them when they play. You want the CD?"

It cost about five bucks. Its ultralimited allure drew me in. I said sure. At the very least, Svart and I could laugh about it after watching a bunch of washed-up has-beens. I pulled out another beer to make some space in my pockets, then stuffed the disc away.

Shortly after, the lights dimmed and I headed up front. Svart joined me. The band hit the stage. Before getting their instruments, they all met in front of the drum kit and stood in a circle, heads bowed. It could have been a prayer. It could have been a huddle.

I recognized them; they'd all been milling around by the bar. Several of them had wispy hair, thin on top and stringy in back. The drummer and bassist had thick black hair that must have been blessed by Michael McDonald or something. The singer had on a partially buttoned Hawaiian shirt and polyester dress slacks. The guitarist looked like he'd just come from an office job: Oxford shirt, pinstriped pants, and loafers.

They started with a bunch of covers. Competent, but nothing too exciting. Svart hoovered down more beers and dropped empty cans at his feet. I moved toward him and showed him the CD cover. The unicorn. The knight and his guitar orgasm. I held it up and we laughed hysterically because the lead guitarist had the exact same expression plastered across his grill as he blazed through "Crazy Train," nose wrinkled, mouth agape, walleyed and squinty. The thinning fringes of his busted hairdo twitched with every note.

After a few more covers, they got into their own songs. Mainly rockers that wouldn't be out of place on a Ratt album. But things changed when the singer said, "This one's for heavy metal, my one true love."

It was a metal epic. Eight minutes to go from soft to loud and back again. The guitarist sat on a stool and plucked out an intricate melody on a twelve-string acoustic. And as it went on, the melody transformed, swelled into a titanic behemoth. He switched to a flying v and dry humped it through a wild and undulating shredfest.

The singer more than kept up. His voice straddled all the octaves. And after a few verses recounting the tale of a guitar-slinging knight in pursuit of a metal dragon, the singer shook his tonsured mullet and wailed his way to the main point of the song.

It wasn't that the knight killed the dragon. Or saved a princess. Or even that the dragon transformed into a princess who then fellated the knight into submission with a long reptilian whip of a tongue. It was that the knight couldn't kill the dragon. His battle guitar just made the dragon stronger. Because of its metal heart.

And so the song ended with the singer declaring, in utter sincerity, though the guy probably had to work the morning shift at some Limburg aluminum smelting plant, though Unicorne were wrongly robbed of their one chance to dethrone Ostrogoth as the true masters of Belgian hair metal, though "hair metal" itself was no longer an accurate descriptor for a band plagued by such extreme hair loss, these words of absolute truth:

> The heart of the dragon . . . is metal
> The heart of the dragon . . . is true
> The dragon of metal loves you.

At the end, the singer just kept going, saying "and you and you and you," pointing to everyone in the audience. It wasn't a big audience. I'm sure he pointed at some people more than once. And for a moment there, he pointed straight at me. And right then, no shit, I shed a tear. A steely metal tear, of course, one that flowed strong and true, but a tear. Maybe a few tears. Because, at that one moment, I believed him. Even though all my recent experiences had shown me that the dragon of metal did not give one burnished bauxite turd about me.

As I wiped the tear away, I realized Tomi was right, too. About this band. These Unicorne dudes had something; they made me feel something.

"Fucking Unicorne rule!" I shouted to Svart.

The songs continued, too. Over to my side, even Svart got into the action. In a high-speed rocker about a motorcycle vixen ("I got what needs you fixing"), Svart clapped along to the beat, his inverted crosses waving along with the music.

They ended with their big song, the Jesus ballad Tomi had told me about on the train. My family wasn't religious. Only nominally. If having a Christmas tree and an Easter basket makes you religious, then sure, call me that. But not really. So

I was surprised by my reaction to the song. It was one thing to be moved by the dragon of metal. I believed in metal, even if I didn't believe it existed in dragon form. Even my move to foreswear metal was evidence of my belief in its outsized power. And midway through this power ballad, it was clear that the singer believed what he sang. His belief in Jesus was so strong it made me believe, at least for the duration of the song. His belief was so strong it even made Svart believe, judging from his rapt attention, his hand at his heart, clasped around his inverted crosses.

The singer reached toward the sky and ululated a falsetto cry: "He is the one. The one who died for me." It drew forth a physical response, pulled it out like a splinter. I felt an actual emotion, a confusing mix of joy and sadness, a jumble of emotions far stronger than anything produced by a song about infernal rites and demonic retinues.

Svart bumped up against me and tousled my hair. For a moment, it was just one cavernous Svart armpit all around me. He grinned, then shook his big melon up and down in an exaggerated headbanging. Drops of sweat shook off his frizzled hair, but his bone crown stayed secure.

An exhilarating sense of joy at the miracle of life overlapped with a deep sadness. A sadness for me, for the singer up on the stage, for doofy-ass Svart, for everyone in the club, because all of us were doomed, at some point, to certain death.

I felt yet another tear welling in the corner of one eye. I felt like I was going to bust out laughing at the ridiculousness of the whole thing, Svart's damp embrace, a crescendo of guitars, and presiding over it all, a wispy haired middle-aged dude pointing his finger up to the heavens, his voice the crystal cry of a Disney princess.

24.
They Almost Scored a Yngwie Solo

After the show, I was hot and heavy for Unicorne. The lights came on as the last sweet guitar lick of their epic Jesus ballad faded away and I felt refreshed. Sweaty and Svart-mauled, but calm inside. The whole world, I thought, needed to hear these songs. Especially "The Heart of the Dragon." World peace, saved whales. We could have it all if everyone just listened to the Unicorne CD I had in my pocket.

The good vibes had rubbed off on Svart, too. He was talking with some old couple—a guy with a paisley bandana tied around his head, a lady in mom jeans and a pink Mötley Crüe tank top. I don't know what they were talking about, but at one point, Svart slipped them each a beer and I watched, amazed, as this random and very un-Svartian act of kindness went down.

We wandered around, still in a daze. Svart took the lead and marched backstage like he belonged there. No one stopped him. I followed in his wake.

We found Tomi sitting on a folding chair, holding court backstage like he was the one who'd just rocked the Belgian hinterlands. The singer dude was there, too. His name was Luc. The real hero of the night. He was sitting on a table, a towel around his neck. He hunched over a little, his hands on his knees. The Hawaiian shirt did little to cover his paunch. He still had a weird fucked up mullet. But after that show, I regarded him with awe.

"You're the guy," I said, star struck. I stepped up to him and put out my hand. He shook it and I felt thankful that he deigned to acknowledge my lowly existence. The king's touch. I thought I'd never wash again. I thought maybe, just maybe, his touch would flow from my right hand and over to my left hand and vanquish my warts with whatever force allowed him to sing with such intense power.

The other Unicorne dudes came in and out of the room, this one hauling a cymbal, that one rolling up some cables. The guitarist ambled up to us, his Oxford shirt now untucked, another button undone. "Amazing," I said, star struck. And he shook my hand, too.

Another guy, short and round, joined them. He had a stack of stickers for his label. Tidal Force Records. He fingered the tip of a long and unruly moustache that dangled past his chin. Occasionally, he resettled his wire-framed glasses on his nose. When this guy showed up, Tomi got right to business. He introduced me and Svart as the rest of Desekration. He praised the guy's taste, told him that helping us, helping Unicorne, was a surefire way to build his label.

The guy, Rolf, seemed nice enough. He'd listened to *Infernö*. He could talk about Unicorne's songs at length. He took out some paper and a pen so he could jot down what we'd get and what he'd get each time some poor soul bought our version of *Infernö*, the "correct" version, *Total Infernö*. Importantly, he had no theories about spiritual rifts torn in the universe through the most devastating heavy metal sounds. He gave no indication that a plague-shriveled spirit dwelled somewhere within his pudgy belly. Or that, by producing and selling a CD, he was enacting a Nietzschean scheme to reverse the customary morality of civilizations.

He just liked heavy metal. A lot. And had no moral qualms about releasing a bootleg version of an album that already existed.

Tidal Force the label had grown out of a zine by the same name. And his zine came out of his extensive tape trading. The longer he traded tapes and published reviews of demos from all kinds of metal subgenres, the more people hit him up for copies of those tapes. More and more, he said, older tape traders were paying him for ancient demos they'd lost or missed out on. On top of that, a bunch of newer traders and zine readers, ones who started out rabid for grindcore and death metal, started hitting him up for copies of all the old shit they used to make fun of. Like Unicorne tapes.

"This label thing isn't planned out," he said. Like Svart, Rolf lived with his mom. But unlike Svart, he was no sponge. The label grew from his zine, and the zine grew out of his tape trading, because Rolf realized all the little bits of money people sent him slowly added up.

"You ever get letters from Nekrokor?" I asked, partly out of genuine curiosity and partly to suss out the full extent of Rolf's metal connections.

"Of course," he said, without missing a beat. "Many poorly written curses," he went on, and laughed.

Apparently, Rolf would review anything metal in his *Tidal Force* zine, including Christian metal. And that hadn't sat well with Nekrokor, who'd once found an Astrampsychos demo reviewed on the same page as a Tourniquet album. To impel even more virulent Nekrokorian hate mail, Rolf had a soft spot for two things that Nekrokor detested: power metal and positive lyrics.

"Now that he's dead," Rolf said, "you know how much I can get for one of those letters? I just sold an envelope—not even a letter—for something like," and here he closed his eyes for a second, stifled a burp, and then counted on his fingers.

"I made something like 200 dollars on that one envelope. And the thing was all rotten. Blackened with mold or something."

Blackened with infectious spores, I thought ruefully and rubbed my wart finger.

Despite his globally rhizomic network of tape traders and zine subscribers, Rolf didn't look like a metal obsessive, though. His hair wasn't long. He was wearing a plaid shirt tucked into beige pants. Unlike Svart, his whole neck wasn't freighted with mystical medallions. He looked like a computer salesman. Occasionally, he put his fist in front of his mouth to silence a burp. And as we all talked, it became clear Rolf had an encyclopedic knowledge not just of metal, but also of pop music, forgotten gems of early psychedelia, and just about anything else anyone mentioned.

When I said, more snobbishly than I meant to, that I'd only been listening to classical music, Rolf didn't bat an eye or act remotely cowed by my pretentious claim to "culture." Not like Svart, anyway, who farted and cracked another brew. Instead, Rolf launched into an exposition of his favorites: EMI records, the intricate complexity of Glenn Gould's mid 1950s recordings of Bach's Goldberg variations, and the ineffable awesomeness of Olivier Messiaen's *Catalogue d'oiseaux*.

I stood there, arms crossed and awkward as he firehosed out his superior knowledge. I felt like a poser. A classical music poser. I felt like one of the teenage Astrampsychos devotees that I loathed, but also hoped to psychically manipulate into purchasing *Total Infernö*.

When he asked me about my favorite composers, I scratched the back of my head and muttered sheepishly, "Bach." And then, to further burnish my credentials, I added, "The Bachs." He let that one slide. Didn't ask me to clarify which ones I meant.

Luckily, that's when Luc changed the subject. For someone who sang with such uplifting clarity, dude was kind of a downer. But from the stories he told, I guess it made sense. By all objective measures, he should have been ensconced in an LA mansion, some expanse of glass and concrete set into a hillside, and not sitting in the back of a community center. He should have already made it, not wasting his time to negotiate the re-release of an album that never got released the first time around.

"Classical music," he sighed. "A few years ago, and that would have been us. Surrounded by an orchestra. We were all set to record something with the Berlin Philharmonic. Even better, we were all set for a guest solo by Yngwie fucking Malmsteen."

The way he explained it, all these things had been scheduled and more. Unicorne had been on the European subsidiary of some big American label. Unicorne had been on the cusp of greatness. A stadium tour around the world. Japan and Australia. Opening for Def Leppard on this tour, since they'd proven their worth opening for Def Leppard in Antwerp.

Unicorne had been on the cusp of greatness. Until they got dropped.

Luc slid off the table and ambled to the back of the room.

"This town still loves us, though," And here he nodded at the guitar player. "Chris works for the city. So they let him store our shit here."

There was a closet with a padlock. He pulled out a set of keys and opened the closet. Inside, cardboard boxes stacked four high teetered up to the closet rod. Each box had a little sticker on the side, a UPC code and product description: "Unicorne-The Heart of the Dragon: 250 units."

"Urgh," I grunted. I'd seen my share of product boxes. But never like that. When I played in Valhalla, Plutonic sent us boxes of CDs and tapes to sell at our shows. But those were always narrow sleeves, the size of a shoebox or something. We'd do a show or two and everything would be gone. I never really had to think about it. Phil handled most of our merch stuff. I guess that's why he was majoring in business and I was hanging around in some closet looking at dead stock. If Plutonic sent along some cool promo—the logo of some band I liked, but emblazoned on a coaster or cast as an aluminum key chain—I grabbed it. Sometimes we traded our stuff with other bands. We always had something new to listen to in the car. Tape for tape, we built our ultralimited empire. But this closet crammed with unsold merch? It reminded me of a tomb. The place where music goes to die.

"This is everything," he said. "We're down to, oh, maybe 5,000 copies left."

"Whoa," I said.

"We sell some whenever we play out. Maybe five here, ten there."

"I bought one," I said.

Tomi piped in, too: "A timeless classic."

"Yes. We sold over ten tonight. It was a good show."

"You think we're old now," Chris joked. He and Rolf hauled a couple boxes out of the closet. "At that rate, we'll have to play gigs until we're senile just to break even."

These were sturdy fucking boxes. U-Haul boxes. Designed for heavy loads. I ducked into the closet and tried to pick one up.

"Fuck, that's heavy," I said.

It barely budged. All the CDs inside clacked together like the claws of a hundred crabs. All the CDs rattled like the bones of a million sparrows slain for Nordikron's magical rites. A dust cloud floated upward like a spirit disturbed from eternal slumber.

I sneezed.

Hunching over the box, I tried to palm it. I planted my legs and heaved. The longer I struggled, the more my post-Unicorne elation gave way to a sense of dread. It felt like someone was stacking box after box of unsold Unicorne CDs on my chest. Boxing me in. Heavy boxes. So many.

With my grip secure, I finally managed to haul that one box out of the closet. I set it on the table, where Rolf had set up a little restickering operation. He put a Tidal Force sticker over the name of the original record company, the big company with all the money. The way he saw it, Unicorne had been ahead of their time. The way he saw it, classic metal was going to come back. That was going to be his niche, he explained. Tidal Force was there to help those bands who got a raw deal.

Tomi went into the closet and came right back out. He grappled two giant boxes, one in each arm. He even nudged Svart into helping. Rolf wanted to mark these all for Tidal Force, get an accurate tally, and start sending this sea of Unicorne albums out to the stores and collectors in his distribution network.

Moving this shit out of the closet loosened Luc up. He relaxed and told us more. The way he described it, Unicorne got dropped while they were recording *Heart of the Dragon*. They were in some big studio in Brussels and they had to make a choice: just leave and stop recording or finish recording and pay for the studio time themselves.

"We decided to pay. We paid for the studio. We even paid the label to make the CDs. Took a lawyer for that to happen. But we didn't care. We figured another label would sign us," he said, accompanied by scornful laughter from Chris. "Of course! We'd opened for Def Leppard! Yngwie Malmsteen was going to play on one of our songs! And the guys at the studio cut us a good deal."

He dumped a stack of restickered CDs back into a box.

"Well, not really a 'good deal' for us, since we were broke. We still are broke. Even more so. But they cut us a deal."

Chris walked past and quipped. "Yeah, I still remember that time we played with Yngwie."

"That would have been amazing," I said. So cool, I thought, and pictured, like, a red Ferrari speeding through the streets of Brussels, then slamming to a stop, Yngwie, his milky white Stratocaster, and a couple of blondes bursting through a cloud of weed smoke as the car doors butterflied open.

But Luc and Chris burst out laughing.

"It would have been amazing," Chris said, "if the guy had actually showed up."

"He didn't show?" I asked.

"What a fiasco," Luc said. He shut the closet door then locked it. Like he wanted to keep the dust, the boxes, the endless stacks of albums, at bay. Keep them from escaping.

"We had the studio time reserved. The label told us they'd pay for it. They told us not to worry. We just needed to show up and the sound engineer would do all the rest. They got one of the best, or so they said. They had some guy who'd worked with Foreigner, Bad Company, Boston. A real pro."

He got some more restickered CDs from Rolf and dropped them in a box.

"We went there. We had all our gear. And the studio told us the label hadn't paid for the time. No Yngwie. Nothing."

As he went on, he spun a familiar tale. Unicorne were too late to the party. The label decided heavy metal was done. I shared my own tragic tale, but on a smaller scale: Plutonic Records, the way my Valhalla friends had abandoned me, Despondent Abyss, the way my Desekration friends abandoned me, too.

Tomi wanted to know how the label had dropped them, but still pressed the albums.

"Yeah, didn't you have a contract?" I asked.

"That contract," Luc muttered. "What a piece of shit."

They had signed a contract but hadn't read it very closely. Not at first. After they got dropped, they did some digging. Somewhere deep within, the contract had a clause that let the company back out, at any time, with no further financial obligation or liability. After the band recorded the album, they went ahead and made all those CDs because the contract said they had to have them made by the company, even if the company no longer wanted to work with the band.

"We thought, we'll just sell them ourselves. We were Unicorne. We had a radio hit. Opened for Def Leppard. No problem."

His voice tapered off. He gestured at all the boxes.

"It was a problem."

We all commiserated. Svart launched out of his chair and raged through a drunken tirade about his stolen band, his stolen royalties. I told them about the blood daubed beer coaster I'd signed as proof of my eternal loyalty to Despondent Abyss, told them about the way that Nekrokor had taken my spot and recorded over all my tracks. Tomi seemed almost embarrassed when he admitted he'd been replaced by a drum machine.

"On that note," Rolf said, and brandished his own contracts, one for the Unicorne guys, the other for us. Even though we'd all spent the past half hour bitching and moaning about contracts and exploitation, none of us—none of the Unicorne dudes, not Svart, not Tomi, not me—none of us read through the short, but dense, page long documents in front of us. And as Rolf handed me the pen he said, "At least you don't have to sign this one in blood."

Tomi and Svart were quiet on the walk back to the train station. Not that this was unusual. Tomi was taciturn by nature. And Svart had long passed the loud and belligerent stage of drunkenness. But this silence as we walked through this empty town felt, to me, like an unspoken acknowledgement we'd all arrived at the same truth: bootleg *Infernö* wasn't going to help us. We'd all signed the contract. And Rolf struck all of us as honest and well-meaning. But we knew. It must have dawned on all of us that restickering a bunch of dusty CDs and selling them to tape traders was no path to success. And doing the same thing with *Infernö* wasn't really going to change anything for us.

That's how I felt, anyway. And I think it was worse for Svart and Tomi. They'd seen some of those initial checks. More importantly, they'd cashed those checks. They'd handled real money generated by Desekration's masterwork. They probably still had some of that money, too. All the beers Svart had consumed that night, mountains and mountains of cans, at least some of them must have been funded from Desekration royalties. But me? I'd seen no money. Before they brought me into this Tidal Force scheme, I'd already made a tenuous peace with my erasure from the band. Or at least I thought I had. A little bit.

The night chill settled around us as we walked through the grassy suburbs of a forlorn and empty town. And then suddenly, Svart just stopped. Like a dog intent on sniffing some random spot of grass.

"Verdomme," he said. "What a bunch of shit."

He grabbed his crown, the little bone crown carefully assembled by Nordikron as some kind of evil crafting project, and yanked it off his head. The fishing wires snapped. Little bones went flying everywhere. Bird bones rained down on the sidewalk, on the manicured lawn of some suburban home.

He whipped out his dick, right there in front of us, right there on the sidewalk, and pissed all over the scattered bones.

"We have to find Mathias," he said when he finished. "We have to take what is ours."

And on the rest of the walk, we talked about how to do that. We agreed we'd do it the very next day. We conspired in the nocturnal silence, we conspired some more once we got on the train. We conspired until Svart suddenly passed out. The beers had finally outnumbered him.

After that, Tomi and I sat in silence. He might have been thinking about Mathias, and money, and the chance to play drums for a band that sounded amazing, but would probably go nowhere. Or he might have been thinking about this lady at work, some sad chick languishing in a dark and, for Tomi, alluring depression.

Svart slumped onto my shoulder. I bowed beneath his weight. The weight of his lumpy mastodon skull. His hair bushed around my chin, my nose, my eyes.

I tried to push him off me. I figured I'd push him over against the window. I buried my free hand in his hair. I couldn't move my left hand. His head crushed against the whole left side of my body. And as I got ready to heave him off me, something hard and round poked into my palm. It jabbed my palm like a pencil or a stick. I pushed him over until his head clonked against the window, and as I pulled my hand back, I freed whatever was in his hair.

It was a bone. Some remnant from the crown he'd broken and destroyed. A bird bone. From a sparrow, maybe, or a rotisserie chicken. I held it between my thumb and index finger; it was about as long as one of my finger joints. I held it against my finger to make a better comparison. It was about the length of the bone going from my knuckle to my hand. The same length as some bird part, too, some logical and reasonable voice told me. But also . . . and here I wondered. But also the same length as someone else's finger bone. The same length, maybe, as Bård's finger bone.

I thought about saying something to Tomi. Get some kind of reassurance. He would set me straight. Tell me I was holding a bone from a chicken and not from a bad tempered and vengeful guitarist. But he had his head against the window, his eyes half closed. I didn't want to fuck with him. Instead, I tried to sniff the bone. Like that would clear things up. But it just smelled like Svart's head. It smelled like a mass of poofy and unwashed hair.

Probably just a bird bone, I eventually determined. But I slipped it into my pocket for safe keeping.

25.
Reinblasphemation

The next morning, sunlight streamed through my curtains. I woke up and stretched out of my creaky and lopsided bed. This is the day when we get Mathias to cough up some cash, I thought. The prospect of confronting that little freak, confronting him with Svart and Tomi by my side, filled me with joy. I made some coffee and sat on the balcony. As the sun rose, the day attained a rare kind of natural perfection: cool, but not cold. Sunny, but not hot. I didn't need a blanket or a fleece or a parka to endure the elements. Just some sweatpants and a stinky Katabasis shirt. A cornflower blue sky, cloudless with a gentle breeze, stretched past the monastery dome beyond the balcony and out as far as I could see.

This, I thought, savoring the heavenly alignment of warm coffee and perfect weather. This. This is the day. Let us rejoice and be glad in it. And I laughed to myself, laughed into my coffee cup, as I recalled the previous night. Not the depressing realization that another Desekration release wasn't going to help anyone, or the other depressing stuff about Unicorne's Icarian flop.

But the fun stuff. I laughed as I recalled Unicorne's cheesy and moving ballad about a heavy metal dragon. I laughed some more as I recalled Svart's righteous anger and the righteous splash of his urine on a bunch of greasy bones.

213

The bones ... thinking of the bones cast the slightest pall, a dark little nimbus, over my otherwise delightful and cloudless morning. The bones that may have come from Nekrokor. The finger bone connected to the hand bone, the hand bone connected to the wrist bone, and so on and so forth, various bits and fragments laced together with fishing wire.

I patted my pocket, where I'd stuffed one of these bones. I still had it. And I intended to keep it. Keep it as a relic, an icon, or just a gross souvenir. I wasn't entirely certain it came from Nekrokor, but I also wasn't certain it hadn't. I felt the outline of the bone in my pocket. It seemed thicker, stronger, than your average chicken wing. Or sparrow leg. But if anyone asked me about it, I'd maintain that I'd found it, that it came from a bird, and I had it out of a deep and abiding ornithological curiosity.

I kind of wondered if customs would bust me for it if—when—I brought it back to Miami. If that happened, I'd claim it came from the in-flight meal. And going back to Miami would happen sooner than later, based on my cash situation. Some DEA dog, trained to sniff out exotic cheeses and Eurodude fingerbones, would probably pounce on me the second I tried to leave Miami International Airport with that thing in my pocket.

The prospect of my imminent brokeness started to bum me out. More than the prospect of keeping a human bone in my pocket. I went back to the kitchen for a coffee refill and came back out with my Discman and my newly purchased copy of *Heart of the Dragon*. It probably hadn't been smart to blow my cash on it, but the five bucks had been worth it because of what I was about to do: strap on my headphones and unapologetically listen to metal again.

I tried to quit metal, but failed. And listening to Unicorne made me realize it was wrong to quit metal. The dragon of metal loved me. Which sounded stupid, but just meant that metal itself hadn't created my problems. It meant that, as long as metal gave me some kind of pleasure, then I should listen to it. And that I shouldn't let people like Natasha try to convince me otherwise.

The disc played successfully for about a minute. One blissful minute of searing leads. One blissful minute of headphones transmitting distorted guitars directly down my ears. One blissful minute of Luc asserting, with total power, "He can fill your cup, He can fill your soul. The blood is shed . . . the blood is shed for you." For that one blissful minute, the religious lyrics didn't even bother me. I thought of Tomi's point—who cared what they sang about? And it was a Sunday; the dragon of metal allowed a special dispensation for Christian lyrics on the day of the Lord.

Religious or not, it was a great song. Whenever Luc sang the word "cup," I took a sip of coffee. But I wondered if there wasn't more to the tale of record label abuse they'd spun the night before. Starting your heavy metal album with a eucharistic rocker wasn't the best way to attain pop superstar status. Even I knew that.

But then, just as I was getting into it, sipping coffee, air guitaring, the CD whirred to a stop. I tapped the Discman a few times. The thing was temperamental. Prone to malfunction. But that wasn't the problem. The battery icon blinked on the display. It was out of juice.

I didn't have any extra batteries. So I finished my coffee and got ready to go to Svart's. His place was closer than Tomi's. I figured Tomi probably had a plan. Some strategy to get that hard-earned royalty money. By the end of the day, I figured, I might not be so fucking broke. By the end of the day, I figured, I might even be able to swing by a nachtwinkel, buy some new batteries.

After all that coffee, I took a massive dump. It was enough time to read the entire *Heart of the Dragon* CD booklet more than once, to contemplate the cover's complex airbrush artistry. When I finished, I washed my hands. As I scrubbed, a flap of skin on my wart finger waved back and forth, like some grotesque tail. The bumps of several small warts—protowarts—

covered the surface of this long and ropy fleshscrap, a good song title. But it clung to my finger at the site of the biggest wart, the mother wart, the one that Mathias had called a "Satanic diamond" marking me as the devil's bitch. It sat on this flap of skin like a spongy paperweight. All around its edges, the skin was pink and inflamed.

I yanked on the flap and jostled it from side to side. It wouldn't budge, though. A little blood seeped out from underneath the biggest wart, but that was all. I gently dried my hands, then got out of the bathroom. I'd given up on BandAids. I'd given up on the wart medicine, too. Fuck it, I figured. God or Satan or the universe wanted to put nasty warts on my hand. And I couldn't really do shit about it. And in my celibate state—Maria gone, Natasha gone—I didn't even care.

When I got to Svart's place, his mom came to the door. She had on a flowered apron over a black blouse. She wore a pearl choker around her taut, tanned neck.

"Goeiemorgen, mevrouw Svart," I said in my most polite voice.

"Goeiemorgen, David," she purred back.

The cinnamon aroma of apple strudel wafted from inside. I asked if Svart was home, half hoping she'd say no and invite me in. Feed me baked goods. Abuse my body. In this fantasy, my wart finger, all my members, were perfect and unblemished.

But, alas, Svart was home. Laid out in bed and soldiering through an aggressive hangover. Mrs. Svart seemed totally oblivious to the obvious cause of his malady. She attributed it to seasonal allergies, even though he'd already hurled a few times that morning. She didn't say it like that, though—about the hurling. She was much more polite. And deluded.

"Poor Jurgen," she said. "There must have been some heavy pollen out in the countryside. It's made him quite sick."

I asked if I could talk to him. She hesitated at first. Didn't want to disturb her little patient. But when I promised I'd be fast, she let me in.

His covers lay in a sodden mass on the floor. His room did not smell like cinnamon and strudel. The air hung heavy, infused with the odor of a soot-gray bath bomb molded out of shit and sweat and bile. His body looked like just such a malodorous bath bomb, or like a malodorous boulder ready to be scooped into hundreds of stencherous bath bombs. Svart, his body a masterwork of pasty flesh and flabby creases, lay across the bed like some gargantuan Lucien Freud nude. He wasn't completely flapping around, though. He had on some kind of man thong, mostly white but freckled here and there with yellow stains. And his occult necklaces, all scattered about. One of them, the Mjolnir, lay wedged in his armpit.

"Dude," I said, and then again," Dude . . . wake up . . . dude."

I reached out and wiggled him by the ankle. Eventually, he stirred, then flopped onto his side.

"Later," he groaned. "Come back later."

He stuck his hand beneath the waistband of his underwear and scratched vigorously.

That's when I left.

And out on the street, the city was even quieter than usual. Because it was Sunday. The day of the Lord. As I put that together, I found myself walking toward St. Baafs. At first, I'd intended to go to Tomi's, but the more I walked, the more I moved across cobblestones and down empty alleys, I realized I had a new plan. I had a hunch, a feeling, more than a feeling, that I could find Mathias. I had a feeling that, with Svart incapacitated for a few more hours, it was my responsibility to track the dude down.

I moved through the arched doorway and into the cathedral. I saluted the statues of Jesus overhead, just for luck. Inside, the martial blast of a brassy processional rocked the sanctuary. All around, light from the perfect and cloudless sky streamed through the stained-glass windows. And yet, despite the pipe organ wall of sound, the images of a thousand saints handling their instruments of demise—a wheel, an arrow, a giant fucking rock, despite the tangible presence of light itself filling this vast space, the sanctuary was nearly devoid of life.

There were some old men in gray tweed. Some old women in slightly more festive shades of gray tweed, too. The lady I'd seen making out with Mathias was there. No Mathias, though.

Despite the vehement antireligiosity espoused by most of the bands I liked (except Unicorne, of course), I felt just fine sitting through the church service. Relaxed. Reflective, even. I drifted off there for a second. The repetitive organ tones of a dreary hymn, paired with the echoes of background sounds, of hymnal pages shuffling, halfhearted singing, and whispered murmurs, put me into a trance. The sounds within the cathedral created the kind of sound tapestry so many of these same bands aimed to replicate in their ambient side projects.

And then I saw him. Heard him, really. I was still kind of dozing when I heard an amplified jostling of paper, followed by a mechanical click, and then his voice. I jolted awake to find him standing at a lectern in front of the congregation. He had his hand-held tape recorder on the lectern, right next to an enormous Bible. He stood there, dressed in a long black robe, his hair combed and covering his shoulders, a big silver cross on his chest. He recited a psalm and he looked right at me as he started reading.

"My soul has a desire and longing for the courts of the Lord," he said, and no lightning rained from the heavens to smite him.

"The sparrow has found her a house and the swallow a nest where she may lay her young," he went on, still without divine retribution.

And then the oldsters assembled finished the verse: "by the side of your altars, O Lord of hosts, my King and my God."

When he finished reading the psalm, he headed back to the organ and slid onto the bench. He started playing and another dismal hymn rocked the cathedral. Even though he was the organist, I hadn't noticed him on the way in. Covered in a black robe, his hair actually combed. Playing hymns unaccompanied by groans and tortured shrieks. Of course I hadn't noticed him.

Right after the service, I hustled up to the organ. I half expected him to just disappear as soon as he played the last note. He turned and smiled.

"So we meet again, David," he said. Then, he added in a sneering undertone, "I can call you that here in the house of your namesake's god."

He grabbed his tape recorder from the top of the organ, then shut it off.

"What the fuck is all this?" I asked. But before he had a chance to answer, his lady friend came over.

They jabbered in Dutch. He thanked her for letting him play. She thanked him for taking the time to help. Not many young people these days, she went on. And then that was it. He stripped off the robe, the silver cross, and gave them to her. Underneath, he had on an old Celtic Frost shirt. *To Mega Therion*. But so faded and worn the design was just a smattering of white streaks and dots.

She left without a single goodbye kiss.

"Dude," I said, and then repeated my initial question: "What the fuck is all this?"

An old guy looked my way and grimaced. I was the one courting divine retribution, not Mathias. So I said, "Het spijt mij," and then whispered, "Seriously, man. What are you doing?"

Mathias just laughed. A high-pitched cackle. He grabbed a satchel lying on the organ bench. He dropped the tape recorder in there, and then said, "Come with me. I want to show you something."

And as we left St. Baafs, I thought of a million excuses to leave. Run to Svart's, pull him out of bed, and track Mathias down. "Come with me." I had no reason to trust him. He's going to lead me to a dungeon or a cellar, I thought. Some isolated den of depravity. According to Tomi, he'd killed Bård, his own brother.

But I kept walking with him. According to Tomi, he'd killed his own brother, and I had the finger bone to prove it. But according to what I'd just seen, Mathias was killing the church organ. And spending his Sunday morning reading holy scripture to a bunch of senior citizens.

"Are you," and here I paused. I felt like I was going to ask him something unseemly, something too personal to express in words. "Are you, like, a Christian?" I finally stammered.

Mathias ran his fingers through his hair.

"You know me," he said. "Do you think I am a Christian?"

I didn't have an answer. He'd been in the cathedral, more than once. Playing the organ. Reading psalms. At the same time, this was Nordikron. Elite practitioner of wailing and gnashing of teeth. Just like it said in the *Infernö* liner notes.

"That lady. That old chick," I said. "I saw you kissing her. That's fucking disgusting."

"I'm not a priest," he said. "I don't have to be celibate."

"Yeah, but," and here I tried to explain. She's super old. Not fit. Many chinned. He scoffed at my reasons. Called me shallow. When I asked again what he was doing at the church, he just answered with a cryptic riddle:

"If the church absorbed the old gods, the old beliefs, then that's the only place where they're still alive. Besides," he went on, "the acoustics are phenomenal. How else am I supposed to get access to the best keyboard in the whole city?"

I didn't have a good answer. The organ—an ancient Casio—Mathias was doing the legwork for yet another Despondent Abyss masterwork.

"Unlike you," he said. "I'm willing to sacrifice for my art."

And he didn't lead me to any dark and desolate place. Instead, we walked back through the city and toward my neighborhood. I knew enough not to let him up to my place, though. I didn't want to end up in my bathtub, dead and drained, my body and blood an anti-communion for the ancient gods of his weird syncretic belief in Jesus, I guess, as just the newest mask over the boundless void that's been the true god all along.

We passed the Record Huis, passed the nachtwinkel with its cracked window, passed the grocery store where I got my fancy beers, and headed up my street, the Rooseveltlaan.

When he crossed the street and headed through the park, I kept my wits about me. They'd found Bård under some trees and floating in a stream. I'd seen enough thrillers to know I was in danger. So I trailed behind him, far enough that I could book it if I needed to. Also, I kept my hand in my pocket, kept a firm grip on the sacred phalange of Nekrokor. At a moment's notice, I'd whip that thing out and jab holmes in the eye hole. Poetic justice. And if that didn't work, I had my key ring. I didn't have a bike, but I still had my bike lock key, and that thing was long and round as a nail.

He approached a mound. A little midden, a dirt pyramid. A bunch of holes, maybe for ventilation, latticed the whole thing.

Another bird tomb, it seemed. I thought of the psalm he had read. The sparrow has found a house, its home a miserable mound of dirt. And inside the mound, we'd find the bird. Interred in a plastic bag to concentrate the noxious fumes of decay. Mathias, sick fuck, grew energized by inhaling the stench of decay. Maybe aroused.

Mathias found a branch and used it to dig. Whatever he'd buried wasn't very deep. Before long, he pulled out a golden box and shook off the remaining dirt. It wasn't, like, a gilt sarcophagus or anything. I recognized the box. You couldn't spend more than a day in Belgium and not. It was a chocolate box. A Leonidas chocolate box. For about twelve pieces, if I had to guess.

He set the box on the ground and carefully opened the lid. It probably wasn't filled with chocolates. I prepared myself for some grim sight, a blob putrefacted by time and dust.

But I was wrong.

Mathias dug his hand into the box. He pulled it out and a tiny sparrow, its body limp but intact, lay in his palm.

I peered closer.

He prodded the bird's side with two skeletal fingers, a move that seemed pointless. If you bury an animal in the ground, it's probably fucking dead. I mean, unless it's an earthworm or something. Its neck, a withered cord, flopped against its body. The head, the skull, hung heavy and still. He did it again, this time holding his fingers against its globular body after he poked.

Maybe he's gauging how much more time it needs below ground? I wondered. Like if you're grilling a steak or something? If it feels as solid as your palm, then its medium rare, good to go. Estimating how much time until he got his bird to his preferred state of decay?

I figured I'd seen enough. First church, now this. I turned to leave. Go get my muscle. Go get Svart and Tomi. I already knew Mathias was a fucked up little dude. Nothing new here. His churchgoing just added a new wrinkle to his many levels of weirdness. He wasn't like me. He wasn't too normal at all.

But then I heard it. A sudden sound. I froze. Turned back.

I heard it again. Like a bell. Sharp and clear above the incessant traffic hum.

A chirp.

I moved closer and peered over his shoulder, where he crouched above the golden chocolate box.

The bird sat in his palm, its head now raised. As I watched, it stood. Alert, it scanned the trees above. It chirped again, then fluffed its feathers.

I crouched in wonder. What would the bird do next? What would Mathias do next?

"Fear not," he crooned, his lips just inches from the bird's head.

This was it, I figured. The moment he'd go full Ozzy and decapitate the sparrow with one swift chomp.

"You are of more value than many sparrows," he said. Then, he raised his palms and cast the bird up, into the air.

I inhaled sharply, expecting to see this bird smash right back into the dirt. Fall back into the Leonidas box so Mathias could let it ferment a bit more. The bird had been through a lot. If that were me, if I were that bird, that's exactly what would have happened. My just-exhumed ass would have flopped straight to the floor.

But that's not what happened. As soon as it left his hands, the bird beat its wings. It flew. Even though it had been buried in the ground. For God knows how long. Even though it had sat, unmoving, a dead blob, just minutes before.

I had no idea what the fuck I'd just seen.

Was this even Mathias? Was this truly Nordikron? Or did he have, like, a non-evil twin? One committed to life and not total death? A pale and poodle-haired St. Francis releasing birds from the tomb. First I'd seen him at church, and now this?

The bird flew away from Mathias, then settled into the trees overhead.

What I'd seen qualified as a miracle. Something that, properly documented, would bring the pope to Gent. Would bring adulating hordes of believers. The thought seemed outrageous and absurd.

I must have laughed. It's what I do when I'm nervous. I can't help it.

Mathias laughed, too.

"Amazing, isn't it?" he asked. The bird still sat on the branch above him. New buds and unfurling leaves festooned the tree, all the trees, and all around, the grass grew fresh and green.

"How'd you fucking do that?" I asked. And at the same time, I realized Svart had been right all along. Mathias was more than a creepy little dude. He was a powerful wizard. A fucking nekrogandalf breathing life into broken bodies. I might have fallen to one knee. The spectacle I'd seen filled me with wonder and fear. Fear because if this dude had the secret of immortality, no way was he going to give us some royalty money.

I felt like I had when I was a kid. When I'd found that boar's head strapped to a tree. I felt overwhelmed. Paralyzed. And just like then, I backed away, slowly at first.

"It is true that I must taste the stench of death. To perform properly," Mathias called after me. "And yet, I also savor the life quiver of the newly awakened. Of those who wake from the sleep of death."

I moved across the grass and through the bushes until I made it back to the real world of cars and parking meters and apartment buildings. And then I ran. To Tomi. To Svart.

26.

The Inmost Sanctum

After serving witness to the miracle of avian resurrection, I hustled straight to Tomi's. I pushed through the growing crowds of shoppers and tourists once I escaped the park and headed toward the city center. In the catacomb of alleys near the cathedral, my frantic footfalls echoed like one of Tomi's most cardio-intensive blastbeats.

I ran to Tomi because I needed his rationality. I needed him to tell me I hadn't seen the zombie sparrow. That there was some other explanation for the undead bird I'd most definitely seen flapping up into the trees. And Tomi obliged me.

Unlike Svart, he had already made productive use of his day. He had on some track pants and a tank top when he let me in. A gym towel hung around his neck. He sipped from a bottle of lime Glucozade. A pile of running shoes sat in a basket by the door.

"Have you been drinking?" he asked when, after he let me in, I breathlessly described the church, Mathias on the organ, and then the bird rising from its chocolate box sarcophagus.

Still, something about my urgency motivated him.

"We must settle this now," he said. He didn't mean the existence of the bird, though. He meant the royalty money situation. He harangued me a little for going to Mathias on my own. He told me I'd blown the element of surprise, even though I

225

made it clear I hadn't mentioned money to Mathias at all.

Tomi didn't believe me. "It was our one advantage," he said. As we left his place and headed over to Svart's, he told me Mathias would know I had some reason for trying to find him. Tomi made the reasonable point that I wouldn't otherwise go to a church service.

Svart was alone when we got to his place. His mom had left for the day. A bike ride out into the countryside. She didn't have Svart's allergy problems. The undead bird had moved with more vigor than Svart, who stared blankly while we filled him in on my Mathias sighting.

My tale motivated him, though. His brow furrowed as he processed it all: his black metal idol in a church, his black metal idol enacting miracles. It confirmed his belief that Mathias possessed powerful magic. And that, if we didn't act fast, he'd use that magic against us. But he shambled from the door and into the kitchen like an eighty-year-old man.

"You should take an aspirin," I suggested.

Svart shook his head and went to the refrigerator. He dug out a can of Primus and cracked it open without comment. The beer had the right effect. Svart disappeared into his room, then came out about ten minutes later in a Kreator shirt and camo pants. Before we left, he grabbed a pair of scissors and stuffed them in a cargo pocket.

"Just in case," he said. Armed and dangerous. For Belgium.

We headed out and marched on Overpoortstraat. The building where Mathias lived sat at the far end of that street. I asked Tomi if he had a plan.

He said, "We go into the building. We find Mathias. We convince him to pay us our fair share."

Svart grunted in agreement. But neither of them could elaborate.

At this time of day, no one went to Overpoortstraat. Only delivery trucks stocking up restaurants and depleted bars. A few drunks from the night before.

The apartment tower stood several blocks away, where all

the bars and restaurants faded into a kind of postindustrial wasteland. A whitewashed rectangle broken only by thin window slits, the building glowered like a Brutalist fortress commissioned by orcs.

We kept walking, and about once a block, Tomi asked, "Are you sure that's the right building?" It was probably the ugliest building in Gent.

"If you were right about his magic," Tomi said, "then Mathias wouldn't live in such a shithole." And then he added, "If we're right about the money, he wouldn't live in such a shithole."

Behind me, Svart let out a wet burp. A light mist spattered the back of my head, followed by an acrid stench. Then, he sprinted ahead and ducked into a nearby friterie. Tomi and I loitered outside. I figured Svart went in there for the bathroom. To barf. But about ten minutes later, he came out with a wet and greasy doner kebab.

When we got to the building, we loitered by the main entrance. Svart munched and he seemed to grow taller and heartier with each mouthful.

Then, the door jostled and clicked open. A couple college guys came out. One of them had a soccer ball. They passed us and we sprang into action. Tomi positioned himself right by the door, so he could keep it open. I put my hands in my pocket and interposed myself between these guys and the door. Svart chewed and didn't barf.

The guy with the soccer ball paused, then tilted his head. He hadn't heard the door latch shut. He turned back, but Svart faced him down with a bout of hostile chewing. Tore into his kebab like a shark into a surfboard. Tomi still held the door open. I did my best to loom menacingly. I hunched my shoulders like I was adjusting a backpack, then clenched my fists.

It worked. The kebab upped Svart's intimidation factor. And then we were inside.

We moved down the hall, examining each door for clues. The doors stood so close together; despite his tales of wealth,

Mathias led a crammed and uncomfortable existence. Because the apartments themselves were so jammed together, the hall was filled with crap. Empty beer crates, waterlogged sandals, umbrellas defeated by the elements. But nothing that hinted at Mathias. No cape. No boots. No empty blood vials.

Svart and Tomi had similar luck. When we got to the end of the hall, we climbed the stairs and tried the next floor.

On the second floor, we thought for sure we'd found him. Ahead of me, Svart stood silent. He had his ear nearly pressed against a battered old door.

He motioned us over. All three of us stood there. At first, I only heard the outside world filtering through the thin walls: the rubbery thump of cars on cobblestones, the thrum of highway traffic in the distance. But then I could make out music. A song. Electric guitars. Heavy metal.

"It's 'Acid Queen,'" Svart said with absolute certainty. And he raised his fist to beat on the door. Of course Mathias jammed out to Venom in the comfort of his shitty apartment.

"No," Tomi said. He put his hand on Svart's shoulder. "It's 'Circle of the Tyrants.'"

Whether it was Venom or Celtic Frost, the sound of antediluvial black metal served as a plausible indicator that Mathias lurked somewhere near. To me, it didn't sound like either song, though. It didn't sound like any song. Like, I could hear with perfect clarity the movement of a car parking outside the building, but the music formed an indecipherable hum of guitar distortion. Until the refrain came through, loud and clear: "Ohh . . . we're halfway there . . . oh ooh . . ."

"Bon Jovi," we all muttered in disgust, and continued our search. We got sloppy. We blazed down the halls. If we didn't find some obvious indicator, a neon sign or a message inscribed in the language of Mordor, we stomped on past.

By the time we got to the third floor, we still had no luck. Feeling defeated, I backtracked, but Svart and Tomi went up another level. Even though I'd seen Mathias come into the building that one night, I had nothing else to guide me. All I remembered was that he pressed a buzzer and then he'd disappeared inside.

And for all I knew, he wasn't even at his place. I'd left him in the park. Just him and a resurrected bird. For all I knew, he'd taken the thing out for lunch. Or they'd had a picnic. Just the two of them. Sitting under a tree and slugging down some sanguinary smoothie.

The junk in front of the apartments didn't help in my quest. And neither did the doorways themselves. They were all equally miserable, just battered in slightly different ways. On this one, a vast expanse of peeled paint the size and shape of Svart's big ass head revealed the acid green color scheme of some long distant era. On another, a cappuccino barf splatter marked everything from the doorknob down. And on a third—I nearly passed it, but then I paused. Just a few doors from the end of the hall. A reddish-brown smudge, head height, marked the frame.

I put two fingers on the doorframe, right where the smudge lay thickest. I held the fingers to my nose and sniffed. It smelled like decay. It smelled like Mathias. I touched the frame again and rubbed a ridge of dried goo and some raised nekrobraille spots. This was the way to the apartment of woe. This was the door to Nordikron's lair. I figured that all out before I heard a Casio melody emanating from somewhere inside. Something simple. Something lame. Something from, like, track nine of *Nekrokorus Mortuus Est*. The glockenspiel setting carried through the air, crystal clear, in ways that a distorted guitar never could.

The keyboarding stopped, followed by some clicks and the whirr of a tape rewinding. I knocked. I heard some shuffling, some paper crinkling, and then the door opened. Mathias stood there; a waft of cold air streamed from his apartment and into the hall.

"May I invite you in?" he asked, putting on the air of the gracious host. Or a psycho ready to murder you in the bathtub.

"Yeah," I said, tentative and fearful. Svart and Tomi were

nowhere to be found.

He turned back into his apartment.

Trash piled all around the floor. I had to shuffle to stay on the tiny thread of trash-free trail leading from the door and into the apartment's main room. Another spur of the trail led to a closed door, probably the slaapkamer. I shivered and the tips of my fingers and toes grew brittle and frozen. Outside, the sun hung high over Gent, but in here, it felt like I was shuffling through snow, not trash. Every shuffle sent me deeper into the heart of winter.

It wasn't dark inside, though. Not like you might think. The bare walls almost gleamed with the blinding white of hospitals and mental institutions. Gobs of dried paint dribbled like wampa snot from the top of each wall where it met the ceiling. An uncovered tube bulb in the ceiling drenched the room in a sickly, flickering fluorescence. The apartment had exactly one window. It had been painted white, too. Paint lay thick across the top half of the pane; a haze of droplets obscured the view through the bottom half. Through the paint droplets, I spied cars passing by outside and the empty sidewalks on this far and forgotten end of Overpoortstraat.

"Welcome to my home," Mathias said. He headed to a wooden table holding my old keyboard and a bunch of recording stuff: a four track, his hand-held tape player, a microphone. A stack of books and papers sat next to the keyboard. A sprawl of pages with his knife slash handwriting covered a hymnal and a leather-bound Bible. An empty vial and a paper bag with powder and fibrous roots lay at the far end of the table. The residue of some nekrobaking adventure, I figured.

It was hardly a home. Besides a bare trail running from the door, trash lay piled knee high everywhere else. Empty candy wrappers, plastic bags, stacks of newspapers. A bunch of envelopes. And page after page covered in words, drawings, and notes. The first time I'd met him, Mathias drew close to me and inhaled the stench of shit and barf wafting from my salmonella-stricken body. It must have reminded him of this nasty hovel.

"You alone?" I asked. "I like what you've done with the place." My command of sarcasm, I determined, would give me the upper hand.

Mathias exhaled heavily, more like the hiss of a beleaguered reptile than anything else, a turtle confronted in its shell. I could see his breath, a tiny yellow fog, coming out of his half-opened mouth, a rash-colored slit filled with sharp yellow teeth.

I patted my pockets, though. Nervous. I wished I'd brought a weapon. A pair of scissors or something. Like Svart had. The only time in life he did something smart. All I had was that bone. More than a weapon, I wished I had Svart here with me. A jumble of movement, the rumble of feet down the hall, vibrated the door on its hinges.

I wondered if Svart and Tomi were out in the hall. I wondered if they would save my ass if things got bad.

"I know why you're here. You miss your keyboard," Mathias said. He walked over to it and fingered a slow arpeggio.

"That's right," I said, even though his bullshit synthesizer tunes ranked low on my list of concerns. The bird. The money. The murder of Nekrokor.

He played a note, then held his brittle finger on the A, the highest one on the keyboard. He held it too long, saying nothing, for at least sixteen beats.

"At a certain point, the note transforms to pure sound. Held long enough, the sound triggers the limbic system, stimulating a physical response described by the metaphysical term 'transcendence,'" He stopped playing. "Or it becomes noise—depends who is listening."

He picked up his tape recorder and hit play. He'd recorded it earlier that day. Mathias on the organ. Fuzzy and muted, though.

"In medieval times, they believed the pipe organ reproduced the sounds of the planets," he said. "Trapped in crystal spheres, the planets gyrated around the earth."

"Medieval times," I quipped and gestured to my chest. "Who told you that? The plague spirit inside?"

I'd paid diligent attention to his nekroevangelizing.

"Is that why you're going to church?" I added.

"The heretic is the truest believer," is all he said. The organ recital continued. A few more loud bumps reverberated through his place. He moved away from the table and spun the volume dial up. He held the tape recorder out at me. Like it was garlic. And I was the vampire. With an organ tape drenched in lo-fi hiss, he walked toward me. Unconsciously, I backed up until I leaned against the door.

"I don't expect you to understand," he said. He reached around me and opened the door. "You are free. Like the sparrow. Free to live. Free to die."

In that moment when he draped around me, his repulsive presence pushing me outside, he stuffed something in my hand—the wart hand—and closed my fingers with his icy touch.

He shut the door and locked it. Before he shut it, though, he said, "Take this seed. Take it home. To your home, your homeland. Take this seed and see if you can make it grow. Then, maybe, you can return."

A few seconds later, the Casio started up again.

I opened my fingers to find a tooth. A chunky molar with spiky roots. A human tooth.

"Fuck," I groaned. I rolled the tooth in my palm. Now I had two Nekrokor relics. A finger. A tooth. I'd stood nose to nose with a murderer and talked with him about fucking keyboards. I wanted to attack. I wanted to be brave. Avenge Nekrokor. Reclaim royalties. I wanted to serve justice and enrich myself, all in one fell swoop. But instead, I just felt afraid. And hopeless. I'd had my chance but failed.

I stood in a daze, my fingers rubbing over the contours of poor Nekrokor's tooth. The whole time, Mathias Casioed away inside. And when I considered just turning around and heading back to my place, Svart and Tomi burst out of the stairwell.

"Did you find him?" Svart yelled. They both ran, but Tomi got to me first.

I showed them the tooth. It was enough to spur Svart into action. He hurled his shoulder into the door. A loud slam shook the hall, but the door stayed in place. Tomi, always so assiduous in his physical training regimen, gently pushed Svart aside and shattered the door with one well-placed Asics blast.

Once inside, Svart kicked the trash all around his feet—he footed an empty soup can somewhere beneath the endless garbage tide.

Mathias stood by the keyboard.

"What the fuck," Svart said. "We know you killed Nekrokor. David showed us the tooth."

Mathias started laughing. Shrill and loud. It shook his paint-smeared window.

"You can't kill someone by pulling their tooth," he said. "Though I wish that I could."

I pulled the fingerbone out of my pocket.

"We have his finger, too," I said. I brandished it like a broken cross.

"And you took our money," Tomi added.

Mathias got a little more serious when Tomi mentioned the money. But he insisted there wasn't really any money to begin with. He started to run down a bunch of costs. He did the same shit the Plutonic Records dudes used to do to me in my Valhalla days.

Tomi stood silent and resolute. He folded his arms as Mathias talked. And then he said, "Murder is a serious crime. This tooth and this finger can cause you trouble if we leave here and take them to the police. But we could also leave here and not go to the police. The path we take is up to you."

It seemed like a fair deal. If he paid us, we'd stay out of it. But Tomi's cold calculation didn't work.

"Is that a bone from some costume?" Mathias asked.

Svart told him it was from the crown he'd made. Svart seemed hurt that Mathias hadn't immediately recognized it.

"That's from a sparrow," Mathias said. "I have been conducting . . . experiments. David, I'm sure, has told you all about them."

Even if he was telling the truth, that didn't explain the tooth. But Mathias told us he had no money to give. He kept to his story, too. Even as Tomi and Svart edged closer to the table.

Tomi grabbed Mathias by the shoulder. Mathias squealed and Tomi told him he'd better use some magic to summon up some money. He laid out, cold and calculating, his own estimates of just how much we deserved.

I stood back by the door. Something jabbed my ankle. Or bit it. I bent down to scratch my sock. A black dot—a flea—leaped off my shin and into the trash all around.

"Gross," I said. "His pet flea bit me."

I leaned down and inspected both legs. My shoes, too. And there, nearly submerged by trash, I reached for an envelope on the ground in front of me. The envelope had a plastic window, the kind they use for checks. It had a Plutonic Records sticker for the return address.

"Dude," I said as I raised the envelope into the air. "Dude. This is from Plutonic."

I shuffled through the trash some more. So did Svart. Tomi held onto Mathias. Before long, we'd excavated a treasure trove of opened envelopes. From a global array of distributors. From major American music stores. I even uncovered one from the Booksalot corporate office. Among all the envelopes and trash, I sifted through endless crumpled pages covered in Mathias's scrawl and scratchy sketches. Some nonsense ravings. "Metal preexists metal" and "the sound of the Nekronomikon's word is death." A drawing of some robed dude floating into a dark forest. Another one of a witch and her spellbook up at the top of the Belfort Tower.

A rustling came from the door to the bedroom.

"You got a girl in there?" Svart asked with a leer.

"Probably more fleas," I said.

Tomi let go of Mathias and headed to the bedroom door.

"No. But I bet the checks are in there," he said. "If he hasn't cashed them yet."

"Yeah, maybe his accountant's in there," I said.

Svart shuffled over to the bedroom door and jiggled the handle. And then it all happened so fast. Mathias bent down. At first I thought he had a flea, too. Or that he was going to finally unveil some sizable check. But when he stood back up, he had an evil knife in his hands. All long and sharp, it had a ring of spikes for a pommel.

He held Nekrokor's knife. The one he pulled on me the first time we met.

In an instant, Mathias lunged at Svart with the sinuous dexterity of the living dead. He sliced at Svart's beer-swollen belly. And Svart collapsed into the door. Hard enough that it popped open.

Mathias stood over Svart and drew the knife back. He was ready to slash him again. But Tomi came right behind and strapped him in a headlock.

Svart groaned. A steady stream of blood stained the trash, the empty envelopes, the lyric fragments, all around him. A steady stream of blood stained his Kreator shirt, now slashed and ruined.

And another groaning, another agonized voice, echoed out of the bedroom.

I snatched the knife out of Mathias's hand and walked into the room. I gasped. The room was just as shitty as the rest of the apartment. It had a desk, a bed covered with a flimsy blanket, and a heater along the far wall. A neat stack of checks sat right in the middle of the table.

But that's not why I gasped. A wheelchair sat in the far corner. Over by the heater. And in the wheelchair, a bent form in a leather jacket heaved and groaned. I recognized the jacket. The spikes. The chains. The patches. It was Nekrokor's. And the thing in the jacket was Nekrokor. Green skinned and groaning, but alive.

This was enough for Tomi to forget his laser focus on the

cash.

"What the fuck did you do?" he asked. He pulled Mathias back, nearly lifting him off the ground.

Svart eased up into a sitting position. I crouched down next to him, setting the knife on the floor and rummaging around until I found a fairly clean towel. As I held the towel against the cut, Svart winced and leaned his head against the wall.

"He's a sorcerer," Svart said. "This proves it."

Nekrokor sat hunched over in the wheelchair. He may not have been dead, but he seemed really fucked up. Occasionally, he erupted into a spasm of grumbling, accompanied by slobbered half words.

"Fish . . . fish," he would say. And then, "Death . . . death."

"As you can see, I didn't kill Bård," Mathias hissed.

"You did something to him," I said.

"Let me go," Mathias commanded. But Tomi refused. He'd seen enough. He wanted answers. We all did.

Maybe it was the headlock, but Mathias let down his front. His undead vampire thing. Even though that's what was at the root of it. His pursuit of undeadness.

"You're the one who gave me the idea," he said when we asked, again, about Bård.

I may have hated Bård. I definitely feared him. But I'd never schemed some way to debilitate the guy.

"Zombichrist," Mathias said. It took a minute for me to register.

"What?" I asked.

"Your song," he said.

"My . . . he's fucked up because of some old Valhalla song?" It was on *Thrones of Satanic Dominion.* Some Plutonic promo tape, too. It was our "biggest" song. About, as the title says, a zombie Christ. One of the Morris brothers wrote the lyrics after an acid tab and a midnight screening of *The Serpent and the Rainbow.*

"A shitty death metal song killed Nekrokor?" I asked, a

belligerent edge to my voice. "What the fuck?"

"Tell us the truth," Tomi said. He tightened the headlock.

Mathias told us that he'd heard the song. Delved deeper into things. Through tape trading, found someone in London who sent him some "zombie powder." He took the powder and it nearly killed him. But he saw the experience as a key to understanding that other time he'd nearly died—that time when he was a kid. When he got so sick he started to believe he had lived—unlived—through his own death. It was in the Bible, he believed. It explained Lazarus. The original voice of the undead.

And then Mathias took it further. The powder fucked up his voice; he'd take the powder and have Bård record him singing in a nearly unconscious delirium. It gave him the sound he wanted. He even went to London to buy the various things he needed. Weird fish parts. Plant stems. Bits of rare mushrooms. The more he did it, the more he realized he could control how deep it took him. The other guys in Astrampsychos once claimed they had buried Mathias in the ground, then dug him out a few hours later. This had been an early experiment. One that almost went too far. The powder slowed his pulse, his breathing, so he hadn't actually died. And the whole thing burnished his credentials as a singer and occult phenomenon. But after that, he started experimenting. Trying to find the right dosage. The "resurrected" bird was just a successful experiment. The dude behind the pink misprints of *Live in Brno*, that was a less successful experiment.

He would have gotten away with it. Except for us meddling kids. And the fact that Bård started taking the powder, too.

"A prisoner of the flesh," Mathias said. "He just wanted to get high."

Tomi kept Mathias in that headlock as he told his tale. Svart moved off the floor and onto the bed. The towel staunched the flow of blood. He seemed in better spirits.

I stood over by Bård. "You okay, buddy?" I whispered and laid my hands on his forearm. I must have grabbed him kind of tight. Tighter than I intended. My grip dislodged one of the scabs, black and scabrous, all up and down his arms. It flecked off and fell in his lap.

Mathias told us that Bård would probably get better. Maybe. He told us that it would take time. Bård took so much of the stuff that only his remarkable tolerance for substance abuse had staved off death.

And it might have ended like that. With Mathias explaining shit and the rest of us going on our merry way.

Tomi got greedy, though. He unhooked Mathias from the headlock, then scooped up the stack of checks on the desk.

By that point, I'd wheeled Bård out of the bedroom. Svart lurched along beside me.

Tomi didn't say anything about stealing that thick stack of checks. He poked around in the desk some more. He opened a drawer and took out a bunch of cash, which he stuffed in his pocket. He opened another drawer and took even more cash.

I was so focused on helping Bård and Svart that I'd left the knife on the floor. As Tomi rifled through the bedroom some more, Mathias picked it up, an evil gleam in his eyes.

Svart saw it before I did.

"Tomi!" he cried.

"Death! Death!" Bård barked from his wheelchair.

Luckily, Tomi used his quick reflexes and caught Mathias by his shoulders. He blasted Mathias across the room. Mathias crashed into the table with all his stuff. Books, papers, even the Casio fell onto his crumpled body.

Tomi rushed out of the bedroom. He hadn't come away unscathed. A sheet of blood poured down his shoulder.

"Get the fuck out of here," Mathias hissed, slowly raising off the floor.

We all ran. Well, not Bård. I pushed him. It took a little maneuvering to get him and the wheelchair through the doorway. It got jammed as I pushed through. The front door smacked back and banged against the wheels. There was some rubber strip at the bottom of the doorway, too. And Bård, completely oblivious, didn't help. He drooled and hit his fist against the door every time it slapped against the wheelchair.

Once I got in the hall, I realized I had a problem. We were on the third floor. And I had a dude in a wheelchair. I paused for a second. Tried to articulate this point to Svart and Tomi.

"Hey . . . uh . . . an elevator?"

They ignored me. They straight up abandoned me. Burdened with checks and cash, Tomi raced like a cheetah straight down the stairs. Svart followed behind, clutching the bloody towel to his stomach.

Mathias came up right behind me. He held the knife over his head. Another second and he would have struck me down. I grabbed the handles of the wheelchair and spun around. Then, I rammed him.

Mathias brought the knife down. It clanged against the side of the wheelchair. I rammed him a second time and he collapsed like a flimsy Halloween decoration. I rammed him a third time and he rolled up in a whining ball.

"Come on, Bård," I said. "Even you don't need this shit."

I raced down to the far end of the hall and found an elevator. I mashed the button constantly. Mathias slowly pulled himself up, grabbed the knife, and stomped down the hall toward me and Bård. As soon as the elevator chimed and the door opened, I pushed the wheelchair in. I frantically pressed the button for the ground floor. As the doors shut, Mathias turned and headed to the stairs.

In the ride down, Bård muttered to himself. "A thousand fish," he said, and then "an invisible city." The shit he'd taken, the zombie powder or whatever, had trapped him deep down in some dream world. His cries and barks described whatever horrors he experienced in his fractured state.

When the elevator door opened on the ground floor, the coast was clear. Unlike Tomi, Mathias did not pursue physical fitness with any degree of rigor. But I knew I needed the head start. I ran and, just as I slammed the wheelchair through the main entrance, Mathias caught up.

Outside, Svart and Tomi cleared the entryway to the building. They turned, then booked it down Overpoortstraat. Bård bucked and flailed. The door banged against his legs; it enraged him. I felt the soft whoosh of the blade passing over my head. And then I was out of the building.

I ran, but Mathias set out in hot pursuit. Weakling or not, he could do some serious damage with that knife. So I pushed ahead, huffing and puffing as I ran. I moved as fast as I could with a mentally incapacitated, but physical imposing, black metal maniac in my charge.

Occasionally, the wheelchair lurched wildly, or tilted up, ready to send Bård out into the street. Every ding and crack in the stone sidewalk threatened to derail our escape. The whole time, he cackled and, like a dog, thrust his nose into the breeze. And behind me, Mathias came on with a burst of speed.

I thought I was done for. But then I saw it. My salvation. A bus for the hospital. Z18: Ziekenhuis. I flagged it down and, even though I wasn't technically at a stop, the bus lurched over to the curb.

The doors accordioned open. I stopped the wheelchair and hauled Bård out of it with a tight bear hug. He murmured in my ear: "The ocean . . . hahaha . . . the bottom of the ocean."

I squeezed him and something crunched like a Dorito. Whether it was my back or his, I didn't care. Mathias moved up the block. I hoisted Bård into the bus and up the steps.

Once inside, I eased him onto the floor and spoke to the driver.

"Het ziekenhuis," I said. "Het ziekenhuis."

Out of the windshield, I could see Mathias advancing on the bus. We locked eyes for a second and he whetted his vicious blade on the edge of a metal garbage can sitting out by the curb. He looked like an emaciated knight, blade drawn and ready to do battle with this lumbering diesel reptile.

I fed all the coins I had into the till. My hands shook, though. A bunch of coins fell on the floor.

The driver muttered something under his breath.

Klootzaak or pokkelijder. I think he meant Mathias, not me, because he shut the doors and the bus heaved away from the curb.

A scrapy metal sound filled the air. It could have been that knife against the side of the bus, Mathias unleashing some bestial nekrohowl, or just the mechanical whine of the bus itself.

Bård had somehow crawled up into the seat right behind the driver, still chattering away inanely: "The fish . . . I am. I am . . . the scales. Become death." I sat next to him and patted his knee.

No one asked a lot of questions at the hospital. An elderly couple helped me get Bård off the bus. A couple of hours later, I climbed the stairs back to my apartment.

When I pulled my keys out of my pocket, my fingertips were wet with blood. Somewhere in there, Mathias must have swiped me. And I didn't notice. The adrenaline, the strange ravings of poor broken-brained Bård.

I knew what to do. I raised my hand and wiped the blood on the doorframe. I left it to brown and fleck away over time. I remembered what Mathias had once told me. The blood, it has protective properties.

27.
The Bard of Unholy Goggles

I stuck around for a couple of months after we rescued Bård. Selling my guitar bought me some time. Tomi came through, too. He felt bad about abandoning me and flowed me some cash from his reclaimed funds. Svart, though—he never apologized. We still hung out, but things weren't ever the same. I spent the most time hanging out with Abdul and Helena; it was easier that way. That bootleg version of *Infernö* came out, too. You could get it at the Record Huis. It didn't make anyone rich, but Rolf dutifully sent me checks every month.

The memory of Mathias and that knife traumatized me. I couldn't shake it. If I heard a high-pitched laugh or the sepulchral groan of a truck, I flinched. It could be Nordikron, I'd think. The voice of the grave. The blade of the damned. At the same time, I held onto something he'd told me. Something he gave me. He'd told me to go home and plant that tooth. Sow it in the soil. Make it give rise to a battalion of warriors.

Well, not entirely. He'd given me a tooth—I never figured out whose—and basically told me to go fuck myself. To go back to Florida and revel in failure. But I'd made peace with things. I planned to go back to Florida after this Belgian summer. I planned to plant that tooth in the swamp, maybe bury it near Natasha's house in Coral Gables, and move on with my life. I'd already confirmed my flight back home.

I never saw Bård again. Or Mathias. The wayward youth of Gent still skulked around in their Despondent Abyss gear. Some sported their Nekrokor tribute shirts, even though the dude was quite alive, taking up space in a government-run mental health facility somewhere in the far north and, if the reports could be believed, slowly regaining his faculties.

After I left Bård at the hospital, it didn't take long for the staff to realize the jabbering mess in their emergency room had already been declared dead. The local news covered that part of the story, but they didn't delve too deep.

And the part about the stabbing, the knife rampage, never came to light. Svart's mom took him to the hospital. He ended up getting a bunch of stitches. Double digits. But when they asked him what happened, he told them he'd cut himself on a beer bottle. They believed him and stitched him up, no problem.

The story about Nekrokor's zombification, about Mathias and his recreational pursuit of near-death states, never spread. This was pre-internet. And at that time, the American papers peddled a frothy blend of white Broncos and ill-fitting gloves that left space for little else.

The whole thing might have spread further, but Mathias was no business guru. Bård had lined up all these sweet international distributors. He'd lined up that Plutonic deal, too. But after the initial influx of money, things quickly died down. It didn't help that, with Bård effectively braindead, all the business shit fell to Mathias. He could formulate esoteric theories on the continuing psychic trauma exerted by medieval ghosts, but dude could not master the skills necessary to move boxes of product to diverse international markets. Mathias wasn't interested in getting records into stores. He wasn't interested in mailing promo copies around the globe. He had little time to talk marketing strategies with the Plutonic Records dudes.

Most of the Despondent Abyss promos went to college radio stations, where unscrupulous indie rockers hocked that shit for beer money. And then, in random used CD stores spread across the land, the occasional isolated misfit blew two bucks on a copy of Desekration's *Infernö* or uncovered a dusty copy of *The Intrapsychic Secret.*

Despondent Abyss produced only one more album after all of this. *Signs of Endings.* It was Nordikron's solo effort. A double disc masterwork of keyboards and pipe organ overlaid with his most devastating vokills. And then that was it. Despondent Abyss went dark.

On one glorious Belgian summer day, I headed back to Le Disque. I didn't go to pick up some ultralimited metal disc, and I sure wasn't there to give Nine Inch Nails another shot. Instead, I stopped at the rack of budget classical discs. They were like a dollar each. Because, like Mathias, I fancied myself an adherent of the true sounds of cosmic harmony, I got a couple Bachs. I dipped into the pop section and grabbed a replacement copy of *Holy Diver,* too.

And as I headed down the escalator, I saw Juan for the first time since that morning after the Desekration fiasco. I saw four or five Juans. On the wall of televisions down by the registers. In the music video for his major label debut. Out of everyone I've told you about, he was the only one to "make it." Juan. The Bard. The Bard of Unholy Desires. That guy. But jumped up and repackaged as CyberBard™.

You probably know that, though. You probably know the video. It lacked the budget of "November Rain," but rivaled it in cinematic scope. It shaped his live shows, too. When he started touring arenas with Nine Inch Nails. When David Geffen himself showered Juan with praise and accolades. His elaborate stage sets had the components of his breakout video.

In the video, he has that same guitar I told you about. The one he'd brought on our ill-fated Katabasis tour. That's what I thought at first. But they'd upgraded it, made a better one. The original guitar had razor blades and random gears superglued to it. The whole body of this one looked like the fuselage of some alien aircraft. The razors were longer, black daggers jagging off the head.

Le Disque had this video on loop. I got to watch it three or four times before I laid out my cash to enhance my classical music collection and reclaim *Holy Diver*. The video started with Juan, with the Bard of Unholy Desires, in his full vampiric costume, each part also redesigned and improved by some team of make-up artists and costume makers. Frilled smock, but frillier than his standard issue smock. A top hat, but taller and almost absurdly conical. Like Tom Petty impersonating the Mad Hatter. Juan wore a black velvet overcoat that nearly scraped the ground. He stood, corpsepainted, at a grave site. He held a dozen black roses.

The music itself had very little to do with Juan and his guitar. It was more like David Geffen gave him a group of trained studio musicians that he could play like a synthesizer. He had a group of people that he could control and command, probably a herd of hired hands fresh off a tour backing Cher. It was a winning formula, though. It led to his pop ascendancy.

Under the brim of his cartoon top hat, Juan wore silver goggles, their magenta lenses as round as John Lennon's glasses, but oversized for the science experiments of a bold new era.

He held the roses to his mouth and sang into them. His voice was processed and whiny, like a petulant robot. Then, he threw the roses into the grave. The camera cut to a shot of them falling before flashing back to Juan as he walked away from the grave. His magic guitar materialized into his hands.

Juan walked through a desert landscape, still whining about his lost love. There's nothing around—just rocks and dust. Stars and purple nebular clouds in the sky. It wasn't filmed in Belgium, that's for sure. Or Miami. And then he came to a full-length mirror, which was somehow standing by itself in the middle of the desert. It had a thick frame, golden and brocaded. The camera shifted to show Juan's reflection, but mirror Bard didn't have a guitar.

And that's when Juan pointed the guitar at the mirror. The

blades on the guitar neck shot off and flew toward the mirror. Mirror Bard held up his hands in mock terror, but to no avail. The blades shattered the mirror, the reflection, into a million cascading shards. That part coincided, in the song, with a resounding Zildjian gong.

The two Bards stood staring at each other, singing at each other, one of them now standing in the mirror-free frame. But it's not the same Bard, the one in the golden frame. Through the power of the razored guitar attack, all his corpsepaint transmogrified into silver and purple body glitter. It looked like he'd dunked his face in the cleavage of a dozen sweaty strippers.

This was the new Bard. Bard Rogers from the 25th century. The Billboard top artist, CyberBard™. Whatever you want to call him, that's the dude who ambled through the frame. He grabbed the guitar from the old Bard, and old Bard stumbled back.

New Bard, CyberBard™, strutted forward. I say "strutted" because the rest of the band followed him out of the empty frame in a jangly synchronized mass. They followed him like the tail end of a beglittered centipede. They followed him in a maneuver that had to require the services of a professional choreographer. And the thing about the band, each one holding an instrument, a keytar, a bass, a snare drum, is that they're all the Bard, too. Or nearly identical looking dudes. Just in different costumes. The one with the keytar had the sand-colored robes of a high-ranking Jedi Council member. The one with the drum looked like George Washington, but with a neon green wig and a Jackson Pollock splattered uniform. They all had the body glitter smeared over all visible skin, and none of them looked like the real people who played the song.

CyberBard™ strummed a few chords, even though what you hear sounds like a jock jam synth riff, sounds like "Get Ready for This," and he eased old Bard, the Bard of Unholy Desires, back to the grave from the beginning of the video. I flinched when I saw what he did next. I almost dropped my little stack of discs. CyberBard™ did to him what Nekrokor did to me: he jabbed him in the chest with the guitar, then kicked him with one of his knee high ultra-buckled cyber boots from the future.

But here's the weird part. The place where logic also plummets into the abyss. As old Bard plummeted, spinning, twisting in the air, he became New Bard, CyberBard™, glitter slathered and, amazingly, singing the chorus as he hurtled through space, then landed, superhero style, in some black-lit fluorescent inferno. New Bard kicked old Bard who transformed into new Bard as he fell.

The song had just enough of a metal tinge to betray its underground origins. This falling, spinning, singing CyberBard™ spit out the chorus in a passable death rasp, for example. Here and there, a crunchy guitar replaced the stadium synth.

And after he landed, the dancing girls streamed in. CyberBard™, singing, rasping, plunged deeper and deeper into the netherworld, his band behind him, a troupe of inferno dancers flocking around him. They pop and lock, drop it like it's hot.

I was totally blocking the line, standing there enraptured, right in the middle of the ground floor lobby, the nexus of home entertainment systems, small appliances, and videogames. The lady behind me mumbled "excuser," and gestured for me to move ahead.

At first, I thought it was a sham, or it wasn't Juan, or that I was losing my mind, mistaking him and his new band of Juanish doppelgangers for, like, UB40 or something. But, make no mistake, it was Juan. And then I wondered how some evil music executive had tricked him, made him put on some new costume, transformed him into an innovator of the hypermedia domain, changed him into a glittery cypher boldly mixing metal with all available popular genres.

But then I realized he'd been training for this all along. You didn't have to work too hard to get Juan to put on a costume. Or to play a new role. He'd done it before. Found a new costume. Found a new friend. Me, Mathias, probably a few talent scouts, and before you knew it, he was homies with David Geffen.

And the idea that someone with money would want to make Juan the spokesweirdo of youthful alternativeness, of what they later packaged as "extreme," still seemed unreal to me as I stood in the middle of Le Disque at some point near the middle of the nineties.

At the time, it seemed laughable, impossible. The Bard as a pop star? It seemed like the fantasy of some wild-eyed futurist, someone who'd changed their name to a barcode. It seemed as impossible as predictions of a company dedicated exclusively to delivering menstrual pads by drone, its delivery schedule synced to the phases of the moon, or some equally crazy, but yes, maybe, possibly possible development that, in retrospect, just seems obvious and inevitable.

When I first saw the video, it seemed impossible, but whoever bet on CyberBard™ cashed in hard. And after I saw that video, I felt better about my situation. I wasn't jealous of him. Or envious. If anything, it convinced me to let go, to enjoy the time I had left in Gent.

I took my change and dropped the coins in my pocket. After bleating out a "dank u wel," I turned from the counter, Bach and Dio in hand. The doors opened and as I stepped from the cool air conditioning and out into the equally cool Belgian summer afternoon, I turned my head and looked back at the row of television screens. On each one, a ray of light pierced the underworld gloom where CyberBard™ pranced with his entourage around ancient stones and marble ruins.

The light illuminated Juan, his hat, his costume, transformed by the glare, made silver and resplendent. The ray spread beyond Juan, overtaking his dancers, the ruins, everything, turning it all into a glittery and gleaming paradise.

Acknowledgements

My family, Andy and Carrie for being awesome and doing so much for indie lit, Bryan Bardine and his metal and literature classes at University of Dayton, Brian Kirkmeyer and his Engineering Global Metal classes at Miami University, Ross Hagen and the International Society for Metal Music Studies, Joshua Wood, Leza Cantoral, Joe Bielecki, Matt Hinch, James Basile, Christopher Lesko, Edward Banchs, David Agranoff, Alfredo Nieves, Sol Pérez-Pelayo and everyone who participated in the Congreso Internacional de Horror y Metal, Dylan, Ray, John, Mark, Duke, James, The Arts Council for supporting local writers and artists, Eliseo Guardado Salguero for expanding the study of metal lit, Benoît for language tips, Ian Lovdahl, Mike Kemp, Pim Blankenstein, Jason Pettus, Vojta of Moonroot Art, and the dungeon synth community worldwide for inspiration.

Dean Swinford likes all kinds of music—death metal, black metal, doom metal, grindcore, funeral doom, power metal, drone, Christian metal, industrial metal, gothic metal, gothic rock, darkwave, hair metal, neoclassical, prog, thrash, dark ambient, dungeon synth, and even, on rare occasions, nu metal. He lives in North Carolina.

Other **Atlatl Press** Books

Very Fine People by Scott Gannis
Heck, Texas by Tex Gresham
Along the Path of Torment by Chandler Morrison
The Joyful Mysteries by Pam Jones
Distant Hills by Lydia Unsworth
Murder House by C.V. Hunt
No Music and Other Stories by Justin Grimbol
Elaine by Ben Arzate
Bird Castles by Justin Grimbol
Fuck Happiness by Kirk Jones
Impossible Driveways by Justin Grimbol
Giraffe Carcass by J. Peter W.
Shining the Light by A.S. Coomer
Failure As a Way of Life by Andersen Prunty
Hold for Release Until the End of the World
by C.V. Hunt
Die Empty by Kirk Jones
Mud Season by Justin Grimbol
Death Metal Epic (Book Two: Goat Song Sacrifice)
by Dean Swinford
Come Home, We Love You Still by Justin Grimbol
We Did Everything Wrong by C.V. Hunt
Squirm With Me by Andersen Prunty
Hard Bodies by Justin Grimbol
Arafat Mountain by Mike Kleine
Drinking Until Morning by Justin Grimbol
Thanks For Ruining My Life by C.V. Hunt
Death Metal Epic (Book One: The Inverted Katabasis)
by Dean Swinford
Fill the Grand Canyon and Live Forever by Andersen Prunty
Mastodon Farm by Mike Kleine
Fuckness by Andersen Prunty
Losing the Light by Brian Cartwright
They Had Goat Heads by D. Harlan Wilson
The Beard by Andersen Prunty